D0065952

POSSESSION

POSSESSION

Elana Johnson

SIMON PULSE

NEW YORK   LONDON   TORONTO   SYDNEY

This book is a work of fiction. Any references to historical events,
real people, or real locales are used fictitiously. Other names, characters,
places, and incidents are the product of the author's imagination,
and any resemblance to actual events or locales or persons,
living or dead, is entirely coincidental.

SIMON PULSE
An imprint of Simon & Schuster Children's Publishing Division
1230 Avenue of the Americas, New York, NY 10020
First Simon Pulse hardcover edition June 2011
Copyright © 2011 by Elana Johnson
SIMON PULSE and colophon are registered trademarks
of Simon & Schuster, Inc.
For information about special discounts for bulk purchases, please contact
Simon & Schuster Special Sales at 1-866-506-1949 or
business@simonandschuster.com.
The Simon & Schuster Speakers Bureau can bring authors to your live event.
For more information or to book an event contact the Simon & Schuster Speakers
Bureau at 1-866-248-3049 or visit our website at www.simonspeakers.com.
Designed by Mike Rosamilia
The text of this book was set in Berling LT.
Manufactured in the United States of America
2 4 6 8 10 9 7 5 3 1
Library of Congress Cataloging-in-Publication Data
Johnson, Elana.
Possession / Elana Johnson. — 1st Simon Pulse hardcover ed.
p. cm.
Summary: In a world where Thinkers control the population and Rules
are not meant to be broken, fifteen-year-old Violet Schoenfeld must
make a choice to control or be controlled after learning truths
about her "dead" sister and "missing" father.
ISBN 978-1-4424-2125-7
[1. Science fiction. 2. Rules (Philosophy)—Fiction. 3. Brainwashing—Fiction.
4. Insurgency—Fiction. 5. Missing persons—Fiction.] I. Title.
PZ7.J64053Pos 2011   [Fic]—dc22   2010034675
ISBN 978-1-4424-2391-6 (eBook)

To my family. I would choose you
over anyone and anything.

1.

Good girls don't walk with boys. Even if they're good boys—and Zenn is the best. He strolled next to me, all military with his hands clasped behind his back, wearing the black uniform of a Forces recruit. The green stripes on his shirtsleeves flashed with silver tech lights, probably recording everything. Probably? Who am I kidding? Those damn stripes were definitely recording everything.

Walking through the park in the evening is not technically against the rules. Good people do it all the time. But walking through the park with a boy could get me in trouble.

When darkness fell, another rule would be broken.

The whir of a hovercopter echoed high above the trees.

In this park, the saplings stood an inch or two taller than me. Some trees in the City of Water are ancient—at least a century old. But the forest is off-limits, and even I know better than to break that rule.

The filthy charcoal shade of the sky matched the impurities I'd filtered from the lake in class today. I imagined the color to be similar to the factory walls where my dad worked, but I had never been there and hadn't seen him for years, so I couldn't say for sure.

People don't return from the Badlands.

"Vi, I'm glad you finally answered my e-comm," Zenn said, his voice smooth, just like his skin and the perfectly fluid way he walked.

"You know my mom." I didn't have to elaborate. Not with Zenn. "I told her I was coming whether she said yes or not." I tried to hide how desperate I'd been to see him, how happy his e-comm invitation had made me. He could've asked me to the moon and I would've gladly gone. And taken whatever punishment followed.

I'd left school during the afternoon break. The Special Forces compound is a two-hour walk south of the City of Water. I'd crossed the border and trekked for half a mile in the Fire Region just to see him. Crossing borders is also against the rules, but Zenn was worth every step.

I watched the hovercopters circle closer, comfortable in the silence with Zenn. Sometimes it said more than we did.

The sidewalks had stopped functioning thirty minutes ago, clearly curfew for this park. As one hovercopter dipped nearer, it took every ounce of courage I had to keep from reaching out, grabbing Zenn's hand, and running.

Before, I might have done it. But there was something different about him. Something that made me think he wouldn't run with me this time.

Another quick glance confirmed it. His eyes. They held no sparkle. No life. Maybe the Forces worked him too hard.

My sweet, wonderful Zenn. I hoped he was okay here. His eyes worried me.

"Well, now that you're here, I've got something for you," he said, smiling.

I angled my body toward him. Zenn's e-comm had said he had a surprise for me—surely something he'd tinkered with until it was absolutely perfect. Like he was.

"The Forces have kept me busy," Zenn continued, reaching into his pocket. He didn't seem concerned about the circling hovercopters, but he wasn't always living one breath away from getting arrested. "But we might not get to see each other again for a while. Your birthday is in a couple weeks, and you're my—"

"You down there!" An electronic voice cut through Zenn's throaty tone. I flinched and took a half step behind Zenn. A one-manned tech-craft, the hovercopter was invented especially for ruining lives. No one ever escapes from one. Not even me.

On the bottom rudder, a red rose winked through the twilight. My breath shuddered through my chest—I'd been caught by this hovercopter before. Maybe since Zenn was a Forces recruit and had invited me here, I wouldn't get in trouble.

Yeah, right. Fairness isn't something the Director cares about.

"Cards!" the mechanical voice shouted. Zenn pulled out his lime green activity card and held it straight up. An electric arm grew from the side of the police vehicle and flew down to scan the bar code on the back of Zenn's card.

I slowly retrieved my own ID. No one in the Goodgrounds can so much as step onto the sidewalk without an electronic record of their activity.

My card was blue for the City of Water. I raised it halfway as the arm jangled at me, trying to get a better angle to scan the bar code. Then I'd be busted for being out of bounds—after dark.

Zenn watched me with a wary eye. "Vi. Don't give them a real reason to lock you up." He stepped close enough for his body heat to permeate my senses. Touching was against the rules, but he'd broken that one lots of times.

I smiled, even though he was right. Lock Up is not a fun place. The stench alone is enough to set rule-breakers straight. Still, I almost threw my activity card into the brambles where no one would ever find it.

Zenn's face stopped me, his mouth drawn into a fine line. My bar code would be attached to his—we were in the park after dark (*gasp!*)—and if I got into serious trouble, he might not be able to advance in the Special Forces. And I couldn't have that weighing on my conscience.

I rolled my eyes at Zenn, something he didn't see because of my oversize straw hat—another rule, one I actually followed. The scanner beeped, and a horrible squeal erupted from the hovercopter.

"What have you done now?" Zenn's voice carried a hint of laughter amidst the exasperation.

"Nothing," I answered. "I've done nothing this time." I'd been good for two months.

"*This* time?" he asked.

"Violet Schoenfeld, stay where you are!" the mechanical voice boomed. "The Green demands a hearing."

"Vi! The Green? Seriously, what have you done?"

"Can I have my present now?"

* * *

Everyone knows the Green is just a fancy name for the Thinkers. They're the ones who broadcast the transmissions and categorize the people. The ones who do the thinking so regular people won't have to.

Zenn would join Them when he finished training with the Special Forces. He'd wanted to be a Greenie for as long as I'd known him, but that didn't stop our friendship. This arrest might—SF agents didn't hang out with criminals.

Inside the hovercopter, large panels with multicolored buttons and complicated instruments covered the dashboard. Glass encased the entire bulb of the body, allowing the pilot to spot rule-breakers from any angle. A window in the floor beneath the single—and occupied—metal chair provided a good view of the ground below. Since I had nowhere to sit, I stood next to the tiny doorway.

I felt trapped in a bubble, with the charcoal sky pressing down around me. My throat tightened with each passing second.

After cuffing me, the pilot scowled. "This return trip will take twice as long. We usually send transports for arrests."

I made a face at the back of his head. Like I didn't know that. Almost as bad as Lock Up, transports are twice as uncomfortable as the cramped hovercopter. And the filth and stink? Nasty.

With my extra weight on board, the pilot maneuvered the craft awkwardly and zoomed back toward the towers on the south end of the Goodgrounds. "I have a break in twenty minutes. I don't have time for this."

Then let me out. I watched Zenn fade to a distant dot, hoping it wouldn't be the last time I saw him.

The hovercopter slowed and the pilot turned to glare at me. "Don't try your tricks on me, girlie."

I had no idea what he meant. I gripped the handle above the doorway as he swung the hovercopter to the left. Toward the towers.

The Southern Rim is only accessible to Goodies with special clearance or important business. I'd never been there, not that I hadn't tried. No one I knew had ever been—water folk didn't make trouble.

True fear flowed in my veins as we approached. Maybe sneaking to see Zenn had been a bad idea. The thought felt strange, almost like it didn't belong to me. It grew, pressing me down with guilt. *You shouldn't have risked your freedom to see Zenn.*

The voice in my head definitely wasn't my own. Damn Thinkers. I shook the brainwashing message away. Zenn had risked his freedom for me last summer.

Below me, fields wove together in little squares, some

7

brown, some green, some gold. Crops grown in the Centrals provided food for those in the Southern Rim and the rest of the Goodgrounds.

The fields gave way to structures standing two or three stories high. Constructed like the other buildings in the Goodgrounds—gray or brown bricks, flashing tech lights, and red iris readers in every doorway.

Windows were blinded off from the outside world. We certainly don't want any sunlight getting in. No, that would be bad. According to the Thinkers anyway. Sunlight damages skin, no matter what color. Our clothes cover us from wrist to chin, ankle to hip, and everywhere in between. Suits for the business class. Jeans and oatmeal-colored shirts for everyone else. Wide-brimmed hats must be worn at all times.

Goodies are walking paper dolls, devoid of personality—and brains.

Yeah, that doesn't work for me. I don't want to be a paper doll. That's why I broke the rules and stopped plugging in to the transmissions.

The pilot swerved and twisted around the tall buildings. I'd never seen the city up close. My eyes couldn't move fast enough from one shiny structure to the next.

The pilot steered toward the last and tallest building on

the border of our land. The one with the symbol that can be seen anywhere in the Goodgrounds.

The olive branch is the symbol of good. It signals our allegiance to the Association of Directors. More like Association of Dictators, if you want my honest opinion. But no one does.

"So now you've seen the Southern Rim," the pilot said. "Was it everything you expected?"

I didn't know how to answer, so I kept my mouth shut—a first for me. That was the Southern Rim? No magic, no golden pathways, no perfect escape from my sucky life. The wall now towered in front of me, closing off any thought of freedom.

The hovercopter hung in midair as a door slid open in the wall. Darkness concealed whatever waited inside. And what would I find on the other side? Could I come back? Maybe I would never see Zenn again. My mouth felt too dry.

"We're going in there?" I asked.

"After I process your file," the pilot said. He made a note on a small screen. A long list popped up.

"I've cited you before," he said, smiling slowly. I remembered the last time: I'd left the City of Water after dark, crossed through the crops growing in the Centrals, and tried to enter the Southern Rim. I'd dressed up real nice in a fancy white dress and old platform shoes—which were the reason I'd been caught. No one can run in shoes like that.

I endured six rounds of questioning until I admitted I'd stolen the shoes from the basement of a house in the Abandoned Area—another off-limits place—another violation of the rules. Wearing contraband (which I didn't know about at the time) from an illegal area, trying to enter another forbidden district, and then there was all that nasty business about lying. Like it's the worst thing on the planet or something.

You see, Goodies don't lie. Ever. Honesty is sort of bred into us, but somehow mine got out-bred. Maybe when I stopped listening to the transmissions. Or maybe because I just don't give a damn.

And I'm a good liar, but that's all been properly documented in my file, which the pilot was now reading with interest. "Mm-hmm," he said. "A liar, a thief, and now the Green wants you. It's no small wonder, Vi."

I absolutely hate it when strangers use my nickname like we're old friends. I ignored him as he eased the hovercopter closer to the wall. A red beam scanned the rose on the bottom and a signal flashed. The pilot steered into a long tunnel with black walls, hardly a wall and more like a building. As we careened through it, panic spread through me—something I hadn't felt since learning Zenn would be leaving me behind to join the Special Forces. I wished he'd given me my birthday present before the stupid pilot arrested me.

When we finally cleared the tunnel, I gasped at the view below me.

A second city loomed behind that wall—an entire city.

People swarmed in the streets. Silver instruments and shiny gadgets winked up at me from the vast expanse below. My stomach clenched painfully, and I forced myself to keep breathing so I wouldn't faint.

The fierceness of the advanced tech burned in my brain. I can *feel* technology, I've always been able to. And this whole new part of the Goodgrounds produced some serious tech buzz. My head felt like it was in a particle accelerator set on high.

"So here we are," the pilot said. "The Institute—the birthplace of tech."

No wonder I felt like throwing up.

Everyone knows prisons have row after row of identical cells where the good-turned-bad live with concrete beds, toilets in the corners, and no projections to pass the time. Mechs escort rule-breakers to meals, and criminals are only allowed outside at certain times. I'd seen all this in school. *Be good, or we'll put you in here.*

But prison wasn't anything like what I'd learned in class. A silver floor stretched into stark, white walls that glared down at me as I followed a wheeled Mech through a door labeled WARD A.

I stopped just inside the entryway, staring down the hall. Numbered doors hid the cells beyond, but I didn't detect any hint of puke. This was far better than Lock Up. In there, it's everyone for himself. Or herself. Girls don't normally get put in Lock Up, but I'd been there four times. The rules are really stupid. Like it matters if I don't lock my window at night. Who's going to come in? It's against the rules to be out after dark.

I had to wait for a hearing. Mechs took me to the bathroom and back. (No toilet in the corner—I'd hit the big time.) They brought me packets of food that I mixed with bottled water, which tasted funny. Metallic, almost. Tech-cleaned. One wall projected the scenery outside, and I wondered if the weather was accurate.

My mother wouldn't come. She'd been notified, but I knew she didn't care. The Southern Rim was a long trip for a daughter she didn't want. I'd broken the rules one time too many the first time. She could have at least sent an e-comm. Even Zenn—trapped in the den of Special Forces agents—did that.

His message was short, only a few lines about how he couldn't get away for the trial, how he was trying to get me out of prison. But he'd signed it *Love, Zenn* and those two words provided all I needed to endure prison and whatever it held.

I don't remember time passing. It was just gone. Finally, I followed a shiny Mech down a wide hall, my heart beating furiously fast. Mechanical whirrings from its wheels scratched against the polished steel floor. The only other noise came from a motionless Mech in the middle of the hall. The oily smell of burning gears filled my nose as the beeps became one constant alarm.

Two guards emerged from the room at the end of the hall. Their gray uniforms almost blended into the surrounding walls. I twisted to watch them deactivate the malfunctioning robot by reaching under the chest cavity. So that's how—

My Mech tugged at my collar, forcing me to turn around. It had rolled out of line and stopped in front of a door. Another robot-guard already waited there, and next to it stood a guy who made my every sense pause.

His sun-stained skin gave everything away. He was bad.

He wore the uniform of someone who'd been in prison for a while. A name had even been sewn on the shoulder: *Barque*. He couldn't be much older than me and stood almost as tall as the six-foot Mech, completely relaxed. Maybe he knew something I didn't.

He looked at me and grinned like we were going to a fabulous party together. Alarm spread through me when my mouth curved up in response. Raising his tech-cuffed hands to his spiky black hair, he tapped his head. "Nice hair," he mouthed to me. One glance from his Mech, and he dropped his suntanned hands and stared forward again.

The shiny metallic doors widened, ready to devour me whole.

"Violet Schoenfeld," a voice boomed. "Jag Barque. Come forward."

The name of the bad boy echoed in my head. What kind of name was Jag Barque? I'd heard stories about how sometimes the Baddies got to name themselves. Surely this Jag guy was one of them. Who would torture their kid with a name like his?

The Mech swiveled forward and stopped at a table as tall as its canister-chest. It opened a briefcase, pulled out a black cord, and plugged it into the podium. The briefcase rotated and the top half flopped back, revealing a touch screen. My picture filled the wall in front of me. My name ran along the bottom, followed by a list of my offenses. *Crossed a border. Illegal electro-comm. Broken curfew. In the park after dark, with a male. Resisted arrest.*

My jaw tightened. I'd climbed that damn ladder to the hovercopter, swaying in the gusting wind. It was a miracle I hadn't fallen to my death. Now I was being accused of resisting arrest. As if all the other offenses weren't enough. What a joke.

It took everything I had to keep my mouth shut. This was court. My Mech representative would speak for me, unless someone asked me a direct question.

A man sat high up in the middle of a long row of seats, a

glossy black counter in front of him. He rested his arms on it and stared down at me with a look. The *don't-mess-with-me* kind. I hated him immediately.

Projection screens filled the wall behind him, and he kept glancing down at something. Probably another list of my broken rules.

Next to me, Jag's Mech-rep lifted a significantly bigger briefcase and plugged two feeds into the silver podium. Jag's picture appeared next to mine. His jaw was strong and square, in contrast to my rounder features. His skin was colored by the sun, while mine remained pale as eggshells. Our hair was practically identical, and my stupid lips curled up again. He had wicked hair too.

Several more projection screens lit up with pictures of Jag, each different. In one, his hair had the black all washed out. His white smile and bleached hair clashed with his brown skin. For some reason, he laughed beside me.

The Greenie in front of us frowned. Another of Jag's pictures showed him with his hair all shaved off. What little remained looked brown, and I wondered if that was his natural color. His shirt was open at the throat, the short sleeves exposing his bare arms. His blueberry eyes sparkled like he'd heard something funny.

My traitor mouth betrayed me again.

"Something amusing, Miss Schoenfeld?" the Greenie asked.

While I tried to straighten my lips out, Jag chuckled again. The quiet sound echoed off the high walls of the courtroom. My Mech-rep looked at me. "Answer him."

"No, sir," I choked out. Another picture revealed Jag passing out phones to Goodies, easily recognized by their umbrella hats and long sleeves. And then I knew. Jag was from the Badlands, and he'd been caught here, distributing illegal tech.

But . . . why was he at my hearing?

"Let's get on with it," the Greenie said. "Full council convening in thirty seconds. Mech-749? Your recommendation?"

Mech-749 had obviously been assigned to me, because it spoke. "Removal, your Instituteness."

"Mech-512?" the Greenie asked Jag's Mech-rep.

"Unrehabilitational, your Most High Institute."

"Not worth the time?"

"No, sir," both Mechs said together.

I had no idea I'd have to learn lame Mech-language to understand the conversation, but the man up front didn't seem confused. I seriously needed to scratch my arm, but my hands were bound in tech cuffs, which sent a shiver of current through my bones.

A door behind the "Most High Institute" opened. Ten green-robed men walked in. They moved behind the MHI and settled into seats on his right. Ten women entered through a different door—decked out in the same green Institute robes—and took the seats on the left.

Yikes, twenty-one Greenies in one room. Whoever this Jag Barque guy was, he was in deep.

In unison, they looked at built-in projection screens on the counter, the glow illuminating their faces.

"Violet Schoenfeld?" they asked in chorus, like they'd rehearsed it a dozen times before.

Then I knew. *I* was the one who was in deep.

"Miss Schoenfeld," the middle Greenie said. "Do you have anything to say?"

I looked at Mech-749. Did I have anything to say? What kind of stupid question was that?

"Not really," I said. "I was just walking in the park with a friend."

"A boy," a woman said, leaning forward.

"Yeah." I looked at her. "Zenn's my match." Surely being with Zenn wasn't against the rules.

"This is the"—the middle Greenie glanced at his p-screen— "seventh time you've been apprehended."

I counted quickly in my mind. Eighth, actually, but I wasn't going to bring it up. My first crime happened before I'd turned twelve and wouldn't be on my Official Record. Not sure if I was supposed to speak or not, I opted for not.

"Violet, you are aware that many on this council find you unrehabilitatable."

"That's a long word," I said, which roused a low chuckle from Jag.

The Greenie creased his eyebrows and scowled at the counter. He typed something that couldn't be good for my case. "It means that you no longer fit in the Goodgrounds." He spoke each word with care, so softly the sound didn't echo in the courtroom. It took several seconds for them to sink in.

I glanced down the row of Greenies, trying to decipher their cold glares and tight lips. "What?"

"When did you stop plugging into the transmissions?" A bald man at the end of the row leaned forward and stared at me, unblinking.

"I plug in," I lied. Another projection screen jumped to life. Not sure what all the red lines meant, I tried to calm my heart and breathe normally.

He smiled like an indulgent parent does when they catch their child eating a chocolate TravelTreat. "Not for a year, I believe."

"Check the records," I challenged. "My comm is linked in every night. Mandatory eight hours."

All twenty-one Greenies touched their p-screens and clicks echoed through the ridiculously huge hall.

"She's right," a woman said. Her voice was low and her eyebrows high. "Still, such a Free Thinker . . ." She made a face like she'd tasted something sour and typed into her notes.

"What happened to your hair?" Another woman fixed her tiny black eyes on me. Her long silver hair lay like a frozen waterfall of tech filaments against her dark skin. She had a large nose with high cheekbones. She looked like a hawk.

"My mother made me cut it," I lied again.

"Why?"

"She didn't think I was plugging in either, even when I showed her the printouts." A projection of the evidence in question replaced my picture on the wall behind the Greenies.

As if. Like I listened to the transmissions. I quit maybe a year ago, maybe longer. I'd figured out how to disconnect my communicator. So technically, I did plug my comm into the transmissions every night. I just wasn't listening.

After that, I wasn't in Their control—but I was tired. I didn't sleep well, living in constant fear that somehow They'd find out. Brainwashed before I could speak, I was terrified of Them. Even now.

"Miss Schoenfeld?" the Hawk prompted.

I glanced at my Mech-rep. "Pay attention. She asked why you had to cut your hair." The robotic voice did nothing to settle my nerves.

"Umm, my mother used perma-plaster to secure the link in place. It got all caught in my hair."

That brought a belly laugh from Jag, and the middle Greenie threw him a furious look. The sound died instantly, but the echo remained.

"So I had to cut it."

"Then you had to dye it?" the Hawk asked.

"Yeah." I stared back at her, daring her to ask another stupid question.

They all started typing like crazy. Whatever. It's my hair. At least that's what I told my mother. As much as I didn't want to, I wished she had come. As much as I wished it wouldn't, my throat burned with unshed tears.

"Mech-749? Do you maintain your recommendation?" the middle Greenie asked.

"Yes. Badlands."

Several of the Greenies nodded, and I wondered what that meant. Would I have to go there to serve my sentence? I didn't even know the Badlands had prisons.

"Jag Barque?"

"Yeah," he said lazily. I looked over, but our Mechs stood in the way, so I couldn't see his face.

"Your opinion has not changed, I presume?"

"Nope." Jag acted like he'd been here countless times before. He shifted his weight from one foot to the other, his hands hanging loosely in their tech cuffs. I wished for his calmness; my heart kept trying to bust through my chest.

"You are required to appear before the Association of Directors," the Greenie said. "In Freedom."

A moment of silence passed, a definite threat hanging in the air. Then Jag said, "I will not," and I imagined the glare he carried in his voice.

"It is your duty, Mr. Barque. You will leave next week," the Greenie said. "The council has some matters to discuss before your release. Violet, I have no alternative but to banish you to the Badlands."

Banished? For walking in the park with Zenn? "What?" I blurted out.

"Permanently."

Everything moved too fast. The walls shifted inward. "What does that mean?" I shouted. "I have to live there? Forever?" I took several steps forward. Two security guards emerged from the woodwork, and I realized I'd crossed a line. The one too close to the Greenies.

"Sir, I think the girl would be more dangerous in the Badlands." The bald guy who'd asked about the transmissions leaned forward. "She is a Free Thinker. Imagine the problems."

"What the hell is a Free Thinker?" I asked.

Mech-749 slapped a patch on my neck. A silencer. Cursing is always silenced.

"Nonsense," the middle Greenie said. "She is more dangerous here, amidst the tech, and given her family history—"

"My family history? You mean my dad? Where is he?" Only silence echoed off the walls. I took another step forward, very aware of their eyes on me. "I'll do whatever you want! Don't send me there!" My words flickered on the projection screens, scrolling across the bottom from one to the next.

The middle Greenie smiled without sympathy. His eyes flashed as he shook his head. I stepped forward anyway.

Don't do it, a voice warned. Hearing voices isn't all that abnormal. But the same voice—and this *was* the same voice as before—meant someone was monitoring me.

The middle Greenie's eyes narrowed, almost like he could hear the voice too. For just a moment, I thought he must be the one infiltrating my thoughts. But his voice had been distinctly higher than the one still echoing in my head. *Don't do it, don't do it.*

I took another step forward.

The middle Greenie raised his hand, causing security guards to swoop in and pull me back toward the Mech. I thrashed and kicked, and even with my soft-soled sneakers, one of them fell. I clobbered another one in the face with my tech-cuffed hands. I desperately wanted to rip the silencer off, but I couldn't get my fingers up high enough. It would've hurt—a lot—but I didn't care.

"I won't go!" I shouted so loud, my throat ripped. "You can't!"

Someone must have pushed a button or raised the alarm, because the courtroom swarmed with guards. Four of them tackled me before I went down. I finally stopped struggling when a taser sparked in my peripheral vision and someone kneeled on my spine. The guard cuffed me a second time, and I winced as the tech burned my wrists. Two pairs of advanced tech cuffs would cause blisters and a severe rash if I wore them for very long. My flesh was already tingling with tech-tricity.

"There's your evidence," the middle Greenie said. "We'll give you one week." He snapped his projection screen closed and stood. The other Greenies mimicked him, and as one, they marched out of the room.

One week for what? I glanced at Jag, my chest heaving

in anger. He held my eyes, studying me like I was a difficult projection puzzle he couldn't figure out. Refusing to look away, I stared at him until the guards yanked me backward.

Just as they pulled me through a door, a man asked, "What are we going to do with you, Mr. Barque?" The voice dripped with disdain, but somehow it sounded . . . familiar.

As I was escorted down the hall, I made the connection: The real-life voice speaking to Jag matched the one that had been talking in my head.

 My sister, Tyson, is the talented one, but she's been gone for years. So my mother never expected me to make it to sixteen, the age when I could really help her with the bills. I'd almost made it. A few more weeks and I could've landed a lame job with the loser algae department in the City of Water.

My only consolation for living that life had been Zenn. My mother allowed our friendship because Zenn's dad—a government official in the teleportation department—had called us a "smart match."

Which meant she thought he could keep me in line. Too bad she didn't know that Zenn planned most of our rule-breaking expeditions. Or that he was more than who the Thinkers had matched me with.

"I'd choose you anyway, Vi," he'd said that day as we lounged next to the lake. "So it's perfect that we'll be . . . that They matched us." He trailed his fingers through my hair. It was still long back then.

"I'd choose you," he repeated.

I smiled and kept my eyes closed, memorizing his words. Because in that moment, it felt like Zenn and I had the world in our hands.

Then he was chosen for the Special Forces. Everything changed. But not how I felt about him. And not how he felt about me.

After the painful removal of the silencer and the tech-cuffs, I fingered my already-raw wrists.

They'd stripped me of my ID card and taken my purse, so all I had were the clothes I wore—a beige long-sleeved shirt, standard blue jeans, my soft sneakers, and . . . yeah, that's it.

I kicked the Mech escorting me, but the silver casings made damage impossible. In fact, my right foot felt like I'd cracked a couple of bones.

The stupid robot babbled in its monotone voice about how empty the place was. "Apparently there aren't too many Baddies in trouble right now," it said, followed by a weird hacking sound. Mech laughter. *Creepy robot-people,* I thought.

Mechs have unlimited power. They can talk and talk and talk. They can run and run and run. Which is why no one ever escapes. How do you beat a robot?

They don't need to eat. They don't need to sleep. And they can sense body heat and bar codes and who knows what else.

I hate Mechs—more than I hate Thinkers. More than the idiotic rules.

I wished this stupid tin can would shut up already. And, miraculously, it did.

The Mech remained silent as we stepped out of the ascender ring and into Ward D. It led me down a row of cells with bars along the front—no privacy up here. It stopped in front of the only occupied cell.

"Oh, hell no. No way!" I yelled, fumbling under the Mech's silver casing for the power button that was surely there.

My fingers found the switch, clicking it off. An alarm wailed. I clapped my hands over my ears just as Jag Barque rolled off the bed, pulling his pillow over his head.

Four human guards appeared. One of them turned on the Mech while another slid the bars open. Several hands shoved me into the cell. Human and Mech laughter mingled together in a horrific medley. At least I wasn't cuffed, and the redness on my wrists had started to fade.

Jag settled back on the bed, stretching out and putting his hands behind his head. "Nice try."

I ignored him as I sized up his cell. A shelf above the bed held a few rare printed books, and his tray from breakfast still lay on the floor where he'd chucked it. This cell had a toilet in the corner. I'd finally made it to the big time. Next to the toilet, a metal sink held a bottle of teeth-cleaning tablets and a tube of green gel.

In an ungentlemanly way, Jag stayed on the bed, leaving the concrete floor as my only option for places to sit. I paced for a minute, but that merely increased my tension as I could only take two steps before turning around.

I stared through the bars, fighting down a stream of profanity and wishing I could fly somewhere far away and never come back. When I turned around, Jag was sitting up.

"What?" I asked.

He grinned. "Nothing."

Didn't look like nothing to me. "Why are we in here together?"

"You have wicked hair."

"Shut up," I said, folding my arms. "I got arrested for walking in the park with a boy. Now they have me living with one. This makes absolutely no sense."

He lay back down, his eyes dancing with amusement.

"You gonna hog the bed?"

"Yeah."

"Fine." I sat with my back against the metal bed frame and flinched when he tousled my hair.

"Don't," I growled.

"I like it. It's just like mine. Very posh."

"Sure, posh."

"Bad," he said, and I twisted to look at him. He managed to shrug with his arms behind his head. "I like it."

I ignored his comment. I'd always longed to be bad, maybe then my mother would have a real reason to hate me, and I wouldn't feel so *bad* about myself all the time. But now the thought of really becoming bad scared me more than I wanted to admit.

"How are we gonna get out of here?" I asked.

"I think you already know the answer to that."

Umm, no, I don't. That's why I asked. He didn't seem troubled by my glare. A superior glint reflected in his eyes.

"I'm not living here with you for a week," I said.

"You can have the bed. I don't sleep much anyway."

The sleeping arrangements were not my main concern. I glanced at the toilet and he laughed. "You can go when they take me to shower."

"How often is that?"

"Every morning."

"Great," I said, turning around and admiring the blank wall three feet in front of me, wondering how long it would take to train my body to use the toilet only once a day.

The night stretched into eternity. Jag let me have the bed, but he paced back and forth, and the constant squeak of his boots kept me awake. Finally I sat up, and he told me about life in the Badlands. People didn't have teleporters in every room because they actually walked to their destinations.

"Really?" I asked. "They walk?"

"Yes, Vi," he said. My nickname sounded natural in his voice, like we were old friends or something. "The Baddies don't have access to your superior tech crap."

"I thought that's why you were here," I said.

"Yeah, but—"

"Yeah, but nothing, jerk. You like our superior tech crap."

Jag did his annoying shrug. He reached above me to the shelf and pulled down a book. He lifted my legs and slid his underneath, leaned his back against the wall, and trained his eyes on the pages.

"What's with the books?" I eyed the two remaining on the shelf.

"It's called reading." He didn't look up. "Surely you know how to read."

"Of course I do. It's just that we don't publish books anymore."

Jag finally lowered the book, his gaze sharp enough to make me flinch. "But you used to. I requested something to read. This is what they brought me."

Maybe they didn't want him to have access to our tech, didn't want to give him an e-board. Whatever. He went back to reading while I thought about what he'd said about the Badlands. Such freedom. I envisioned my dad walking wherever he wanted. Without fear. Without that pinched look he got around his eyes when he went out to develop our "superior tech crap."

He'd hug me good night—yeah, that broke a rule—wearing his jacket. The shiny black leather made my nose tingle with the smell of polish.

And I knew.

He was going into the forest. At night. Two more broken rules.

Rule-breaking must run in the family, said that voice again, the same voice as in the courtroom. I wished I'd been able to turn and see who it belonged to.

I hadn't heard any voices before this. Maybe it was my

proximity to the Thinkers. Or maybe my offenses had finally landed me on someone's to-be-monitored list.

Maybe the Baddies didn't abduct Dad after all. Maybe the Greenies . . . This time, the voice was all mine. I shoved the thought aside and told myself to go to sleep. My dad had worked in the tech department, level ten, top secret. He'd developed the highest-class tech in the Goodgrounds.

He'd had clearance to enter the forest. Anytime he wanted. That's what he'd told my mother when she asked. That he'd gotten the proper approval, that many of his inventions needed power he could only get when the rest of us were asleep.

And I'd believed him.

As I drifted to sleep, I could almost smell the leather of his jacket. Almost feel the gentle press of his embrace.

Almost, almost. But after seven years, everything about my dad was harder to imagine.

Waterfalls and rivers and streamlets and the sound of waves on the shore . . .

I couldn't keep the images of water out of my head, and I seriously needed to *go*. Morning had arrived and Jag still hadn't left to shower.

The luxuriously warm water of a hot spring called to me.

"I gotta go!" I sprang up and took the two steps to the toilet. But I couldn't. I just couldn't go in front of him. He would hear!

I felt his eyes on my back. Didn't he need to go? Turning, I saw his playful smile before he wiped it away.

He closed the book and started banging on the bars with it. "Hey! Get me outta here!"

Slowly, painfully slowly—so painful and so slow, I thought I might wet myself—the guard sauntered down the hall.

"I gotta go," Jag said. "And I'm not goin' with her here." He jerked his head toward me.

My face must have looked absolutely pitiful, because the guard laughed as he unlocked the cell. "You guys working together yet?" He ran a red reader from Jag's shoulder to his ankle and bound his hands with *superior tech crap*.

I stared at the guard. Working together? What did that mean? Jag shrugged and threw me a look that made my heart do a little flop. The guard appraised me for several seconds before escorting Jag down the hall.

And then I was able to go.

4. The first time I got thrown in Lock Up, my mother came as soon as she got the e-comm. If I'd stayed longer, I might not have been so eager to go back (the getting-puked-on came during my second incarceration). My mother droned on about how embarrassing it was for our family to have a rule-breaker, how my sister, Tyson, hadn't died so I could be a vagrant, how I was exactly like my father. Blah, blah, blah.

I was proud of her last argument. I *wanted* to be like my dad. Maybe not living in the Badlands against my will. But at the time, I thought even that would be better than living in the Goodgrounds according to someone else's will.

After the lecture-that-had-no-end, my mother smeared perma-plaster over my link, gunking me up from ear to ear.

She dialed in special transmissions for me, ones about lying and stealing. It started because I told her I'd attend this totally lame Goodie party. And I went to a party, just not that one. Instead, I'd snuck down the street and into the Abandoned Area where I'd hidden an old ID card on another . . . questionable trip.

With the card tucked in my back pocket, I'd snuck to the Central community closest to the Southern Rim. Zenn arrived a few seconds behind me using his older brother's ID.

We had a good time. A little too good. On the way back to the teleport pad, I only made it half a block before a red iris recognizer caught my bleary eye. At least all the good citizens were asleep and hadn't been influenced by my bad choices. Yeah, those were my mother's words.

Now, sitting in prison, I reminded myself that it wasn't my fault Dad had been snatched. It wasn't my fault Ty died. Disgusted that I'd let my mom get to me, I followed a Mech down the hall without trying anything funny.

We met a human guard at the entrance to the showers. "Lucky you," he said. "The guys all shower together."

I tried to get that picture out of my mind as I scrubbed my skin in lukewarm water—in a room that wasn't completely closed off. I kept my eyes toward the doorway and my towel nearby. Maybe now that Jag had specifically pointed out that we didn't have adequate facilities, I'd get a separate cell.

The water turned off as I finished rinsing. I toweled my hair, but I had nothing to make it stand up the way I liked. Jag seemed to get his spiked. Maybe he had something hidden back in his cell.

Maybe they'd put me in a cell close enough to borrow it.

Oh, they did. They put me back with Jag.

The guard threw in another blanket along with a pillow and fixed me with a glare. "Don't try anything *bad*." But he wore a knowing smirk on his face as he shuffled away. Why did I have to share a cell with Jag when the whole ward was empty? They *wanted* me to break more rules. Well, they weren't gonna get that.

Something strange bubbled inside, smoked through my bloodstream. "I'm innocent!" I pressed my face against the bars. The guard turned around, something silver already in his hand.

I jerked my thumb toward Jag. "He distributed illegal tech. I took a walk in the damn park." The foreign feeling seethed beneath my tongue, coated my mouth. Rage.

Jag lay on the bed, a notebook open, his dull pencil hovering in midair. With a curious hint of determination, his eyes warned, *Be careful.*

A blue spark caught my attention. A taser filled my view. Then the guard's cruel grin. "You had a question?"

He wasn't any bigger than me, but that was some serious electricity flowing next to some very metal bars. I swallowed. "Um, no."

"No, what?" A very unfatherly twinkle resided in his dark, slanted eyes.

"No, um, sir."

"That's what I thought." The guard sauntered away, deactivating his taser before stuffing it in his pocket.

The rage waited, coiled in my toes.

Jag went back to writing. The scratch of the pencil grated on my already raw nerves. "What are you? Like, a poet or something?"

He didn't answer, but I didn't feel like being ignored. "Where'd you even get that? You're in the Goodgrounds. We use projection screens and electro-boards."

"And you get controlling messages transmitted to your communicators," he said, still scrawling away. "I think I'll stick to my notebooks, thanks."

If only we could all be so lucky. "Where'd you get all this stuff?"

He glanced up. I wore the same blue uniform he did. Mine didn't have my name blinking on the sleeve. I guess they didn't think I was worth it for only a week. At least I still had my own shoes, and I slipped them on so no one could take them without a swift kick.

"I've been here awhile."

"So? That means you get to have notebooks and hair products?"

Jag watched me intently, and my heart did that annoying flop again. Something passed between us, a feeling so strong, certainly he noticed it too.

"Yeah," he said, his eyes never leaving mine. Determined not to look away first, I waited for him to say more. He didn't.

"Well, then can I borrow your gel?" I asked, spreading the blanket on the concrete.

"Sure." He plucked the tube of green gel from beside him and tossed it to me.

It smelled like *guy*. Like spicy aftershave or musky something or other. Maybe pine needles. I cringed.

"What's wrong?" he asked.

"This reeks."

"What does it smell like?"

"Like a guy," I said. "I don't want to smell like a boy."

"Fine." He snatched the tube back.

Smelling like guy was better than flat hair, and I decided to apologize. Spiking, coloring, and cutting my hair were the only outward gestures that showed my blatant distaste for the rules. My hair was all I had, even if it wasn't technically against the rules to have bluish-black hair. Yet.

"You know, I could show you how to make it cooler." He studied the tube of gel like it was the most fascinating thing on earth.

"What? My hair?" I followed his long fingers as he tightened the lid. He caught me looking, and raised his eyebrows. I shrugged like I didn't give a damn about the gel. Jag didn't buy it.

He made me kneel on the bed and look in the scrap of a mirror hanging above it. Then he stood on the bed behind me. His breath tickled the back of my neck and his hands lingered just above my hair, his fingers almost touching my scalp.

A loud hiss echoed in my head. *Don't let him touch you!* It sounded parental, demanding.

I deliberately didn't move. Hardly breathed. That Thinker couldn't make me follow his rules anymore. I waited.

Jag hesitated. I met his eye, and we breathed in together.

Then his fingers landed against my skin. I jumped. "That's cold!"

He concentrated as he pulled the spikes into place, a tiny crease appearing in his forehead. After he finished, he kept his fingers in my hair, his eyes down.

"Are you done?" My hair looked better than ever.

He hopped off the bed, wiped his hands through his hair and then on his pants. "You clean up nice."

"Prison clothes and a two-minute shower in freezing water. You must be joking."

He shrugged. Something lurked behind that signature gesture, but he wasn't sharing.

I pulled the covers down and stretched out in the bed. "I'm taking a nap. You can have the bed tonight."

"Nice," he said as he settled on my blanket and pillow, pulling the notebook over from where it had fallen on the floor.

I tried to get the feel of his hands in my hair and the image of his straight, white teeth out of my head while I fell asleep.

Yeah, that didn't work.

**5** I don't dream. At least I didn't used to. But now my sister, Tyson, walked next to me, her green eyes sparkling from something I'd said. She always understood my jokes, just like I loved seeing her new inventions. Her honey-blond hair fell over her shoulder as she bent over something at the water's edge.

"It worked," she said.

"What did?"

She sat back on her heels, something gripped in her hand. "I saw this in a dream. It increases algae production." She held the piece of tech at arm's length, like it might bite her. Something dark crossed her face. Finally she dropped the device back in the lake. "Don't tell anyone, okay?" She stood and wiped her hands on her jeans.

"Tell them what?" I asked.

Ty's laughter infused my soul with joy. I tried to hold on to it, because I knew she was gone. The sound floated away, replaced by another voice.

My mother. Blaming me for Ty's death. She blamed me for everything.

"Vi?" Jag's voice interrupted my semiconscious memory. I opened my eyes and found him inches from me. Ty's image faded, and anger surfaced at losing her. Again.

I jerked back. "Why are you right in my face?"

He stepped away, and I pulled the blanket up to my chin.

"You were thrashing and calling out," he murmured.

I hoped I hadn't said anything embarrassing or revealed something I didn't want him to know—which was pretty much everything.

He reached out to touch me but stopped. "You said something about Ty. Who's that?"

"No one," I snapped, sitting up. My sister reminded me of happier times. A life I couldn't get back. I kicked the blankets off and stood up. I had to get out of the cell, but there was nowhere to go.

"Sorry, I just—"

"I said no one. I don't want to talk about it." I glared at him until he sank onto the closed toilet seat.

"And I said I was sorry." His eyes tightened and he held out his notebook. "I wrote something I want you to read and take to a friend of mine in the Badlands."

I ignored him. The cell seemed much smaller than it had a few hours ago. The walls pressed closer, smothering me. One wall flickered and moved a tiny bit. It wouldn't surprise me if it was programmed to shift, a control tactic to mess with my mind.

I could reach out and take the notebook from him without even taking a step. He shook it, rattling the pages. The sound set my already frayed nerves on edge.

"I don't want to be your messenger," I said.

"You've got to stop attacking me. We have to live here together."

"Like hell we do." Maybe if I caused enough trouble, I'd get my own cell. Isn't that what They wanted? More trouble?

I turned and started banging on the bars. "Let me out! I gotta go!"

A Mech whirred down the hall with a guard, and together they cuffed me before taking me to the bathroom. I took a long time washing my hands, using the hottest water possible and three doses of stinky prison soap. The plastic started to wilt, and I pulled my hands apart hard. *Please, please break.*

As soon as I thought it, the tech popped with electricity. Shock waves splintered up my arms, and I stifled a cry. I dunked my hands under the faucet and yanked harder. With more soap, the cuffs slid easier. The thin electrodes seemed to stretch in the heat and suds.

Someone banged on the door. Tears leaked down my cheeks. I was so close! I imagined the tech broken, lying limply in the sink.

The metal fibers cutting into my wrists broke, sending a spray of scalding water in my face. Blood dripped from my arms and I hurried to press hydro-dryers onto them. But HD's are made to absorb water for recycling, and the blood merely congealed on contact. Some of it plopped on the counter and bounced.

"Just a minute!" I called.

Just as I'd imagined, the defeated tech sat in the sink. I swept it into the garbage can with the jiggly blood. I hastily wiped my wrists on the inside of my shirt. When the bleeding stopped, I laced my fingers in front of my body before pushing the door open with my foot.

The Mech waited next to the door, but the guard stood down the hall, talking with another man—the bald Greenie from the hearing. This was so not going to work. Not with mind-reading Baldie here.

The Mech whirred toward the cell, stopping next to the two men. I continued past them without glancing over. I focused on taking one step at a time, thinking that I wasn't doing anything wrong.

I waited outside the cell, the air too thick to enter my lungs. *Keep talking*, I thought. *I'll wait.*

The murmur of Baldie's voice wafted down the corridor. I relaxed enough to inhale.

Jag still sat on the closed toilet seat, the notebook gripped in his hands. "Hey," I hissed. "How do I get out of here?" I wiggled my fingers through the bars to show him I was free.

His eyes widened as he dropped the notebook. "How did you . . . ?"

I growled. In Vi-talk, that means, *Really? I don't have time to explain.*

Good thing Jag understood Vi-talk. He glanced at the guard, still talking to Baldie. "Go down those stairs at the end of the hall. There're no prisoners in Ward C. No guards." His eyes sparkled the same way they did in the pictures, like he was thrilled. For a brief moment, his fingers lingered on mine. Then I ran.

I flew down the stairs like they were already moving, my soft sneakers hardly making a sound. Ward C loomed dark and empty. Halfway down the first corridor, footsteps boomed behind me on the stairs. I made it to the end of the row, stopped, leaned against the wall, and tried to quiet my rising panic.

Which was pretty much impossible.

I could hide from the human guards. Mechs would cause more of a problem as they can sense body heat.

When the guards had run further downstairs, I took several deep breaths and found the showers. They were in a circular room with twenty faucets, just like Ward D. I turned the water on cold on every showerhead. The icy spray made my breath catch, and I shivered at the thought of cold-water torture. But Mechs had to be able to detect a distinct difference in temperature to locate a human, so it was self-inflicted freezing or getting caught. Plus, I had no idea where to go next, and I needed a minute to collect my thoughts.

I chose a spot in the middle of the chamber where the least amount of water sprayed. The air around me frosted my throat and lungs. After only a minute, my body shook and my teeth chattered.

Minutes passed. Or maybe hours; I wasn't counting. All I knew was that my skin was clammy and my insides felt like they'd been sucked into a glacier.

Yeah, the Mechs found me as I was still trying to figure out the next step of my lame escape plan. With frozen fingers, I managed to switch off the first four. Their shrieking alarms screamed, echoed, ratted me out to the whole world.

I couldn't believe I'd tortured myself for no reason.

6.

Tyson disappeared a week before my twelfth birthday. Despite being barely fourteen, she'd been offered a job working with the water rangers, near the border of the Goodgrounds. My mother had been *so* happy, like everyone should be thrilled to have an *early job* with the *wonderful* water rangers.

Which is true, I guess. Rangers are the highest-ranking people in our society. There are different types of rangers, all at the top of their class, all supersmart, all well liked. I could never be a ranger. They're the kind destined for greatness, you know? The kids who always get straight A's without even trying. Popular, with parents who adore them. No, the rangers were not for me. But Ty? Yeah, Ty was born to be a water ranger.

And she loved it.

In the few months before her disappearance, she improved the tech purifying the water so much that a man came from the Institute. His skin was naturally dark, but he still wore the covering clothes and wide-brimmed hat. He spoke with an accent, yet every word burned in my ears.

In his lilting voice, the man told my mother what a wonderful daughter Ty was, and how proud she should be, and hey, maybe the Greenies would take her from school a few years early. My mother followed along, nodding and agreeing—until the taking-her-away part.

"I need my daughter," she said, her expression suddenly stony. "My husband is gone, and I don't have anyone else."

I happened to be sitting in the room when she said it. The black-hearted man glanced at me. "You have another daughter right there."

I hadn't done anything wrong at that point in my life. I went to school, hung out with Zenn, skipped rocks in the lake—okay, that *is* against the rules, but everyone does it.

"I need both my daughters," my mom said. The man spoke into old tech, something that recorded his voice so he could hear it later, and pressed a letter into my mom's hand. Even at eleven years old, I knew that paper held something huge. Our communications are usually sent through e-comms.

She read it after he left, tears pouring down her cheeks. They came for Ty the next day.

Human guards—six of them—escorted me to the cell without allowing me to dry off. The thin prison garb clung to my body, and I was terrified it would be see-through. I wondered how I could cover myself in case Jag took a peek, which he surely would. He is a bad boy, after all. My mother told me all they want is sex. I didn't know if that was true, but I wasn't going to take any chances.

Before pushing me back in the cell, one of the taller guards tech-cuffed me—twice. The techtricity caused spots to appear in my vision.

"Hey!" I said. "How am I supposed to do anything with these things on?"

"I don't know, girlie. Figure it out." He glared down at me before turning to his buddies.

"My head rings for hours when those blasted Mechs go off," another guard said as the group shuffled away.

"Me too. How long did it take to catch her? Thane will want an exact—"

Jag pressed his face against the bars, but the door had closed behind the guards, silencing the rest of the words.

"What's up with you?" I asked.

Jag didn't respond as he bent over to pick up the book he'd dropped.

My stomach growled, and I looked for the two trays of food that had been there before my pathetic escape attempt. They were gone.

"Great," I mumbled as I sloshed over to the toilet and sat down on the lid. I checked to see if the wet uniform was transparent. It wasn't, thankfully.

"Vi, I've never met anyone who can get out of tech-cuffs. That was wicked awesome." He smiled—one of his Jag-winners.

"I got caught, didn't I?" And I didn't know how I'd gotten those tech-cuffs to break. Soap and water shouldn't have been enough. A cold prickle crept over my skin, like someone was watching me. I glanced around, through the bars, up to the ceiling. But there was only Jag.

"Yeah, but tech-cuffs!" He took a step closer, eager to hear the story. "And you've been gone for, like, two hours."

I shook the creepy feeling away, focusing on Jag's face instead. "Yeah, and I'm soaking wet. And freezing cold. How long until dinner?"

"Coupla hours."

I groaned with disappointment. "I'm starving."

"Sorry. They took your food without asking my permission."

"I'm sure they did." His chill attitude bugged me. Didn't he wonder at all about why we were in here together? "Why are we still here? What do they need a week to plan for?"

He shrugged, not alarmed by my snarl that followed. He settled on his bed with that infernal book.

After I dried out, I joined him on the bed, resting my back against the smooth wall. He put his book down and looked at me, which I took as an open invitation to ask more questions.

"So how'd you know about Ward C?"

"I don't read and nap every day. I've . . . done some exploring."

"Meaning you've tried to escape," I said.

"A few times." He watched me, like I should do something with this information. But I didn't know what.

"They brought me the books so I'd quit making life so difficult for them," he said.

"Ah, so that's all it takes to keep you in line. A pencil and a paper. Noted."

He looked like he wanted to laugh, but he didn't. "I make my own decisions," he said, as if I didn't know.

"I do too," I shot back.

He leaned very close, his eyes flitting back and forth between mine. "That's why they need a week to figure out what to do with us." His voice carried an urgency I'd only heard from Zenn. And thinking of Zenn made my heart crack a little, made me realize Jag wasn't my match and I shouldn't get too attached to him.

I shifted away from Jag and wrestled with myself to find a new topic of conversation. "So tell me about your family," I said, my voice only slightly strained.

His mouth tightened for a second before he told me about his older brother. Everything Jag knew, he'd learned from Pace. Every entrance to the Goodgrounds, every exit, every change in guard, every piece of tech the raiders used. The calming sound of his voice made my eyelids heavy.

When I woke up, Jag's arm was coiled around me and my head rested against his chest. It rose and fell in an even pattern as he slept. I liked how his hand felt on my upper arm. Without moving, I closed my eyes again and tried to silence the screaming (*You're matched with Zenn!*) in my brain.

Like that worked.

The smell of dinner preceded the food cart. I jumped up and pressed my forehead against the bars. The guard was moving so slow he could've been walking backward. I twisted my aching wrists in the tech-cuffs, willing him to hurry.

Jag let out a loud yawn and joined me.

"What is it?" I said, salivating. I would have eaten anything at that point, even though this meal smelled like the boiled cabbage my mother made.

"Must be ham tonight."

"Ham?"

"Yeah, it's meat."

"Oh." I wasn't quite sure what meat was, but I didn't want to admit it. I'd grown up on potatoes, carrots, beans, and anything else that grew in our garden. We supplemented our vegetable diet with vitamin and protein packets mixed in water.

The guard uncuffed me with a nasty glare. The release brought instant relief to my swollen wrists. I lightly traced the ugly rash that had formed while he pushed a tray through the slot.

Whatever ham is, it was delicious. The potatoes and carrots felt heavy and fibrous in my mouth, like they'd been grown in hydro-soil. The fizzy drink had already been mixed. Definitely vitamins, but they tasted stronger than the ones I'd had at home. Maybe because the water added its own flavor. And by flavor, I don't mean something tasty. More like metal.

I ate everything in about three minutes. Jag stared at my empty tray and laughed. The sound made me happy. He created a calm inside I hadn't experienced before. Not even with Zenn.

A pang of loneliness—and guilt—accompanied the thought of Zenn. For a minute I imagined how he'd looked in the park.

His playful smile, his lifeless eyes. I pushed the memories away as I watched Jag eat. His tan hands and long, slender fingers moved methodically. Every bit of his brown skin glowed. The sun is supposed to drain a person of life, allow for more sicknesses, yet Jag appeared perfectly healthy. He radiated life like no one I'd ever met.

"Did you grow up bad?" I asked as he wrapped his bread in a napkin.

"Yeah. But I'm not really bad, you know. That's what you guys call us. We're really just like you."

I thought about his comment for a long time. After he stashed his leftovers on the bookshelf and showed me how to play word games in his notebook, I still thought about it. Long after he fell asleep on the floor—very gracious to let me have the bed again—the thought of him not really being bad bounced around in my brain.

What if I had been born in the Badlands? Would I be a different person? Would I be bad instead of good? Who am I really? A Goodie or a Baddie? Can a person be both? Does it matter?

Of course it matters, the voice whispered. *It matters very much.*

I ignored the words, even though they rang true. The intrusive voice ignited a fire in my stomach. I hated having someone in my head. Hated the lack of privacy. Even worse, I hated that sometimes I agreed with the Thinker.

I never talked back to the voices, as that only seemed to encourage them to keep invading my head. But, hey, I break rules, even ones I make for myself. *What do you want with me?* I asked, thinking he surely wanted something. Something that took a week to plan.

Of course no one answered.

I'll go to the Badlands, I thought. *No problems, no fights. Promise.*

But the thought of living in the Badlands terrified me, because I'd never see Zenn again. My heart thrummed faster, squeezing up into my throat until I couldn't breathe. And not just because of Zenn, but because I didn't think They'd really let me go to the Badlands. Not after my fine display of disobedience.

To calm myself, I rolled onto my side and watched Jag sleep. My pulse slowed, and the air became lighter. He was right—he wasn't bad.

He was perfect.

Sometime later, Jag nudged me. I moaned and rolled over, right onto the cement floor. "Ow," I groaned, wishing I could rub my shoulder, but I'd been recuffed before bed. They didn't want me to "try anything bad" during the night. My shoulders burned, and stabbing pains arced up my arms from the techtricity.

"We've got another hearing," he said, running the water in the sink and pulling his wet fingers through his hair to re-form his spikes.

My throat turned dry. I was used to getting myself in trouble. But Jag? I didn't want to be responsible for causing more problems for him.

"Do mine," I said. He re-wet his hands and reached up, pausing when he saw my wrists.

His cool fingers traced along the cuffs. "Tech rash." His voice held a knowing tone, like he wasn't surprised the tech burned me. He finished my hair and I turned around.

"Nice." He brushed his hand across my cheek. "You have such great hair."

"You're a freak about hair," I said, turning away from him to examine my spikes in the mirror. I almost expected to see a trail on my cheek where he'd touched me. "Most people don't even notice it, because of our hats and all." That's how I'd kept my new short do from my mom for almost two weeks. Zenn hadn't said anything, he'd just raked his fingers through the short locks when I told him why I cut it.

"No hats in the Badlands," Jag said. "Hair is like status there."

"What does that mean?"

"Everyone will love yours. It means you're like, *the* bad guy, you know? Except you'll be the bad girl." He stepped close enough for me to feel his body heat through the thin prison clothes. The charge of energy pulsed through me, a feeling of familiarity so strong, so overpowering, I almost asked him if we'd met somewhere before. But that was ridiculous. I'd never met a bad boy before.

"I don't want to be bad," I argued.

"Too late, Vi. You're worse than me."

I spun around, ramming into him with my shoulder. "Take that back."

Face flushing, he stepped away.

"I am not bad," I said.

"Okay, fine. You're not bad." He studied the cement floor. "But you really are," he added under his breath. I might have taken a swing at his pretty-boy nose if I wasn't double-cuffed. But three Mechs and no less than twelve heavily armed guards appeared, and I thought the timing was a little off.

The Mechs swiveled around me, one in front and one on each side. They were the switchless kind, way high-class, so I couldn't turn them off without a decoder.

Jag walked ahead of me, uncuffed, with two guards next

to him. The other guards clustered around me, their tasers activated, ready to fire if I so much as sneezed. Like a fifteen-year-old water girl could take down ten fully grown men with muscles and weapons.

We marched through the abandoned halls. We didn't wait for the Greenies to call our names before entering the shiny courtroom, which was likewise empty.

Jag and I stood together, without Mech-reps. I'm sure this was a violation of my rights—oh wait, Goodies don't have rights. We link to the transmissions, work the jobs we're told, marry who They match us with. In return, we're provided with a good life. Or so the Thinkers wanted us to believe.

The Thinkers had also brainwashed me to believe the Badlands were just that—bad. After talking with Jag, I wasn't so sure. Again, I wondered if my dad had been banished. The Badlands couldn't be awful if he was there.

A doctor hovered nearby, his eyes trained on my wrists. He didn't look surprised as he typed on an e-board and left.

Moments later, the Greenies swarmed through the door like vitamins fizzing in water. They buzzed among themselves, pointing at their p-screens. The middle Greenie entered last and sat in his previous spot. Even with bloodshot eyes and a stubbly chin, he radiated coldness.

"Remove her cuffs," he said. The guard who moved to

comply didn't look happy about it. I sighed in relief at the release.

"Violet," the middle Greenie said. "What are we going to do with you?'

"Do, sir?" I asked innocently.

Several Greenies exchanged looks and raised their eyebrows as if to say, *Toldja about her heinous attitude.*

The middle Greenie took a deep breath. "By order of Thane Myers, you must appear before the Association of Directors."

I didn't blink. Didn't move. Didn't understand.

"Who?" I asked at the same time the middle Greenie said, "You will both be implanted with tags."

Tagged. Marked for life. In the Goodgrounds, that's really, really bad. Every scanner, every reader, will pick up the tag. Alarms will wail. Everyone will know what you are. A loser. A criminal.

My future with Zenn faded into a white horizon, where I could hardly see it.

Jag stiffened next to me. "No way. You will not touch me with your Goodie tech crap."

"You do not have a choice, Mr. Barque. You came here illegally, distributed contraband tech from the Badlands, and attempted to steal our technology."

"I wanted to leave six weeks ago."

"Six weeks?" I whispered. Jag ignored me, his cold blue eyes really frosty now. He and the middle Greenie seemed locked in a silent battle of wills.

"Perhaps. But you would have come back, with more of your Badlands hype. Now that you two are together, we have no other choice."

My mind lingered on *together*, and what the middle Greenie meant by that. He'd put us together—did that mean we hadn't done what he wanted? Or that we had?

"I'd rather die," Jag said.

"No!" I whispered. They'd really do it. They had no qualms about killing. I should know—Ty is dead.

"The Association won't take no for an answer this time. Sorry," the middle Greenie said, sounding anything but apologetic. "Thane has authorized your transportation for the day after tomorrow." He turned his attention to me. He was thinking that I wasn't worth the trouble, and he should just get rid of me as fast as possible. Sometimes the eyes can't hide everything. "Dismissed."

We were herded upstairs to the cell where Jag did a most surprising thing.

He lay down on the bed and cried.

7

I hadn't pegged him for a crier. His eyes were always so bright, so full of life, like he lived for trouble.

Ty had been that way too, except she lived for the water, the adventure of being herself—of *finding* herself. The day the black-hearted men came to take her, my mother tried to stop them. But a single taser blast caused her to sleep the rest of the week away. She missed my birthday and everything. Not that she would've done anything to celebrate, but still.

I'd hugged Ty and she'd wiped my tears, promising to visit. She whispered that she'd see me again, and hey, we'd walk around the lake and laugh at how we cried like babies when she left. She only came home once. Then the dark-skinned government guy told us she'd died working on a new piece of tech that backfired.

After that, he'd had to use his submission tactics on me, or I might have killed him. That's when the real trouble had started.

As I watched Jag's shoulders heave, I felt the same mix of anger and grief as when Ty left. Finally I knelt on the bed and placed my hand on his back. I patted awkwardly, hoping that was protocol for when someone is sobbing their eyes out.

"Hey." *Pat, pat.* "It's okay. We'll bust out of here before they tag us." *Pat, pat, pat.* I felt lame.

He pushed himself up and wiped his hand across his face. He avoided looking directly at me. "Do you really think you can get us out of here?"

Of course I couldn't. Didn't he remember my last pathetic attempt? I hadn't even made it out of the bathroom. But his lovely eyes, not so cold anymore, the perfectly curved arch of his mouth . . .

I'd tell him whatever it took to make him stop crying. "Sure," I lied. "We'll go tonight."

He threw his arms around me and pulled me down onto the bed with him. His laugh filled my soul, and I wanted nothing more than to feel that sound reverberating in his chest. So I laid my cheek against his breastbone as the last echo faded away. Startled by his embrace as well as my own actions, I withdrew quickly and lay on the floor, refusing to meet his eyes.

I warned you not to touch him.

I jerked at the sound of the voice, hitting my elbow on the wall behind me. Once again, I was in direct opposition of the rules. Because I craved the human touch. I always had. I shook away my traitorous thoughts.

"Sorry," Jag said, his fingers trailing along my shoulder. "Didn't mean to freak you out."

"It's okay. I—I don't know."

"Do I scare you?" He leaned over the side of the bed.

"Course not."

He smiled, making my heart skip a beat. "Nice." He said that a lot. It was like his shrugging thing.

"How come you've been here for six weeks?"

"Rehab," he said. "They tried transmissions, but I wouldn't wear the comm. So they tried counseling with one of your Goodie mind doctors. That didn't really work either. They don't want me to be here, but they thought it might be better than letting me go back to the Badlands. I didn't think they'd send me to Freedom."

"Where is Freedom?"

"Back east. Vi," his voice dropped to a whisper, "we can't go there. We'll never come out. Thane . . . well, we just can't go there."

I waited for more of an explanation, but he clammed up.

"Because we're Free Thinkers," I said, as if stating a fact. Baldie had called me that at the first trial. That's why Jag and I were in the same cell and why I felt such a strong connection to him. "Why won't we survive in Freedom?"

In the dim artificial light, his eyes reflected fear. "That's where the Association is."

"Yeah, so?"

"They're the good guys," he said.

"Like—"

"Like, really good guys," Jag repeated. Which meant they'd be pretty bad for me.

"Who's Thane Myers?" I asked.

"Nobody," Jag answered, the lie written in all three syllables.

"He's controlling everything," I whispered. The guards. The Greenies, maybe even Jag. I'd heard his name enough to know.

"Forget about Thane," Jag said, his voice oddly powerful. "Let's figure out how to get out of here."

I rolled away, trying to think of how a Goodie could get out of prison.

Then it hit me.

Be bad.

We didn't go that night. I promised Jag we'd try after showers in the morning, buying myself some time by telling him I had something to check in the bathroom. Really, I just needed to think of something a Baddie would do.

Instead, he told me stories about the Badlands and how he hadn't been to school in three years. He said everyone got to choose their clothes. Long sleeves or short. Blue or red or purple. Didn't matter. No hats, unless you wanted to wear one for "fashion purposes." (I didn't even know what that meant.) I couldn't fathom that kind of freedom. Every morning my closet spat out a pair of blue jeans and a drab long-sleeved shirt.

Jag told me that most people are happy being bad because they don't know any different. He only knew because he came to the Goodgrounds on a regular basis. He knew the tech we had—saw how the Badlands could benefit from our purification systems and comforts of life.

I couldn't argue. It felt totally unfair—except for the brainwashing part. I could leave the links and transmissions behind pretty easily.

I wondered if I'd ever been happy being good. I mean, I didn't know any different either—at least not until I stopped plugging in. When I mentioned it to Jag, he said, "It's just a control tactic, Vi, to make you believe one thing over another."

I knew that, I did. But a lifetime of labels is hard to overcome. Maybe I just needed a new label, one that was neither good nor bad. Because Jag seemed good enough to me, no matter where he'd been born. In fact, he was the complete opposite of everything I'd been raised to believe about Baddies. Disease-ridden, losers, undeserving of help—just plain bad people.

Nothing about Jag meshed with what I'd believed about the Baddies. I harbored such negative feelings for them. Because I blamed them for Dad's long absence.

But now . . . yeah, now nothing made sense.

Finally Jag slid the pencil into the spiral binding of his notebook and shoved it under his pillow. I sat next to him, staring through the bars into the corridor. How could I get us out of here? I swallowed my doubt, determined not to give in yet. I would think of something.

Jag threaded his fingers through mine and leaned toward me. The tension drained from my body as I enjoyed the same comfortable silence I'd only experienced with Zenn. I forced the thought of Zenn away. Tagged and sentenced to the Association, my past life was just that—in the past. I only wished it didn't make me feel so empty.

"You do smell like a guy," Jag whispered, his voice soft in my ear. His breath trickled down my spine. His fingers filled the spaces between mine perfectly.

"Shut up," I managed to say, but my voice sounded breathless. Surely he noticed the effect he had on me. I wasn't that good at hiding it. We'd only been living in the microscopic cell together for two days, but I felt a connection with Jag somewhere inside—somewhere I hadn't known existed until I met him.

I slid off the bed and settled onto the floor, my hip bone grinding painfully into the unyielding cement. Jag leaned over the side of the bed. "Vi?"

"Yeah?"

"I'll help you." His hand rested on my shoulder as I fell asleep.

For the first time in, like, forever, I might have been able to sleep all night, but the whirring Mechs roused me before it was light. Jag didn't stir, even amidst the creepy Mech-chatter—unusual for his light sleeping habits.

The Mechs (three of them) escorted me to an elevator

(totally old tech) and we rode to level one (at least I'd fallen asleep with my shoes on). I couldn't have managed a descender right then, so I was thankful. The doors opened into a room flooded with the whitest of lights. I squinted as the advanced tech-buzz assaulted my senses. Way more than cloudy vision, this was like going blind because someone was hacking with a sharp object from inside my head.

Several white-coated people loomed over me because I'd fallen to my knees. Something snapped in my brain, but by the time I realized what was happening, I couldn't react. They bound me at the ankle and wrist, strapped me to a stretcher, and wheeled me under even brighter lights.

They were tagging me.

"Don't move," a doctor said through a face mask. "This won't hurt if you stay still. Otherwise, I promise it will hurt."

Not afraid of trouble but terrified of pain, I stayed still. The damn transmissions had made me a chicken by the age of six.

Cold hands unstrapped my left wrist and drew a line around it with a black marker. The ink absorbed my flesh. That doctor was the foulest liar on the planet. Because the surgery skin boiled away a one-inch strip of skin. And that hurts.

Willing myself to look, I saw my tissues, tendons, and bones. No blood spilled out, controlled with the surgery skin and a hemal-recycler one of the doctors dabbed on my wrist. The blood congealed into little globs that he shook off into a tray.

Gloved fingers snapped the tag around my wrist like a bracelet, securing it with a tiny knot next to the bumpy wrist bone. Blinking sensors and a long bar code took the place of my skin.

Permanent jewelry from hell.

"No one will see it," she explained. "Only our tech. We don't want to make your life completely miserable."

"Too late," I growled.

Another doctor approached with a long needle. That did it. I thrashed and kicked and cursed. Hands restrained me, and someone slapped on another silencer.

I squeezed my eyes shut and rolled my head to the side. My heartbeat strummed in my ears and mouth. The needle stabbed hot into my wrist and the regrowing skin itched as it covered the tag.

Five minutes, and I was marked for life.

I wondered how much of this tech my dad had invented. Probably all of it. He'd had to sign off on all new inventions before they were used on the general public.

The last time I'd seen him, he'd smiled. But it had been filled with sadness and had painted pinched lines around his eyes.

He'd gone into the forest a few nights before, but he wasn't wearing his jacket when he'd hugged me good night. His long-sleeved shirt smelled like onions from dinner.

"Good-bye, V," he said.

I hadn't noticed that he'd said "good-bye" instead of "good night." I remembered the next morning when I woke up—and he was gone.

I'd searched the house for his jacket. I was late for school because of it.

The jacket wasn't there. I never did find it.

In fact, by the time I got home from school, the house had been purged of everything that belonged to my father.

But not my memory.

I could still see him if I closed my eyes and concentrated. His green eyes twinkled with sparks of gold. His trim brown hair. His ivory skin. His warm embrace that comforted me at night.

I heard him tell me he loved me. His voice was low and crackly, and filled with emotion.

A tear ran down my cheek. I made to wipe it with my tagged hand and winced at the flash of pain.

A doctor checked my wrist where the skin was still regrowing. He made a tiny note on a big electro-board and moved away. I turned my head toward the back wall.

An exit sign hung above a door radiating some severe tech energy. Jag's haunted voice filled my head. *"They're the good guys."*

I couldn't go to Freedom. Which meant I had to get to the Badlands. Somehow. Maybe I could find my dad.

He made his choice, the voice whispered, carrying a hint of empathy. Something I definitely didn't want.

I didn't care about choices right then. I didn't need that stupid Thinker to feel sorry for me. I wanted to be left alone.

Shut up! I commanded. *Get out of my head!*

The voice didn't return. At least I couldn't hear it through the swirling desperation, ill-conceived hope, and anger coursing through my body.

Doctors checked my wrist every ten minutes, making notes. Finally one of them removed the silencer and said, "Look."

My flesh had returned. I ran my fingers over it, feeling the miniscule knot that could've been part of my wrist bone. The techtricity in the tag sent a dull ache resonating up to my elbow. But whatever. I'd learned to live with the slight buzzing in my ears from the comm too.

"Learn your place, and we'll never need to use that tag," the middle Greenie said. I hadn't recognized him without the Institute robes on—but his voice was ingrained in my brain. He pulled off his face mask and glared down at me.

73

"And you're not to return to the Goodgrounds. Ever."

"I don't want to come back," I spat, the last thread of hope that I'd marry Zenn drying up with my words. But I'd be okay. I always am.

"The boy now?" another doctor asked as I was escorted away.

"No, Thane wants to do it himself. Besides, that boy won't be awake for a couple hours at least, and I'm beat. Let's rest. Then we can—" The elevator doors slid shut, cutting off his voice.

Back in the cell upstairs, Jag still hadn't woken. I lay on the floor and stared under his bed, the cement as hard as ever.

I clenched my teeth and growled, "No way in hell Thane— whoever he is—is tagging Jag."

8 Tech is an interesting thing, full of power—for good or bad. Unlike Ty and my dad, I don't have the inventing gene. But I can certainly recognize good tech when I see it. Or rather, feel it. And I'd seen and felt it in the tech-lab downstairs.

I couldn't stay here and do nothing.

Yes, you can. The voice carried a patronizing air. I really hated that. I sat up and pulled my knees to my chest, listening, hoping the Thinker would implant another thought, desperate to identify him. His voice sounded so familiar.

When no one spoke, I got up and shook Jag. He didn't respond. With horror, I realized why that doctor had said he wouldn't be awake. They'd drugged him.

I turned on the faucet and threw cold water in his face. He jerked and opened his eyes. They were bloodshot and glazed over. He said nothing, barely registering that I stood in front of him yelling his name. His eyes drooped closed again.

"No! Jag, you've got to wake up. They're gonna tag you!" I opened his gel—the smell alone could wake the dead—and waved it under his nose. "Wake up!" He stirred again, and I threw another handful of water on him.

"Finally," I said as he sat up.

"Ugnh." He rubbed his hands over his face.

"Can you stand?" I checked the corridor for guards. Empty. It had to be very early in the morning, maybe still the middle of the night.

The bed creaked as he lay down. "Give me a break," I muttered, pulling him back up. I could barely hold his weight in his drugged condition. "No. You've got to wake up."

"I don't feel so good."

"Well, too bad. They're coming to tag you, and I can't get out of here by myself." I spotted the bread he'd saved from dinner on the shelf and grabbed it. "Here, eat this. We gotta go."

As he ate, he seemed to throw off some of the fog surrounding him. I helped him stand and pace in the tiny cell to get his blood moving. *He's not sick. Everything's fine,* I thought on every turn.

He stopped and looked at me, his eyes brightening.

"How do you feel?" I asked.

A strange look crossed his face, something between wonder and fear. "You . . . I'm . . ." he said, and then shook his head. His face closed off again.

I didn't have time for his issues with, well, whatever. "Come on," I said. "You've got to pretend you're sick so you can go to the bathroom. We've got to get to the elevator."

"It won't be pretending." He sat on the bed. "We're using the elevator?"

"Yeah, I explored a bit yesterday." I didn't want to waste time explaining—or for him to know—that I'd already been tagged. "You'll have to help me with the guard."

"Sure, whatever," he said as he pulled on his shoes.

"Hey!" I yelled toward the guard's office. "Jag's sick! He's gonna blow chunks! You gotta come get him!" I shouted for ten minutes before a bleary-eyed guard came out, tucking in his shirt as he walked.

The color had returned to Jag's cheeks. He bent over to hide his grin. My face relaxed into a smile. I wiped it away as the guard slid the bars to the side. Jag shuffled forward, clutching his stomach and moaning.

The guard put his hand under Jag's arm for support. "What's wrong with him?"

"How would I know? Do I look like a doctor?"

Jag moved slowly, giving me time to edge out the door. I stood outside the cell before the guard noticed. By then, it was too late.

In one motion, Jag straightened and punched him in the nose hard enough that the disgusting crunch of bone echoed in the corridor. The guard doubled over, clutching his face as blood dripped through his fingers.

I grabbed the keys and taser from his belt. I hesitated, unsure if the taser could kill him. Jag locked his hands together and brought both fists down on the back of the guard's head. Jag dragged him into the cell, and I locked him in with shaking hands.

After exchanging a glance, we ran down the hall. I punched the down button for the elevator. It was so low-class, we didn't even need the ID card Jag had snagged from the guard.

When the doors opened to the laboratory, we pressed against the side of the elevator. With my heart in my throat, I held the Door Open button and waited.

An alarm would sound if the door wasn't allowed to close, so I took a chance. I stepped out of the elevator, crouched down, and scampered behind a long metal counter. Jag followed me, his breathing ragged. When I glanced at him, he was glowing. There I was, terrified, making stuff up on the fly, and this guy acted like he was on vacation.

"Now what?" he asked.

Thinking fast, I nodded toward the exit, at least thirty yards away. The security tech coming from the door caused bright flashes to cloud my vision.

"Where does that go?" he asked.

"Out."

"I love you," he said, and my heart stopped. He peered toward the exit, his eyes still dancing with life.

A joke. Not a funny one.

Before I could respond, Jag chuckled. "This is the most fun I've had in a long time."

"Fun? This is not fun."

Another low laugh. It reminded me of his shrug and how he said "Nice." All three were growing on me.

He cut the sound short when the elevator beeped.

As one, we stood and darted silently between operating tables and surgical carts. He had some serious sneaking skills. After we were safely hidden in the shadows beside a large bookcase, I took a deep breath, every cell in my body on fire. Three doctors entered the room, carrying electro-boards and talking softly to each other. As they moved closer, I slipped behind the bookcase. Jag followed, effectively sandwiching me between his body and the wall as well as blocking my view of the lab.

We waited for several minutes, each one notching up my nervous factor. "What are they doing?" I finally whispered.

"Sitting."

"How far away?"

"Maybe fifty feet."

"We can't wait, Jag. They were going to come get you in a couple hours."

He turned, his hands encircling my waist in the cramped quarters. I stiffened as his breath washed over my face. "How do you know?" His murmur sounded strange—smooth and rolling, with a slight pleading tone. The truth floated to my lips. I swallowed hard against the word-vomit.

"I . . . uh . . . I heard some guards talking after you went to sleep." When he didn't respond, I said, "We've really got to get out of here."

"Let's go then, but that door's gonna wail." He stepped to the door and pushed it open. An ear-splitting alarm rang, but I still heard the mental command to *Stop!* loud and clear, and I wasn't strong enough to fight the brainwashing. Both Jag and I turned back to the lab.

The middle Greenie stood next to the lab counter, wearing a frown of disapproval. I cocked my head, almost daring him to try to control me again.

He took one step before another man stood and held up his hand. He was clearly in charge here. His skin shimmered with an odd, pearly quality. I couldn't see his eyes because of the dark sunglasses he wore. His mouth moved, but I couldn't hear the words over the siren. Instead, they echoed in my mind. *Make the right choice.*

I took one step closer, recognizing the voice in my head, the voice of—

Just as I was about to think his name, it fled. My thoughts swirled. I closed my eyes, trying to retain what I knew. But no matter what I did, black spaces appeared in my memory, and when I opened my eyes, I didn't recognize either of the two men standing in front of me.

Be good, the voice said, filling the empty spaces.

I took another step, ready to join Them, prepared to do whatever They wanted.

Someone yanked on my arm. "Don't listen to the bad guys," a boy said.

I turned to look at him. His blue eyes sliced through the confusing thoughts. His bad suntanned skin screamed at me to run away. *He* was the bad guy here.

"We're leaving now," he told them. He pulled me out the door and into the crisp morning air. "Vi, come on." The use of my nickname brought back the last two days with Jag. He wasn't the bad guy here. I inhaled deeply, using the cold air to help lift the fogginess still lingering from the extreme control. My mind still felt sluggish, but at least I could think my own thoughts again.

I exited to muddy ground, my blood surging with an angry fire. My sneakers absorbed a lot of water and gunk, making my feet heavy. I slogged through a swampy area to the street, which was deserted. The sky lay silent and silver, but it brought no relief to my rage.

"Hurry, Vi." The urgency in Jag's voice told me that we didn't have much time before a search party would be dispatched. Every step ignited another angry spark in my head. I really, really hate Thinkers.

As we fled, the alarm faded. Then it stopped completely. I followed Jag as he wove between buildings, maintaining a northern course toward the Centrals. By the time we reached the border of the Southern Rim, my breath came in gasps and my back hurt. I'm a water girl, and the most I've done is (leisurely) row a boat to collect (lame) algae samples.

I clutched my side as the air pressed down around me. Surely that Thinker wouldn't just let us run away. Would he?

I ran my finger along my wrist bone, and the tiny knot of the tag jutted out like a boulder.

"Are we going to the Badlands?" I asked, coming up beside him as we ran.

"Yeah," he answered. "We can gather some supplies and head to Seaside."

"Seaside?"

"Yeah. Seaside offers political asylum to those . . . like us."

"And the Badlands doesn't?"

"The Badlands aren't completely free," Jag said. "We're loosely monitored by your government."

"Not free." The words felt foreign in my mouth, as if I'd never said them before.

"We'll be safe in Seaside, granted we get asylum."

I wondered how far away Seaside was. But safety—and gaining political asylum—sounded more than great. "We should head for the Fire Region. The heat will mask our body heat."

"Copy that."

I didn't mention the heat would also obscure the signature of the tag, which seemed to throb with the omission. "So who was that guy? He took my memory. But I know him. I swear I know him."

"That's Thane Myers."

"And who exactly is that?"

"I don't know," Jag said. It was the worst lie I'd ever heard.

"Yeah, right. You know the guy's name, but you don't know who he is?" I rubbed my forehead, wishing I could cling to the pieces of memory wafting in there. "I've heard that name."

"No, you haven't."

"And you're a terrible liar," I argued.

Jag turned toward me, frowning. "I am not. I'm a really good liar." His words rang with truth, with power. Jag Barque was more than a really good liar—he was an *incredible* liar.

"You'll have to teach me a trick or two," I said, in complete awe of his lying talent.

For some reason, his face fell. "Yeah, sure. Let's go."

A guard station and a fifteen-foot fence with sharp teeth along the top separated us from the fields of the Centrals, and only Jag had the stolen ID card from the prison guard. We dodged from building to building, and Jag kept holding me back with his arm. I swatted his hand away.

"Do you have a death wish?" he hissed.

"Do you? Stop pushing me or I'll kill you."

"Vi." He turned toward me. "You're impossible."

My irritation flared. "Thanks." I peeked around the corner and prayed we'd be able to make it through the guard station. He joined me, chuckling.

"Stop laughing at me," I said. "It's annoying."

That only made him laugh harder, and though he was quiet, his whole body shook next to mine. Our shoulders touched, and after a minute he put his arm around my waist.

If we weren't on the run for our lives, if I wasn't tagged and worried about how we were going to get to the Badlands and then all the way to Seaside, I might have been terrified at the thought of kissing him. Slowly, I placed one hand on his chest.

"Freeze!" a woman yelled.

**9.** Jag and I jumped apart like we'd been caught making out by my mother.

Two Greenies approached, their hands empty. The Hawk and Baldie.

"Perfect," Jag whispered. "You take the woman."

Instead of taking on anyone, I sprinted toward the guard station, with Jag right behind me. I found the lack of personnel odd, but maybe this area wasn't manned so early in the morning. Or maybe those two Greenies made sure there wouldn't be any witnesses to our deaths. I ran faster.

Jag passed me and swiped his stolen card across the gate reader. We squished through before it opened fully, and Jag tried to jam it while I sprinted toward the terraced crops in the Centrals. Curses and clangs caused me to glance over my shoulder. My hopes of losing anyone were dashed by the sight of Baldie running a few yards behind me and Jag still wrestling with the gate.

I made a sharp turn to my right, heading toward the imminent drop-off. I jumped at the last second, which made my landing that much harder. Rolling, rolling, I finally came to rest in a plot of bean plants. I didn't have time to feel the pain throbbing in my spine.

From the bottom of the terrace, I saw Baldie—still at the top—swipe a large stick at Jag's legs. I sprinted up the non-moving stairs, both desperate and disgusted that I had to save him.

By the time I reached the top, Jag was kneeling with his hands laced behind his head. I sparked the taser, wondering if I had the guts to use it. The blue electricity caught Baldie's attention, and Jag dove at him. I dashed forward as they wrestled. Jag threw Baldie off just before I discharged the taser into Baldie's shoulder.

He screamed as he fell. Silence. A twitch, then he lay still. I stared at him, my stomach lurching. I may break rules, but I'm not violent. My chest tightened. The air around me evaporated.

"Vi, let's go." Jag pulled on my arm. I turned and ran. Very far to the west, across the rolling wheat and beans and golden-tipped corn, the flames in the Fire Region created an orange horizon.

I started down the staircase first, only to hear a strangled grunt behind me. Then Jag smashed into me.

I'd never felt such pain, not even when the surgery skin had melted away my flesh. My head hit on the sharp corners of the steps, my back crunched against itself. Blood flooded my mouth and I gagged. Jag swore with every collision, and I would've joined him if my jaw didn't feel splintered.

Above it all, the Hawk laughed. I finally stopped at the bottom of the staircase. Silver and black flashes swam in my vision. My head felt heavy and soft at the same time. I wanted to move, but couldn't. Time slowed into breathing and pain.

"The taser." The Hawk leaned over me. I managed to lift my head. Blood ran down my face, but at least I didn't have to inhale the hot, coppery scent anymore.

Jag moaned but didn't move. Blood covered most of his face, and his left sleeve was completely stained red.

"The taser," the Hawk repeated, her hand outstretched. She towered over me, one step up on the staircase. Her silver hair shone in the moonlight.

Give her the taser, the voice commanded. *You don't need it.* My injuries made my attitude dormant, and I couldn't muster the energy to tell the Thinker that he had no right to tell me what I did and didn't need.

But if I gave up the taser, Jag and I would end up like Baldie. Unconscious. Who knew where we'd wake up—if we woke at all. But I couldn't use the taser again. Baldie's scream still echoed in my ears. His vacant eyes . . .

Give her the taser, the voice ordered again.

"Jag," I pleaded. "Get off me."

Using the sturdy metal stairs for support, he stood and wiped his bloody hands on his prison uniform. He watched me slowly extend the weapon toward the Hawk, understanding spreading through his eyes.

"No!" he yelled, hitting my arm. The taser flew in a magnificent arc into the terrace behind us. The Hawk swore and kicked Jag in the chest. He landed with a soft *thump* and didn't attempt to get up again.

Anger surged through my desperation and pain. I shook Jag's shoulder as the Hawk leaned over to inspect him.

"Vi, leave the bad boy. You're a good girl. Your father would've wanted you to be free." Her words sounded rehearsed, but she'd just given me the label I craved: free. But if being free meant leaving Jag, I couldn't do it.

Choices, choices. The voice mocked me now. In my mind, I saw the Thinker, with those dark lenses hiding his eyes. A cruel smile graced his features. He clearly controlled the situation. The Goodgrounds. The Hawk. Everyone and everything.

But not me. And not Jag.

Jag rolled over, with the tiniest curve in his lips. I ground my teeth and thrust my elbow back, right into the Hawk's beak.

She staggered backward. I grabbed Jag's arm and hauled him to his feet. I half-dragged him through the fields between the two terraces and up the steps on the other side. I didn't turn back until we made it to the top. The silver Hawk was on her feet, searching for the taser.

Like I was going to wait and see if she found it.

I ran. More like stumbled. In my delirious I've-lost-too-much-blood state, I didn't know Jag had stopped until he called my name.

I turned too fast and fell down. As far as I was concerned, it would be fine to stay there for the rest of my life. Something cold touched my head and probed in my hair. I faded out as Jag dabbed at the blood with a cloth. Then he said my name in his soothing voice. It sounded so restful, so calm.

"Don't," I slurred. "I'll fall asleep."

He stopped talking. When I opened my eyes, I wished I'd kept them closed.

"You look awful," I said. Blood oozed down his face and dripped off his jaw. He wiped it with the piece of cloth—one of his sleeves he'd ripped off.

Even though his face was smeared with blood—probably mine and his—it caused my stupid heart to pump a little faster.

"Come on," he said. "We can't stop here."

We clung to each other as we made our way toward the Fire Region. I thought it odd that hovercopters weren't circling but didn't say anything. Maybe They would just let us go. After all, I was tagged. They could find me easily if They wanted to. At least until we made it to the Fire Region and the heat obscured the signature in the tag.

The sun had crested the mountains when we came upon a lonely farmhouse in the middle of a rolling wheat field. I collapsed against the bricks, my breath burning on the way in and out. Jag unrolled a hose and sprayed himself down, yelping and dancing around in the cold water.

I wanted to laugh because he looked like such an idiot, but the thought of it made my insides hurt. When he turned the hose on me, the burning in my lungs wasn't my biggest problem.

"Hey!" The water ran red, sickening me. After my "shower," Jag traced his finger along my hairline.

"Not my hair," I said dryly.

He chuckled in his soft, sexy way. "Of course it's ruined, but it's this gash that concerns me."

"You don't look so great yourself." A long cut ran behind his left ear.

He nodded toward the back door. "You up for some rule-breaking?"

"Always," I said. "I'll get food and first aid. You get clothes, okay?"

Jag moved up the stairs and paused next to the door, peeking inside to assess the situation. He reminded me so much of Zenn, the way he took the lead, the way he seemed to have a plan for everything.

"All clear. I think this guy must already be working in the fields." Jag cracked the door and slipped into the house. Unlike Zenn, he didn't wait for me to follow, and I entered the kitchen to find it empty. I couldn't even hear Jag's footsteps—the guy had broken into houses before.

I collected the first aid kit from its regulated place under the kitchen sink. After checking it to make sure it was fully stocked, I grabbed two handfuls of protein packets and shoved them in the foil bag with the medical supplies.

The farmer didn't have any dehydrated food, so I took two bottles of water and retreated to the back porch to wait for Jag. He emerged seconds later with a backpack, and I loaded my stolen goods into it.

My head ached, and I had to wipe a trickle of blood away every so often. I leaned on Jag more than I wanted to, but he seemed to be relying on me just as much.

I thought about the night Zenn and I spent in the Abandoned Area last summer, and the way we kept each other awake by making up stories about what life would be like if we were in charge. How I missed him, but at least thinking of him helped me to keep going.

Finally I stood on the edge of a wheat field. If I took a single step, I'd be on cement. In front of us, small huts dotted the landscape, made completely of stone. No grass, no vegetation. Besides the blazing heat needed to manufacture tech, the Fire Region consisted only of concrete and technology. A buzz started behind my eyes, pulsing along the cut in painful zings. Waves of heat shimmered in the air.

Jag scouted ahead and found a small shelter next to an inactive Burning Element. We scooted inside just as the street swarmed with fire workers wearing shiny, yellow jumpsuits.

Littered with broken equipment and garbage, the shack didn't have much room for anything else. Jag kicked debris around, clearing a small space in the middle.

He knelt down and opened the backpack. Then he let

out a soft moan of satisfaction. "I'm changing right now." He pulled out an off-white shirt with long sleeves. Then he pulled out a pair of dark jeans and smiled his Jag-winner. "Be right back." He left, and I wondered where he would change.

I rummaged to the bottom of the bag, and pulled out another shirt. I cast a quick glance at the door, then pulled off the prison top and slipped into the much thicker shirt that covered my arms down to my wrists. Even with the sweltering heat, it felt like freedom. I threw my bloodstained prison pants in the corner with a pile of garbage. The shirt was cleaner, thanks to Jag's hose-down, and I tucked it back in the pack. After pulling on the slightly too-big jeans, I felt like a normal good girl. Except I was bad now. But whatever.

Jag came through the doorway and he looked fine. Really, really *fine*. His jeans looked like they'd been made especially for him and settled down around his hips. His shirt was untucked, making his waist seem much lower than it really was. His arms were bronze and muscled—and bare, because he'd pushed the sleeves up above his elbows. His skin looked warm and smooth.

He wore a necklace. Jewelry is against the rules in the Goodgrounds. Yeah, I broke that rule too, after Zenn gave me a watch for my birthday. I wished I would've worn it the day I went to see him. It would've shown him that I loved him.

But I'd never seen a boy wearing jewelry. The necklace didn't hang down onto Jag's chest, but barely encircled his throat. It looked like it choked him—almost. The white rocks were shaped like cylinders with different colored jewels alternating between them. Red, blue, purple, and orange. The gems sparkled even without a light source. Almost like an internal glow radiated from within.

He caught me gaping at the necklace. "You like?"

"It's nice, I guess," I said, struggling to remain nonchalant. "Where'd you get it?"

He laughed, the sound truly happy. "I have secret hiding places."

The heat rose to my face. I wished it wouldn't, and I covered my embarrassment with a fake coughing fit. No one should be allowed to look that hot.

A wave of guilt engulfed me. I'd been matched with Zenn. I shouldn't be looking at another guy like that. Especially not a bad one.

But my future with Zenn was as good as over. I couldn't enter the Goodgrounds again. And I doubted Zenn would leave his position of authority in the Forces and follow me to Seaside, even if I could send him an e-comm to let him know that's where I was headed.

That hurt. A lot.

Jag scanned me from head to toe. "Nice."

"What does that mean anyway?" I asked, annoyed at my stupid racing heart and how I couldn't tear my eyes off him.

He shrugged.

Damn him. Damn him to hell. I turned away and pulled out the first aid kit. I spread some cream over my cut, feeling the cooling powers of excellent meds. Wordlessly, I offered the tube to Jag and zipped the backpack closed. Lying down, I used it for a pillow and thought about how screwed up my life had become.

A lost future with Zenn.

A possibility of finding my dad in the Badlands.

And the excitement of a different future. With Jag.

Someone grips my shoulders. "Don't let them control you, son. You have no duty to them."

I blink, and the brown-haired man in front of me is whisked away by three men wearing black suits.

Someone else touches my arm. "Let's go, Jag."

I follow my oldest brother. "Blaze! What happened back there? Wait!"

But he's so much taller than me and can move faster. *It's not fair*, I think, sprinting to catch him before he rounds the corner.

I skid to a stop next to Blaze. He puts his arm around me, and I know something is very wrong. "Run home, Jag," he hisses out of the corner of his mouth.

Another man approaches. He has pale, pale skin. Like the men who just killed my father.

"Blaze, you must come with me." The man has no hair. His voice doesn't sound menacing, but filled with urgency.

I grip Blaze's hand. "No," I whisper. What if he dies too?

"Jag, go tell Pace," Blaze says. He takes a step forward, trying to shake my hand out of his.

Fear and panic combine with the hurt inside. "No!" I shout. "You can't leave!"

He turns and crouches in front of me. His eyes are glazed over. He sighs and draws me into a hug. "I must. You'll be okay. Just tell anyone who bothers you to go to hell. You'll be fine."

"Blaze," the bald man says again. "Please, you must hurry."

Blaze wipes my tears. Smiles. "Tell Pace good-bye. I'm sure I'll see you both soon enough."

"When?" My voice sounds so high. So childish. My chin quivers. Tears leak out of my eyes.

"Soon."

I watch him walk away with the Goodie. And something breaks apart inside. Something that can never be put back together.

* * *

I rolled over, gasping, feeling the pieces of Jag's shattered life as if I still lingered in his nightmare. His arm jerked and he muttered something. Something that sounded very much like, "Blaze, don't."

I sat up, drawing my knees to my chest. My hands trembled as I laid my head in them. How did I get inside Jag's head?

My stomach clenched. My head throbbed. I stumbled to the door and leaned against it.

I hated having people inside my mind, and that's when I was awake and could control what they heard and saw.

What I'd done (unwillingly, but still) was so much worse. Jag could never know.

I took a deep breath, shaking as it shuddered through my chest. I held it for a moment, before letting it out slowly and turning back toward him.

An unmarked book, bound in plain brown leather, lay on his chest. Only Jag could find time to read while on the run. I wondered how long he'd stayed up—and how he'd managed to find a book out here. I picked it up and started reading where he'd marked his place.

Technology isn't that hard to invent. All it takes is a little imagination and a lot of money. True, money can be a problem, but not in the Goodgrounds. They want the tech, and they'll pay for it.

Badlanders can invent tech too, and they should try. Maybe then the good and the bad can be reunited.

Reunited? Had the Baddies and the Goodies lived together before? Why were we separated now? Who did it? I closed the book and found the author's picture on the back cover. If his name hadn't been printed under the photo, I never would have known it was him. A strangled cry escaped my mouth and I dropped the book on Jag's chest. He jumped and grabbed my arm, his fingers closing over the tag.

I jerked away from him, covering my wrist where he'd gripped it. The ache in my arm matched the one in my heart. "Where'd you get that?"

He glanced around wildly for a second before realizing where he was. He looked a little guilty as he picked up the book. "I saw it poking out from under that farmer's bed." He studied my face. "Why?"

The answer wouldn't form. I sat all the way up, trying to get more oxygen. The shelter had grown stiflingly hot. The walls crowded in around me, the air choked on the way down.

"Vi?" he asked, sitting up and cupping my chin in his

hands. "What's wrong?" He used the soothing voice, the one that made my eyes heavy and the truth float to my lips.

"That's my dad," I said, finally getting the words out.

He examined the picture. "Lyle Schoenfeld." He looked up. "What's the problem?"

I shook my head, the mass in my throat choking me. I held the tears back as long as I could. But there were just too many, pushing, fighting their way out. I turned away from Jag before closing my eyes and letting them fall.

Jag had told me a bit about his family and life in the Badlands. He answered every question I asked and some I didn't.

I, on the other hand, had flat out refused to reveal anything about my missing father, my dead sister, or my cruel mother. And now I'd fallen apart over a book. Just great.

"Hey, it's okay." Jag grasped my shoulders and twisted me back around. I slumped into his chest, sobbing. He held me, just like Zenn used to when the world stopped spinning and I needed someone to tell me that life would go on.

10.

"Vi," Jag said when I finally stopped shaking. "Where is he?"

I pushed away from him, angrily wiping the tears that wouldn't stop. "I don't know."

Jag frowned. He opened the book and scanned the front page. "Well, this was published last year. He has to be alive."

"He's an inventor—my mom told me he went to the Badlands to search for a piece of tech. I'd always thought . . . well—" I couldn't tell him my theory about the Baddies abducting him. Because I didn't believe that anymore. "I think the Greenies must have taken him or something. I mean, that picture doesn't look like him at all, yet this was published recently."

Jag cleared his throat.

"Tell me," I said, brushing away the last of my tears.

"The Badlands published this book."

I stood up and paced toward the door. I needed time to think, to reason through what this meant. My first thought was to message Zenn. He always knew what to say when I had family issues.

"This makes no sense," I said. "If he's in the Badlands, why—why?"

"Maybe he didn't want to come back," Jag said.

I blinked, his words slicing into my heart. "If your precious Badlands are so much better, why wouldn't he take us too?"

"Maybe They wouldn't let him."

"But *why*? They wouldn't want him to invent tech for the Badlands."

"Maybe he's hiding."

"Yeah, and maybe you don't know what the hell you're talking about. My dad loves me." I glared at him, daring him to say something else that started with "maybe."

His face hardened as he clenched his jaw. He shrugged before lying down, flipping the book open and finding his place. I didn't want to fight with him—I needed him to survive in the Badlands and find my way to Seaside.

I also needed air that wasn't filled with Jag and his maybes that morphed into facts. Without speaking, I left the shack and turned away from the street. Behind the building, away from prying eyes, I composed an e-comm to Zenn.

> I miss you. I miss you so much my lungs have forgotten how to breathe. I can't tell you much, other than I'm alive and I just found out my dad is too. Or at least he was last year. This guy I'm traveling with thinks my dad left the Goodgrounds for the Badlands and lives there now. But why, Zenn? Why would he do that? Why would he leave me behind?

I erased it as soon as I finished it, knowing I couldn't message Zenn. Not only would it make him look bad, it could be traced to my location. But how I longed to hear his voice again, even if it was only in my mind.

And so I imagined what he would say in response. *Vi, I miss you like crazy. I'm glad you messaged, but you worry too much, beautiful. I'm sure your dad would come get you if he could. I dunno about the Badlands, I'll look into it . . .*

The fake conversation only served to remind me how much I'd lost, so I cut it off and took a deep breath to rid my head of the lingering fantasy. My head ached along the cut, and I felt like I could easily sleep forever. Once I returned to the shack, I dabbed some more ointment on my cut.

"Jag?"

He lowered the book, his beautiful eyes guarded.

I held up the tube. "You want me to do your cut?" That's Vi-talk for "I'm sorry." Good thing Jag understands me. He put the book down and sat up.

I spread the greasy cream onto his wound. He watched me the whole time, like he was trying to get inside my head. Surprisingly, I didn't find it irritating.

"Thanks," he said when I finished.

I picked up the discarded book and studied the picture of my dad. He had wrinkles around his eyes I didn't remember. His hair had grown as long as my mother's and a scraggly beard covered his face. He didn't look like my dad at all. Jag gently took the book from me. "We'll find him, babe. If he's in the Badlands, we'll find him."

My mind stalled on the word "babe," but I refused to let the heat rise in my cheeks. I leaned back into his body, and he wrapped his arms around me. He smelled like strength and comfort.

"Did I ever tell you about my parents?" he asked, barely above a whisper.

An image of his father blipped in my head. I couldn't tell him I'd somehow invaded his dreams. "Not much."

"They were killed by Goodie raiders. I was five." His

voice remained flat as he told me. Jag had gone shopping with his parents. In the square, Goodie raiders were scanning everyone. His parents matched what the Goodies were looking for that day.

"I should have stayed home with my brother Pace, but I convinced my parents to take me," Jag said, his voice turning hollow, frail. "My oldest brother, Blaze, was mad; he wanted to go shopping with my parents alone. When the raiders arrested them, I went wild. I shouted things, bad things. My dad broke away from the raiders and grabbed me by the shoulders. I'll never forget his eyes. Panicked and stern at the same time. He said, 'Don't let Them control you, son. You have no duty to Them.' Then he was yanked away, his hand stretched toward me still. He shouted, 'I love you! Stay true! Be yourself!' And then I watched him die."

I didn't know what to say to erase the hurt in his eyes or make his voice sound normal. So I said, "I'm sorry," and hoped that's what you say when someone tells you they watched their parents die. It didn't seem like enough, but I didn't have anything else.

Especially since I'd already seen this—in Jag's dream.

That night we went as far west in the Fire Region as we could to keep the signature of my tag concealed.

The part of me that belonged to Zenn died when we crossed into the City of Water, leaving behind a hole even wider than the one that had opened when he left the first time. Because now I was leaving him. And this time felt permanent.

Hovercopters circled above the Centrals as well as the City of Water, their spotlights sending a shiver of fear over my skin.

"Coming west was a good idea," Jag said as he knelt next to a stream.

"Yeah, no tech out here." I peered into the dense forest, hoping there weren't any wild animals either. Or rangers. Or search parties on foot.

He filled our bottles and dumped in the protein packets. He handed me one, and while I guzzled, he cupped his hands and drank from the stream, dripping water down the front of his shirt. He stood and ran his hands through his hair. I tried to focus on something besides how sexy he looked wet. My thoughts landed on the permanent jewelry in my left wrist. If the hovercopters dipped too close, nothing would mask my tag from the readers. And then Jag would know.

Wet and cold—again—I hacked my way through the wild forest, shielded from the rising sun by the taller trees. They weren't the ancients I'd read about in school, towering hundreds of feet, but stood tall enough to cast shadows and provide cover from the occasional hovercopter.

When the sun crested the horizon, Jag found an outcropping of rock, and we crawled underneath to sleep the day away. I let him hold me, telling myself it was for warmth. Yeah, I can lie to myself too.

Listening to Jag's steady breathing, I composed another e-comm to Zenn.

I'm leaving, Zenn. I'm going somewhere safe, where I can be free. If you can, come join me. We can swim and watch the sun set into the waves. I only have to make it past one more checkpoint, and then the tag won't matter. I love you.

Before I could start to cry, I deleted the message. Only the walk through this forest and the Northwest guard station separated me from the Badlands. Jag said our government monitored his homeland, but surely it'd be easier to hide there. Surely They'd be happy just to be rid of me.

That evening we drew closer to the Badlands, and Jag's enthusiasm seeped into me. I thought of my dad and what it would be like when I saw him again. Of course the sun would be shining, a golden backdrop for our reunion. He'd smile, his eyes crinkling the way they always did. Then he'd hug me the way he used to before I went to bed at night. He'd ask me about school. I'd tell him everything. How much I'd learned. How Ty had been chosen as a water ranger. How Zenn and I had been matched. Dad would listen like I was the only person who mattered, just like he always had.

And I grew excited. For the first time, leaving the Goodgrounds felt right. With these happy thoughts came hatred. Toward those who'd stolen my dad from me. Toward those who'd taken Ty. Toward that guy Thane, who'd tried to control me. I tried to push away the debilitating feelings and focus on my dad again, but I couldn't.

At least I hadn't heard any voices for a couple of days. I imagined what life would be like without rules, without a taunting voice inside my head, without scanners and readers in every doorway. The Badlands sounded better and better with every step I took.

"Tell me about your city," Jag said as we walked under the cover of trees the third night. "I feel bad we're not going through it. You could have shown me where you lived."

"You don't want to see it. It's wicked lame."

He chuckled and slid his arm around my waist. He'd been doing that a lot lately. I pressed my shoulder into his, glad he couldn't see my face through the filtered moonlight.

"Sorry I'm so cranky about it," I said. "I hated living there.

I got into a lot of trouble and broke a lot of rules trying to escape my life."

He inhaled the scent of my hair. "Mmm," he whispered. "Sorry you don't like your life."

"Didn't," I corrected. "I like it fine now." My step faltered. Had I really just said that out loud? And was it true?

He stopped walking. "I think that's the nicest thing you've ever said to me."

"Shut up. I'm nice to you." Feeling brave, I put my hands on his chest. He held my gaze as he slipped his hands under the backpack I wore and around my waist.

"I don't know what it is. You're . . ." I couldn't think of the right word that wouldn't reveal my longing. "Different."

He dropped his hands and pushed past me, his eyes reflecting a glimmer of moonlight.

"Are you mad?" I asked.

He didn't respond.

"Jag?" I trotted to keep up with him. "What did I say?"

"I get it now," he said, his voice harsh. "You only like me because I'm bad—"

"That's not true."

"—and I'm a new adventure for you," he continued, ignoring my protest. "But guess what? I'm not a pet. I'm not a sideshow. I'm not just your next rule-breaking expedition, *Violet*."

He slapped me with the use of my full name, and I stopped walking. He stomped off through the trees, leaving me in pitch blackness.

Alone.

Did I mention it was dark?

11.

On my fifteenth birthday, my mother plunked a plate of steamed cabbage in front of me. "Only one more year."

I guess that meant "Happy birthday," in cruel-mother-talk, but I didn't understand it. So I wolfed down the "meal" and escaped to Zenn's.

He gave me a watch. Not a piece of tech with alarms and cameras and voice recorders, but just a watch that I could wind when I needed to. He'd found it in the Abandoned Area and fixed it up. The arms were shaped like arrows and pointed to numerals plated in gold. It only told time, but his gift meant more to me than any expensive tech-thing. I must have started crying, because he wiped my cheeks and slid his hands up my sleeves and over my bare arms.

A forbidden touch.

His hands felt rough from his training in school. With his skin on mine, a thrill zinged through my body.

Then we kissed, sealing our commitment to each other. I remembered how warm his lips felt pressed against mine.

Why I was thinking of kissing Zenn while lost in the stupid forest in the City of Water, I don't know. Maybe because of how he'd always protected me. Or maybe because he understood my need to live an uncontrolled life.

Or maybe because he loves you.

My heart leapt in my chest. In fear. Number one, because the same stupid voice was back. Number two, because I wanted to believe it. And that hurt too much.

The day Zenn left for the Special Forces, we snuck to the edge of the forest before the sun rose. Every step was painful, because each one brought us closer to good-bye.

But he didn't say it. He crushed me in a desperate hug. I cried into his neck, staining the collar of his starchy new uniform. He cupped my face in his hands and leaned his forehead against mine.

"I'll come back," he whispered. "I promise we'll be together, okay?"

I didn't answer, because it seemed like he was trying to convince himself as much as me. He kissed away my tears and repeated himself. I thought he'd tell me he loved me. He didn't. But it was etched in the lines of his face. I felt it in his touch.

I turned around and headed back to the Special Forces compound. Back to Zenn. But every step felt wrong. The voice hissed that it was right, and I stopped.

"Shut up. Leave me alone." My words sounded so loud in the empty forest. "I'm making my own decisions now."

I stood there, breathing in and out, in and out. I closed my eyes and filled my thoughts with Zenn. His angular jaw. His warm hands. His mischievous smile.

His image was replaced by Jag and then my dad.

And I knew.

My dad was waiting for me in the Badlands. I could feel it the same way I'd once felt Zenn's skin against mine.

And Jag was, well, as close to free as I'd ever felt. I wanted to feel that way all the time, and that meant leaving the Goodgrounds.

I pivoted and ran back the way I'd come. Next week my sixteenth birthday would be in the Badlands. Possibly alone, but hopefully free.

I am going to the Badlands, I told the world, the Thinkers, anyone who was listening. Then I imagined what birthdays might be like in the Badlands. How people could make their own choices. I thought of Seaside and how I could finally be free.

Lost in thought, I stumbled and fell. Pain engulfed my knee, matching the strumming loneliness in my heart. The sun would rise soon anyway, so I curled into a ball and tried to push away the agonizing memories of my life before Zenn had been chosen for the Forces.

Sometime later, my stomach woke me. I filled my water bottle and emptied some protein granules into it, leaving just three more packets. But nothing could fill the hole inside—the one Zenn used to fill. Or the one Jag had created when he left.

A bird called, shattering the still evening air. I inhaled deeply, enjoying the crispness of the forest, the thrill of being in a forbidden place. I wondered if Jag was coming back or if he'd leave me to cross the border by myself.

Pushing him from my mind, I packed my stuff and stretched. My whole body ached from sleeping on the hard ground. The eight hours I'd spent walking, running, or sneaking every night didn't help.

I reopened my pack and dug through the first aid kit. I stuck the pain stick in my mouth. It tasted awful—bitter and chalky, though Ty had said this was a side effect because of my sensitivity to tech. But I sucked the meds for the full ten seconds. By the time I'd applied more ointment to my cut and had my bag repacked, the aches were receding.

I approached the Abandoned Area as the rising sun painted the sky gold and pink. I hurried down the hill and crawled into a decrepit mansion before the first rays of dawn peeked over the mountains.

The air inside the house smelled musty. I climbed into the attic and looked out the window toward the Badlands, half-expecting to see Jag striding forward to help me. I finally gave in and admitted that I missed him.

The earth appeared red and brown in the shadows but shone golden in the sunlight. No green fields, no major sources of water, the buildings old and broken down. Beyond that, a glimmer of sun bouncing off glass marked the real edge of the Badlands. No one lived in the settlement closest to the Goodgrounds. They don't want our transmissions infiltrating their minds.

I shivered, but for the first time it wasn't from fear of the Badlands. No, just thinking about what someone must be like to be a Thinker unsettled me. The blazing, controlling eyes of the middle Greenie flashed in my memory.

Yeah, Thinkers are not my cup of tea. At least I have that in common with the Baddies.

* * *

A guard tower on the edge of the Abandoned Area barred the way between the Badlands and the Goodgrounds. I had no ID card, and the tag would scream *Fugitive!* if I got too close to a scanner.

So, chicken that I am, I stayed in the mansion another day, brooding about Jag.

Did I really only like him because he's bad? No way I believed that. I spent most of the afternoon staring at the Badlands, thinking about him, his tortuous nightmares, and what it meant to be bad.

"It doesn't matter," I said out loud to the house.

It was so low-class, it didn't answer back. Thankfully, neither did the voice, which surely would've argued that it *did* matter.

The next night I prepared myself mentally to leave. Never to come back. Never to see my sweet Zenn again. Never be a Goodie again. If I ever had kids, they'd be bad. I almost turned around right then, prison or not.

The guards faced north into the Badlands, but the only road leading west ran right behind the station. I slipped behind it, only a few yards from the boundary. This was the closest I'd ever been to the Badlands, and my heartbeat strummed in my ears.

Just when I thought I was in the clear, an alarm sounded. The door banged open, making the beeping louder. I sprinted down the road and into the western ruins of the Abandoned Area. The buildings crowded close to the cliffs on this side of the old city, but I didn't want to hide. I had to leave, now.

Directly in front of me, the ground sloped almost straight down into a dry riverbed with a nearly vertical climb up the other side. If only I could jump ten yards, I could leap over the chasm. Yeah, I don't have any superpowers.

I also had no idea how to get down this ridiculously steep hill without breaking my neck. I started on my feet, which I found is not the right way to start. After one step, I landed hard on my butt. A landslide of rocks and dirt accompanied me down the slope. The noise added to the panic already swirling inside. My heart pounded *Get-up, get-up, get-up*.

I didn't wait for the red flashes of iris recognizers or the buzzing pack of hovercopters. I heaved myself up and climbed the other side of the hill. Rocks and dirt and dust showered to the ground behind me. My fingers bled and sweat dripped down my face. But I made it to the top.

I'd made it across the border.

I ran until I collapsed in my *I'm-invisible-and-you-can't-find-me* state, repeating the words as I tried to catch my breath. My muscles refused to move. I must have fallen asleep, because the next thing I knew, something licked my face.

12. Ty brought home a dog once. That's all it takes with my mother. She reported the incident to Them. They came and took the dog away.

Pets are against the rules, of course. Animals require care, and They only want you to care about who They tell you to care about.

Ty cried for a few days, and then she told me she didn't want a dog anyway. We were sitting next to the lake, Ty shredding a fern leaf and me feeding ducks—both illegal activities. I didn't believe her. She did want a pet. The real Ty did anyway. That night, after she fell asleep, I unclipped her link and plugged it into my comm. The brainwashing voice articulated the evils of pets and, hey, did you know dogs carry diseases?

My transmissions had been about helping my neighbors, serving my community and those weaker than me. That night I learned the transmissions are tailored for each person, each subject.

Each slave.

This dog looked exactly like the one Ty had found. Short brown fur matted with golden dirt. His pink tongue hung out of his mouth, almost as low as his floppy ears. He scratched behind one and yawned. Stinky dog breath billowed in my face. I pushed the dog away, disgusted. The transmissions said . . . I shook my head, fighting for control of my own thoughts.

I called the dog back over. "Where'd you come from?" I asked it, feeling lame. First I was talking to houses and now dogs.

The dog panted and sat.

"Nice," I said, wishing I'd chosen a different word. "Nice" belonged to Jag.

The sun had drifted a quarter of the way through the sky. I'd have to risk traveling during the day. I had to eat something soon or I would die out here. Then nobody would find me and I'd be a nobody-Baddie that nobody missed.

That's too many nobodies, even for me.

I got up and started trudging through the dirt. The dog

trotted next to me, unconcerned about lingering dust trails and possible hovercopters—which never came. We headed toward the Badlands, me talking to the dog like he understood the English language, and the dog sitting when I sat and walking when I walked. He wouldn't have abandoned me for calling him "different." Didn't Jag know different was good?

Obviously not.

I pounded my anger into my footsteps as I passed building after derelict building. Most of them sported charred wood and twisted metal. This area had been abandoned during the fires and never rebuilt. In a few places, the fire ranger rings still shone on the cracked stones.

The powdery red dirt coated my shoes and the back of my throat. Without a hat, my face was burned by the time evening settled in. Without food, my legs trembled and the horizon blinked between white and sunset.

Lights shone a few miles ahead when I found a stream. Forgetting about purification, I practically inhaled that water. It felt cool against my inflamed neck and ears, and I decided that wearing a hat was actually a decent rule.

Green shoots poked through the soil. Dirty purple bulbs came up, and I hardly rinsed them before crunching them down. They tasted like soap and Jag's hair gel, with a little onion thrown in.

I didn't complain. I lay on my back, looking at the sky. When I was a child, my dad had told me stories about how he used to wish on the stars. I'd been mesmerized and wanted to wish on the brightest one.

"Can I fly up there and touch it? I could make a wish on the way back down."

"You can't, V," he'd said. "Nobody can fly. And there's no use wishing for things that won't come true."

"Who says they won't come true?"

"Violet," Dad said, crouching down and looking into my eyes. "You must learn to be satisfied with what you're given."

I just looked at him.

"Sometimes life doesn't allow us to be free to fly wherever we'd like. Do you understand, honey?"

"Yes," I said, my voice small. Dad smiled, took my hand, and walked me home, careful to let go before any of the neighbors could see and report that we'd broken the no-touching rule.

But now I wasn't satisfied with what I'd been given. I wanted more. I wanted to be free to wish on the stars and eat ham (if I could find it).

In memory of my dad, I wished on the brightest star. A single tear trickled over my cheek. Just as quickly, I wiped it away, determined to find him here in the Badlands.

If you can, the voice whispered in my ear.

I sat up, fear pounding in my ears. Suddenly, under this wide-open sky and without any transmissions hanging in the air, I paired the voice with a person. The man who'd spoken to me in the lab where I'd been tagged was the same man who'd been inside my head since the day I went to meet Zenn.

Thane Myers had followed me. The darkness settled over me like a thick blanket, and it took a long time to fall asleep.

The next morning I woke up alone. Great. Dogs couldn't even stand my company. I chomped through a couple of bulbs, filled my water bottle, and by afternoon, stood on the edge of the Badland city. I wondered if Jag would saunter by with his real friends, his sun-stained skin glinting in the petering light, his mouth curved up in his trademark smile.

He didn't.

My hair was wilder than the teens here. Sure, theirs was on the short side, and they didn't hold back in the color department. Red, orange, bleached, they had it all. No wonder Jag liked my jet-black do—no one had hair exactly like mine.

I watched the Baddie teens roam the streets, living their own lives, free from the imposing rules of a Thinker. From anyone, really. What would it be like to live that way? To live without the guilt of breaking rules and disappointing my mother?

I didn't know.

Bad girls wore plenty of earrings. Guys could keep the gel factories in business by themselves. Couples held hands, and one boy pulled his girlfriend close and kissed her on the cheek. She tucked her hand in his back pocket as they walked down the street.

Standing on the outside, I realized something. The Baddies aren't bad because of their skin or the way they do their hair or even because of the revealing clothes. They're bad because they're uncontrolled.

They're bad because that's what I'd always been told.

A boom rocked me from my thoughts. My inner criminal urged me to run. I hid behind a cluster of rocks on the outskirts of town, expecting hovercopters, red iris recognizers, and a swarm of Special Forces agents to descend around the plume of smoke rising into the sky.

Of course nothing like that happened. A car approached, with its orange lights blinking lazily. Two men wearing blue uniforms with low-class tech lights on their sleeves questioned a few people before cleaning up a blackened mess of burnt wrappers. One said, "Firecrackers," but I had no idea what that meant.

No intimidation. No threats. I'd been arrested for *walking in the park*. Apparently in the Badlands, you can blow things up and then get a coffee. I wasn't sure if this signaled freedom or chaos.

I crouched behind the rock until the officials drove away. My joints and muscles groaned as I straightened. Tonight looked like another starry sleep.

Until I heard a voice behind me. "Vi! You made it!"

13.

Jag grabbed my hand and pulled me forward. He hugged me, smelling of soap and fresh summer air. I wanted to bury my face in his chest and inhale him right down to my toes. Instead, I pushed him away. The light was not so gone that he couldn't see my glare. I certainly noticed his perfectly styled hair.

"I'm so glad you made it across the border." I folded my arms and focused on the horizon. "By yourself."

"Come on, Vi, don't be mad." He smiled slyly, like he knew I wanted to slobber all over him.

"You're a high-class jerk," I said. "You *left* me!"

He had the gall to shrug.

"Don't you dare *shrug*!"

He took an uncertain step forward that he should have taken backward.

"Stop," I said. He'd left me in the woods—alone—to cross the border into the scariest place of my life—alone. "You. Promised." I shoved him in the chest with every word. "You. Said. You'd. Help."

"Vi—"

"Don't 'Vi' me," I snapped. "Why don't you use my whole name?"

Jag opened his mouth to say something, then shut it.

"Spill it, Barque," I said.

His mouth opened again. He squeezed his eyes closed and clenched his fists. "Look, you said I was different." When he opened his eyes, his glare could've cut holes through me.

"You are." I stepped closer to him, and this time he moved back. "It's not a bad thing, Jag."

"It is to me."

"Well, maybe you're mental."

"Maybe *you* are." He paused, and I took a swing at his pretty face.

He grabbed my wrist before I made contact. "Violet, don't." His voice became soft and full of apology. "I've been looking for you for two days."

"That sure makes me feel better." I tried shaking off his

grip. He chuckled, but I wanted to stay mad. "Jag, don't you get it? I told you my life was better, because of—and then you left me."

"I know, I came back. You were already—"

"What was I supposed to do? Wait around for you? You deserve to . . . to . . . I don't know what, but something really, really bad." My voice cracked, totally ruining the threat.

"Please don't be mad." His words wrapped around me like a quilt. My anger faded, replaced by relief. Jag was here. He'd find me somewhere to sleep and something better than gel-flavored tubers to eat. Everything would be okay now.

He released my hands as we sat on one of the rocks. The silence was comfortable. It seemed like no time had passed, we'd never been apart, and he hadn't abandoned me to cross the border by myself.

"You want me to fix your hair?" he asked. I interpreted this as Jag-speak for, "Please forgive me, you're the most beautiful creature I've ever met. I'm so, so sorry, and I'll do anything if you'll let me kiss you later."

"Sure." I sat on the dusty ground in front of the rock with him behind me, his knees gently pressing into my arms. Jag's touch sent a thrill from the top of my head to my throat, where my breath caught. When he finished, he put his hands on my shoulders.

"I'm sorry." His words in my ear made me shiver.

"Me too," I said, getting up before I turned to total mush. "I didn't know different meant bad."

"Let's just forget it, okay?"

"Forget what?"

He laughed—exactly the way Ty used to when I did that to her—and took out the first aid kit. "Let me doctor you up."

As he spread cream over my burnt face and checked the status of the cut along my hairline, I watched him. Conversations passed between us, things we couldn't say out loud but that patched up all the holes in the silence.

When he finished, he carefully laced his fingers through mine. "Come on, I'll show you what my city is like."

Holding hands with Jag was nice. He'd touched me lots of times, but he'd never taken my hand and held on skin to skin. The transmissions are crystal clear. No human contact past age eight, until you're married. That rule is the first imprinted, starting at age three, when the transmissions become mandatory.

I'd hugged my dad before he'd left. He broke the rules, at least when no one else was around. And Zenn had held my hand and kissed me. But always in secret.

Jag pointed to things with his free hand while we walked. People sat on curbs or benches, chatting. Some of them ate at outdoor cafés, or loitered on emerald green grass with blankets and pets and friends.

In the distance, houses stretched in neat rows of straight streets. Orange lights showered each corner, continuing as far north as I could see. There were more Baddies than I'd ever imagined, but the people milling about didn't seem that bad to me.

I kept glancing from face to face, hoping to find one that looked like my dad. No one paid any attention to me, and none of them looked remotely familiar. I gave up the search and tried to decipher the things Jag said. Some of it made sense, like, "That's where I used to sit and feed the ducks when I was little." He pointed to a small white-brick building. "That's where we get mail."

"Like e-comms?"

"Yeah, but no. We have some tech, phones and computers and stuff, but nothing like your comm. Mail is like, a message on paper."

Several people came out with white paper squares in their hands. A girl with spiky red hair laughed when she looked at hers. Then she ripped it open, and I looked away. Didn't she know how many trees it took to make paper? Didn't she know most of the trees had burned in the fires?

Even as I thought these things, I wondered if they were

true. I was making a judgment based on projections I'd seen in school about papermaking and logging. But I'd also been shown what prison was like, and that had been wrong. Maybe everything I'd been taught was a lie.

Could everything be different from what I knew? *Different, different, different.* In the Goodgrounds, I'd longed to be different. Here, I wanted to blend.

Without thinking, I reached over and traced a fingertip up Jag's arm. He stopped speaking midsentence and gaped at me. The shocked look on his face felt like a slap. I pulled away. Good girls don't touch boys, not even good ones. And Jag wasn't good.

He reached out and tucked my hair behind my ear. "Hey, you just surprised me. You can touch people here. It's okay."

Something inside crashed and burned. I don't know what. Maybe it was the shock of leaving the only life I'd ever known. Or maybe because deep inside I've always wanted to be a bad girl, but actually becoming one hurt too much.

I shook my hand out of his. He looked like he'd been punched. I wanted to apologize, but the words wouldn't form in my mouth. Somehow he understood, because he flashed his Jag-winner smile and clasped his hands behind his back.

I fell in step beside him. He continued talking about the buildings we passed. "We sometimes watch movies in there."

Pictures—printed on paper—adorned the bricks. I stared at women wearing tops with no sleeves, men with guns, and two people who had their hands all over each other. I couldn't look away.

"Movies?" I choked out.

"Yeah, they're like really long TV shows."

"TV shows?"

Jag's face shone with happiness, and the next thing I knew, his hands slipped around my waist. We stood too close, touching all along the front of our bodies.

"Like your projections," he said softly, tipping his head down. He moved his hand to my wrist and pushed my sleeve up as far as it would go. "Virgin skin," he whispered.

Jag pushed the other sleeve up, staring at that arm too. The last of the sun warmed my skin, and I liked it—too much. I'd stopped listening to the transmissions. I'd walked in the park—with a boy—after dark. I'd pulled plenty of pranks, but I had never allowed the sun to touch my skin.

I felt dirty.

Now Jag was touching my bare skin, rubbing both his hands up and down. They felt as dangerous as the sun. A shiver ran through my body.

"Sorry," he murmured, stepping away. I quickly pulled my

sleeves down, feeling the heat from his touch build in my face.

"You're almost one of us, you know." He shoved his hands in his jeans pockets. "All you need is a new shirt and some tanned skin."

He was right. People stared at me in the Goodgrounds because of my hair. Here, I stood out because of my covering clothes and the milky skin they hid.

Two girls walked by, their fingers flying over their phones. Something beeped, and one girl squealed. She showed the screen to her friend. Both of them threw their heads back and laughed in a way I'd only heard from Jag. Uncontrolled.

The girl who'd gotten the message started typing in a response. She wore a short skirt and knee-high boots. Her sleeveless shirt revealed golden skin that didn't look as rough as Jag's. Every strand of her shoulder-length hair was a different color. Bleached, brown, red, black, even a streak of purple.

The other girl had bright pink hair. I liked it and wondered what she'd used for dye. Her beige shorts could barely be counted as a piece of clothing. She'd tied the bottom of her green shirt in a knot. Her dark skin was natural, not tanned from the sun.

"You gonna walk by without saying hello?" Jag asked.

The girl with the multicolored hair looked over, and her face split into a grin. "Jag!" She launched herself at him and he caught her around the waist, her legs wrapping around his torso as he lifted her off the ground. They seemed to blend into one person. I watched, torn between envy at their relationship and longing to see Zenn so I could hug him like that.

"You got out," she said once he set her down. She pocketed the phone and kept her hand on his shoulder.

He shrugged. "This is Vi," he said, indicating me with a wave of his hand. It lingered for a moment, like he expected me to grab it. I didn't. The girls appraised me, scanning from my blue-black hair to my sunburned face to my ridiculously long sleeves.

Jag pointed to the girl wearing the hideous boots and sporting the rainbow-colored hair. "Vi, this is Sloan," he smiled at the pink-haired girl, "and Indy. My friends."

The smile Indy gave him in return looked a lot more than friendly.

"Hello," I said. (Yeah, I can be polite when the situation calls for it.)

"A Goodie? You brought another Goodie with you?" Sloan's wide eyes flicked back and forth between me and Jag.

"Shut up, Sloan. She's almost bad," he said, defending me.

He spoke in a voice I'd never heard before. Casual, light. No pleading tone, no sexy undercurrent. Nothing that would cure insomnia. He wasn't the Jag I knew at all.

"*Another* Goodie?" I raised my eyebrows.

Jag shrugged again. I walked away, my polite-meter on empty. When I reached the end of the street, Jag, Sloan, and Indy had formed a tight triangle.

Jag gestured with his hands, his eyes wide and his mouth moving fast. He was spilling. Maybe I'd misinterpreted his Jag-speak earlier.

I expected him to have friends, but I didn't think they'd be girls. Jealousy burned in the back of my throat no matter how hard I swallowed. With it came the disturbing thought that maybe Jag hadn't told me the truth. Certainly not all of it.

My anger uncoiled, rocketing into full-blown rage when Thane spoke in my mind, *He's bad, and you're not. You made the wrong choice.*

I almost believed him. Which infuriated me even more. I narrowed my eyes and looked down the street, thinking that somehow I'd see Thane standing there.

People crowded onto the sidewalk as they left the movies, and I lost sight of Jag.

"Hmm, you look different," someone said from behind.

"Different" echoed in my ears as I turned around. "Different" definitely meant bad.

The bald man stood in front of me. The man who took Jag's brother.

The same man I'd tased and left for dead. Judging from the look on his face, he remembered.

14.

"No," I said, backing away.

Baldie's face broke into a cruel smile. "Where's Jag?" He scanned the crowd, his plastic grin cemented in place. I edged into the mass of bodies, pretty sure I could lose this guy in a footrace. Baldie flipped out a red iris recognizer and activated it. I squeezed my eyes shut and shoved my tagged wrist in my pocket as I turned and ran.

Screams and pounding feet echoed around me as the Baddies scattered. Yeah, the glare of a recognizer has that effect. People bumped into me, and I opened my eyes. An unearthly crimson glow illuminated the street in front of me.

My dad had told me about Moses parting the Red Sea so the Israelites could pass through on dry ground. That's what I thought about as I pushed through the crowd. Miraculously, they cleared a path. I ran through the gap, willing it to close behind me so Baldie couldn't follow.

Jag and his friends were gone.

The buildings along the unmoving sidewalk were dark and the sky bled that unsettling shade of charcoal. What if I couldn't find Jag? Sleeping alone in the forest in the Goodgrounds was one thing. Sleeping alone in the Badlands with a maniac Greenie after me was quite another.

Deciding alone was better than caught, I joined two guys as they sprinted toward the stream.

"Vi!" Jag stepped forward and pulled me into a doorway on the outskirts of the city. Sloan and Indy had disappeared.

"That bald guy is here!" I crumbled into him.

"Shh!" He peered around the corner. The light grew brighter, turning his face the color of blood.

He pushed me further into the shadows. The bricks were cool and biting, even through my thick shirt. Jag stepped in front of me, the red light almost upon us. Recognizers can't detect temperature, only irises and electronic devices. I could only hope Baldie wouldn't pass by close enough to pick up the bar code in my tag.

"This is bad," Jag whispered. Without warning, his body

pressed against mine, all the way from foot to shoulder. "Don't move." He looked over his shoulder, the red light pulsing now. My heart sped up. I closed my eyes and inhaled sharply. Both good things.

Because he kissed me. He wrapped his arms around my body and rubbed my back. The tag was sandwiched between his stomach and mine, also good. His body heat combined with mine, and everything felt too hot.

Maybe the temperature rose when he ran his hands through my hair. Or maybe because of the salty taste of his lips on mine. He kissed me long after the danger from the recognizer had passed. I had no complaints. In fact, I kissed him back, my free hand automatically moving to touch his cheek.

When he stopped, I took a deep breath.

"Nice," he said breathlessly.

Yeah, that didn't even begin to cover it.

"I think it worked." Jag moved to the corner of the doorway. I forgot about the red light of death. What did he mean by "it worked"?

"Come on." He stepped into the street and squeezed my hand hard. "Can you run?"

"Do you think I arrived on a hoverboard?"

He cocked one eyebrow before leading me through darkening neighborhoods. He turned down a deserted sidewalk with a small screen at the end.

"Hey." I slowed in front of the terminal. "This sidewalk used to move."

"Yeah," he said. "That's why I was in the Goodgrounds last time they caught me. You saw the picture."

I frowned. "That one with all the Goodies around you?"

"Yeah."

"Did you get the tech to fix this?"

"No. Come on, my place is just down here." He turned toward a single-story house with a sliver of golden light falling through the crack in the door. Jag suddenly stopped at the top of the steps.

"Oof," I said as his muscled arm whacked me in the ribs.

He pushed lightly on the door with two fingers. It swung in too easily, revealing a long hall with all the lights on. Bright tech lights. Voices floated toward us, soft and slurred.

Jag didn't breathe. "Stay here."

"Yeah, right." I clutched his arm as the white spots crowded in my vision from the increased tech.

Jag's eyes softened and his lips turned upward. "What? You'll miss me too much?"

Blushing, I looked away. The darkness seemed thicker since I'd been staring at the lights.

"Vi, this is my house. It's fine. My roommates are just having a party."

"You're wrong. You go in there, you won't come out."

He smiled, the way a parent does when their child says they've seen a ten-foot monster covered with brown fur.

"I gotta have my phone. I'm dying without it. We need supplies for the trip to Seaside. I'll be right back. Promise." He wrenched his hand out of mine and stepped through the door.

That's pretty bad. You should never go into the light. Especially tech-induced light.

15.

As I stood in the darkness, watching Jag disappear into the light, I remembered the time my dad told me about light and dark and how God had separated them. I didn't get what he meant then.

But as Jag's front door swung closed with a loud click, the light was separated from the dark. That's when I realized that someone can't be both good and bad, just like darkness can't exist in the light.

Which meant I had to make a choice.

Bad or good? looped endlessly in my mind. Another voice joined mine, taunting.

Leave me alone! I commanded, and Thane's voice receded. The thought of him possibly listening to my every thought unnerved me.

I sat on the steps, determined to keep Thane out, to regain control of my own mind.

Noise-that-must-be-music filtered from the back of the house. Jag's roommates had a serious party raging. I waited through four songs.

Then five. Then six.

Jag didn't come back.

So I allowed myself to freak out. Which basically means I crept around the side of the house with my heart leaping in my chest. The music grew louder, with people gyrating and laughing in the backyard. I crouched below the only lit window. I took a deep breath and peeked inside.

I knew Jag shouldn't have gone in. Because now the stupid boy was tied to a chair.

I stared a lot longer than I should have, mostly because his bare—and sculpted—chest distracted me. After that initial shock, I noticed the two round labels secured on either side of his breastbone. Tech monitors. A green light flickered on one. So far, whatever he'd said was the truth.

His kiss still lingered on my lips, and his scent was

embedded in my Goodie shirt. I wanted to help him, but I had three great reasons not to.

Baldie, the Hawk, and a Mech.

The Mech must have sensed me, either my body heat or the bar code in the tag, because an alarm wailed.

I ducked and ground my teeth together. Stupid Mechs. I was so sick of them ratting me out for merely existing. I hated that they could sense body heat. I despised them for their ability to read bar codes. For everything.

All the anger and fear and desperation raging inside flooded to the surface. I focused on the mechanics of the robot now standing at the window. The siren pounded in my brain.

Stop! I screamed inside.

And it did.

I suddenly felt like I needed to puke my guts out. But I didn't have time for that. Baldie's shout mingled with the Hawk's as they burst out the back door.

Ignoring Thane's voice in my head, which said, *Leave Jag. Save yourself. Don't make the wrong choice—again,* I crawled through the window. Thane's encouragement to leave Jag made me that much more determined to stay together. Maybe Thane needed us to be separated before he could make his next move.

Maybe I'm not the monster you think I am.

Thane's words jumbled up my feelings. He could clearly control others, and I'm definitely not a fan of Thinkers. But with Thane on the inside, protecting me . . . having him on my side would be beneficial.

In the room, I fell hard on my knees next to the despondent Mech, overwhelmed by the amount of tech in the house. It felt like someone had thrown a bucket of ice water in my face. My breath didn't fill my lungs. A hand scrabbled on my backpack and I jerked away.

"Stop!" I commanded. Baldie's eyes glazed over, fogging as if made of glass. I saw the Hawk's big beak before she turned and moved toward the backyard.

Scrambling across the room, I punched the low-class lock on the door. So useless. One good kick would bring it down. And I've seen the way the Hawk kicks.

"Jag?" I knelt and began untying his hands. "Holy tech overload." My fingers fumbled on the tight filament knots. The air-conditioning billowed over my neck, mingling with the tech-burn inside my chest. I felt like I was trying to undo knots of thread with winter gloves on.

"You were right," he said.

I didn't answer. Of course I was right.

"How did you know?" he asked.

"I'm a Goodie, remember?" It doesn't take a Thinker to figure it out. Oh, and all the tech buzz was a dead giveaway. The sound of the machines grinded in my head. The smell of Jag's spicy gel was so strong, I thought I might vomit.

I finally released the knots on his hands and he started working on his feet. I tiptoed over to the door. Footsteps approached.

"Hurry!" I hissed, passing him as he stood. He opened the window all the way and pushed me through headfirst. That didn't hurt nearly as bad as having Jag land on my stomach, forcing all the air out of my lungs. Or his boot on my thigh as he pushed himself up.

"Ouch!" I complained. The door rattled and the Hawk's angry shout filtered through the window.

"Come on!" He didn't have to tell me twice. We ran as the door splintered open.

I gripped Jag's hand as we wove through backyards and deserted streets. After a few minutes he grunted as he ripped the electronic patches off his chest. I expected a siren to wail or red lights to flash, but nothing happened.

Pretty soon we left behind the houses and streetlights and ran under nothing but trees. If it could be any darker in the forest, it was. Jag half-dragged me beside him as he somehow maneuvered over the uneven ground. Branches and limbs scratched my face and clawed at the mostly empty backpack, but I pushed them away.

I'd spent days in the woods while crossing through the City of Water, but the forest here felt scarier. Darker. Dangerous.

My lungs burned, and my legs felt detached from my body. "Jag," I gasped, leaning against a tree trunk. "I gotta stop."

"Just a little further," he whispered.

I shivered as the chilly air brushed my face, turning the sweat into liquid ice.

Jag pulled me against his bare chest; his heart thumped against my arm. I tried to calm myself. The woods frightened me, but what I felt was not fear. More like pure anticipation for the next time Jag would kiss me, hold me like he'd held Sloan, put his feet in between mine so our knees touched and we connected along every point of our bodies.

Yeah, I was falling for Jag Barque.

He led me to the largest pine tree on the planet. By way of instruction, he gestured up. As if that were adequate.

"We're climbing a tree?" I asked.

"Only about halfway."

Heights are not my thing. Privileged to have a teleporter on our block, I never needed to learn how to ride a hoverboard. The only time I'd been in the air was in the hovercopter, and that wasn't a memory I wanted as I climbed this very tall tree.

Jag moved faster than me but waited as I struggled to find footholds.

"No, try that one," he whispered, tapping on my left elbow and pointing to a branch I couldn't see.

We progressed up the tree little by little until I felt like the air was too thin to breathe. On the next reach, my hand hit solid wood. A tree house.

"Did you make this?" I was whispering. Because someone is always listening.

"My brother did, a long time ago." He sounded tired as he stepped onto the platform.

I wondered which brother—Blaze or Pace—but of course I didn't ask. The tree house had four walls and a roof, but no windows and only a small opening in the floor for the entrance. Jag could stand upright in it, though. He pulled a blanket from the corner, shook it, and lay down.

He opened his arm for me to join him, but I remained standing near the entrance.

"It's gonna get cold and there's only one blanket," he said. I translated that to, "I'm a nice guy, but not that nice."

I wanted to sleep next to him. Too much. But good girls don't throw themselves at boys. Especially bad ones. How did

Jag feel about me? He'd kissed me, but only so the recognizer couldn't scan our eyes. Right?

And what did a kiss mean in the Badlands? Because in the Goodgrounds it meant something. It meant you'd committed yourself to someone. The way I'd pledged myself to Zenn.

I pulled my backpack off, found the blue prison shirt, and tossed it to him.

"Hey, you kept this?"

I gave a shrug he didn't see because he was pulling the shirt over his head. I couldn't get my voice to speak coherent words anyway.

He yawned and lay down again. "Vi? Come on, please? I know I'm gross, but—"

"You're not gross," I said, sitting down next to him. My skin itched to touch his, and his plea indicated that our kiss meant something to him. Still, my mind screamed to maintain a respectable distance.

"Well, I've been sweating up a storm for an hour."

"I want to, I'm just . . ."

"Nervous?"

More like scared as hell. "I guess."

He pulled me down next to him. "That's rubbish," he said, his lips in my hair. "You stood in a cold shower for two hours. You elbowed that woman last week. You crossed into the Badlands by yourself without getting caught. You don't get nervous about anything. You can lie next to a sweaty guy."

I tried to tell him that wasn't it. That I really wanted to lie next to him, sweaty or not, but the words wouldn't come.

"Ah," he said, throwing his other arm over me and adjusting the blanket so it covered us both. "You're warm." He spoke in a drowsy tone, comfortable, happy.

His lips were so close—right at my ear. A shudder that had nothing to do with the cold ran through my body. Jag pulled me closer, nestling his arm under my elbow.

"Jag?"

"Mmm?"

"What's gonna happen now?"

"We're going to sleep." He sounded like he was already halfway there.

"Yeah, but what about tomorrow?" What I really wanted to say was, *What about finding my dad? What does Thane Myers want with us? When are we leaving for Seaside? We can't stay here.*

"It's not important."

I twisted to look at him but found only blackness. "How can you say—?" His mouth met mine, cutting me off.

"Only you're important," he murmured, his breathing deep

and even on my cheek, his thumb tracing circles on my arm.

The bad boy is right, the voice mocked. *You're very important. What will you choose to do?*

I silenced it, determined not to answer Thane, the stupid Thinker who still believed he could control me.

Yeah, he can't.

**16.** I pace as I wait. The room is all polished wood and red velvet. *Where is he, already?*

My brother, only a few years older than me but with long silver hair, laughs. "Relax, Jag."

"I *am* relaxed, Pace," comes out of my mouth in a growl.

A door opens and there he is. Blaze. Older. Wiser.

Shock coats my brain. "Blaze." My feet force me to move forward, and then suddenly I'm running.

"Little bro!" Blaze crushes me into a hug. My breath leaves my body, taking with it all my fear and pain. "Wow, you're huge."

I chuckle. "And you're not as tall as I remember."

"Well, you've grown over the past eight years. I haven't."

"Sure, whatever." I take in his dyed black hair, his square

jaw, his blue robes. "What's with the costume?"

"I'm Assistant Counselor. Didn't Pace tell you?"

I glance at Pace, who swipes his hand across his face real quick. "No, he didn't mention it."

Blaze places his arm around my shoulder, just like he used to when I was a kid. "Don't worry. We're still active in the Resistance. In fact, that's why Pace brought you here." He slides me a quick look. "How about you move here?"

The thought of living in Seaside—with Blaze—has me giddy. I try to straighten my smile and find I can't. Pace has accepted his position in the tech rangers and feeds me regular reports. Blaze is safe in Seaside, almost a full-blown Thinker. His information will be invaluable. And my friends in the Badlands . . .

I sigh. "I can't. With Pace gone, I'm leading the Resistance now."

Blaze drops his hand and pivots to face Pace. "What? He's twelve years old."

"Thirteen," I say.

"He can't lead the Resistance." Blaze folds his arms, his voice firm and parental.

I open my mouth to tell him to go to hell, that I can do whatever I want, when Pace says, "He's been doing fine for the past eight months."

"Yeah," I say.

Blaze faces me and squints, like he's trying to see through me. "You'll die if you don't get out of that place."

"He's already established a spy in the Goodgrounds," Pace says. "The other members aren't much older than him, Blaze. Let this go."

Blaze's fists clench. He's about to go all older brother on me. "Like Pace said, I've got contacts in the Goodgrounds no one else would've been able to get. *Because* of my age."

The fight leaves Blaze's eyes. He puts one hand on my shoulder. "You're thirteen." He means more than that. He means he misses me and wants to protect me. He means he's sorry for abandoning me after Mom and Dad died. He means he wishes it didn't have to be this way.

I put my hand on his shoulder. "I know."

Blaze studies the floor and then focuses on me. "Who's the spy?"

I grin. "Cool cat by the name of Zenn Bower."

"No!"

Blaze's shout didn't wake me. Mine did.

Meager light filtered into the tree house. My heart pounded in my chest, my ears, my mouth.

I couldn't get Zenn's name out of my head. Or Jag's voice saying it.

Or the words "the Resistance." Zenn never mentioned anything about any Resistance. And I didn't think we kept secrets from each other.

But I couldn't e-comm Zenn—and asking Jag? No way. I was determined to keep my jaunts into his private memories filed away in the corner of my mind labeled *Classified*.

A shiver shook my shoulders, as much from the cold as from the lingering weirdness of entering Jag's mind. I rubbed my hands over my arms, trying to warm up.

I jumped when Jag rolled in his sleep, muttering. Grateful I wasn't living his nightmare anymore, I tucked the blanket around his shoulders.

After he settled back to sleep, I couldn't get a breath that wasn't full of his scent, of Zenn's name coming out of his mouth. I had to get out of there, so I climbed down from the tree house. I stretched, yawned—and felt the tech buzz. My mouth watered, like I'd eaten something sour. This was a new tech side effect. And the cause came from more than just a cell phone.

I rubbed my hands over my arms, trying to decide what to do. Going toward the tech-buzz seemed suicidal. But retreating to the tree house where I'd be susceptible to Jag's innermost thoughts wasn't an option either. *Choices, choices,* I thought. I was so sick of making choices.

I crept toward the tech, keeping close to the trunks of the trees. Daylight filtered through the forest, and I could smell the pitch from the trees, hear the scuttling of insects in the leaves, and see the dust hanging in the sunlight. My skin crawled with anticipation.

When I finally peered around the last tree, my breath caught in my throat. The sun was just rising over the mountains. It would hit the valley last. Where the facility stood.

The tech facility.

My mind raced. What if my dad was down there? He surely knew of this place if he'd come here for a piece of tech. The structure looked at least seven years old.

Only one road led to the building. One way in = one way out = easier to guard. A tall fence surrounded the property, with towers in each corner. Badlands or not, a facility like this would have guards equipped with the latest weapon-tech and dressed in various shades of beige. Heat-sensing optical-alterations would be mandatory, as would the willingness to tase before asking questions.

Without realizing it, I'd stepped out into the open, staring, shocked. Until I heard a voice, coming from further down the tree line.

". . . still here, Elli. Where else would they go?"

"Cam, look. We searched all night. We can scan for them inside."

I scooted behind the tree real fast when I recognized them as Baldie and the Hawk.

"We won't be able to," Baldie snapped. "Jag didn't get tagged, and Vi's isn't activated yet."

I rubbed my *inactive* tag, wondering what that meant. The alarm at the border had gone off, I assumed because of the tag. But if it wasn't activated, what would've triggered the alarm?

"Whose job was that?" the Hawk asked, adding her question to mine.

"Thane wanted to do it. We didn't know she could get out."

The Hawk tossed her silver hair over her shoulder and stopped walking. "Everyone should've known about her. She broke the tech in the bathroom. Advanced tech. And she *broke* it with water. Her file from the Association is very specific. How could Thane, of all people, underestimate her?"

I leaned into the tree further, ignoring the bite of the bark against my palms. I'd always known Thane was the one in charge. Why did he want to personally do everything? Surely he had minions for that. Yeah, he had a specific purpose for me, and I wondered what juicy tidbits I'd find in my file. I didn't even know I had one at the Association, which surely wasn't a good thing.

Doesn't plug into the transmissions. Cuts and dyes her hair. Can feel tech. But her match—

With the thought of Zenn, I wished he was here so I could ask him about the Resistance, about Thane, about everything. He always had the right answers.

Maybe Thane needed me to get to Zenn. Maybe Thane needed me to get to Jag, to the Resistance.

Maybe his purpose for me isn't bad. I couldn't believe I'd thought that all by myself, but there was no voice, no Thinker, in my head. Maybe my tag hadn't been activated on purpose so that I could escape easier.

With all my inner musings, I didn't realize how close the Hawk and Baldie had moved, until I heard, "We must take our time, get them to trust us—" Baldie cut off and looked over his shoulder.

I slinked further around the tree so they wouldn't see me. Baldie pushed the Hawk into the trees as another voice registered in my ears.

Jag. Calling my name.

Stupid boy. Moving through the forest was not a silent business. I couldn't run for it, meet Jag, and tell him to shut up already. The Hawk and Baldie hid only one tree over. I wished on a star, even though there weren't any out. *I wish they would leave. Please let them leave.*

"Come on," Baldie said. "Now's not the time." He and the Hawk ran toward the edge of the hill and disappeared over the ridge.

I thrashed through the undergrowth toward the sound of Jag's voice. "Hey!" I hissed, coming up behind him.

"There you are." His eyes harbored panic. "Don't leave like that." He pulled me close, rubbing my back. "Well, I mean, just let me know where you're going."

I pushed away from him to study his face. The fear melted away. He slid his hands under my long sleeves and rested his forehead against mine.

"Come on, we gotta go. I've got some things to tell you." I clamped my hand on his and we walked back to the tree house. I spotted a small sack of nuts lying on the floor and my stomach rumbled. "Man, I'm hungry."

He handed me the nuts and I tried not to inhale them. Yeah, that didn't work. But Jag had seen me hungry before and never said anything about my disgusting eating habits.

I told him about Baldie and the Hawk and the facility. For once in his life, he didn't shrug. Instead he looked like I'd hit him with the latest stunning-tech.

"Pace might be there," he said, getting up and wiping his hands on his low-riding jeans. "He's a tech ranger. Show me."

"Wait, there's more." I held out my wrist and took a deep breath. "I got tagged."

Jag stared at my wrist, and he didn't breathe for a full minute. Fear shone in his eyes, then anger, then something else. Maybe regret? I hoped it was *for* me and not *because* of me.

"Why didn't you tell me?" He ran his fingers over my wrist until he felt the tiny bump. He massaged it, as if that would somehow take it out.

I had to admit it. "I was scared."

He smiled sadly. "You're wrong," he whispered, still looking at my wrist. "I wouldn't have left. Not because of this."

"I would have. Anyway, I overheard Baldie talking, and he said it hasn't been activated yet. They'll have to scan it with a special coding device before it'll work. So it's like it's not even there."

"Nice." His fingers circled my wrist in slow motion. "What else did they say?"

"They said everyone should have known I could break those cuffs. They mentioned Thane." I let the name hang there, an open invitation for Jag to finally tell me the truth.

But he didn't. Instead, he asked, "How do you know so much about tech?"

"What do you mean?"

"Like, you know they'll need a special device to activate your tag. How?"

I swallowed hard. "My dad invented pretty much everything They use in the Goodgrounds." Basically, I was saying that my dad was responsible for killing Jag's parents, raiding the Badlands, and everything else I hated about advanced technology.

"My brother Pace does the same thing," Jag said, and it sounded very much like a confession. He strung his fingers through mine. "Funny that you can break tech, right? I mean, your dad makes it, you break it."

I didn't know what to say, and Jag's voice had taken on that haunted quality again, the same one I'd heard back in the Fire Region when he told me about how his parents died. I felt like he was teetering on the verge of telling me about his Resistance, and I leaned forward.

"I mean, who can break tech?" he continued. "It's wicked amazing. And I bet you used your gifts to get across the border too. I came back . . . I felt so bad . . . anyway. You know your abilities, so—"

"Actually, I don't," I said, disappointed that he hadn't spilled any secrets. "I don't have any abilities." To cross the border, I'd fallen down a rocky hill and clawed my way up the other side. No special talents there.

"Sure you do. You can feel tech, for one. I'm sure you have others. I can sense them in you."

"I don't know what they are," I said, wondering if those same things Jag could sense were written in my file. Was feeling and breaking tech a good enough reason for Thane to chase me to the ends of the earth?

"Pace has been gone for four years," Jag said, the sound barely carrying across the small space between us. His breath shuddered through his chest. "I miss him."

I understood his emotions for his brother. Because I felt the exact same way about Ty. It's crushing, desperate, unwelcome—the loneliness that comes from losing a sibling. And even though Jag hadn't said so, I knew he'd lost two brothers.

"He's gone, and I'm all alone," Jag whispered as tears coated his cheeks.

17.

Everything was screwed up. If my dad were here, he could fix it. Dad knew how to turn regret into something positive. He was smart, inventive, able to reason through problems like no one else. I ached for his advice, the same way Jag ached for his parents, for Pace.

When Jag's sobs subsided, he turned away from me and folded the blanket.

This silence sucked. "So, what now?"

"I'm tired," Jag said.

"And I'm still starving."

He rummaged in the pack and tossed me a black-wrapped bar. A TravelTreat—a really old one. Before peeling back the wrapper, I wondered when he'd last replenished his hideout food supply. As soon as I bit into fruit and nut bar (disgusting), I knew it had been a very long time. But it tasted better than emptiness. Jag lay down while I crunched my way through the bar. He didn't seem to be in a rush to go anywhere.

But I was. "We're getting the hell out of here. I'm not living in the forest in a microscopic tree house."

Jag smiled, but it didn't carry its usual winning quality. "It's better than prison."

I snorted. "Marginally."

Jag closed his eyes.

A lurch of panic hit my stomach. Was he seriously taking a nap? "We're not safe here."

"Probably not."

"And that's okay with you?" Where was the leader of the Resistance? I couldn't make the Dream Jag who'd seemed so in charge mesh with this Melancholy Jag in front of me.

He opened his eyes. They had a spark back. Finally. "Of course not. What do you suggest?"

"Anything! Anything would be better than sitting here in the forest waiting to be caught."

"You said that tag wasn't activated."

"That's what Baldie said. But I don't trust him, just like I don't trust anyone."

Jag's mouth twitched with a tiny smile. "Not even me?"

I hesitated. Did I trust him? Could I? Jag opened his mouth, but I spoke first. "I trust you."

"Took you long enough."

"Sometimes you're an—"

"We can control people," Jag interrupted before I could get the insult out. "Whole cities of people. So yeah, we're not safe. We're wanted now—by Thane and his Association of Directors."

I could control other people? I tried to work up enough saliva to swallow. I put my hand on my face, and it felt too hot. I sputtered when I realized I hadn't been breathing.

Jag put his hand on my back. "You okay?"

Unable to speak, I nodded. The TravelTreat waged war with my insides. I didn't want to run a city. I didn't want to be in control of anyone.

"It's duty or death," Jag said, leaning back and closing his eyes. "Controlling people, I mean. That's the world we live in. Duty or death."

"So . . . you're saying they want us dead or on their side."

Jag shrugged, which I interpreted as a yes. He was right—both of those weren't stellar options. No wonder Thane kept whispering in my head. At least I knew he didn't want to kill me.

"So, uh, do you hear voices?" I asked.

His eyes snapped open. "No. Do you?"

I might have told him, if he didn't look and sound like hearing voices was the absolute worst thing that could happen to a person. "No, no," I said, maybe a little too quick. "I mean, I did in the Goodgrounds—sometimes—with all the transmissions floating in the air." I hated lying to him, but I'd just spilled about the tag. I could tell him about the voice later. Much later.

"Well, let's get out of here," I said. "How far is Seaside?"

"Night is the safest time to travel. We should rest while we can. It's a long walk to the oceanic region. Probably a couple of weeks."

When I fell asleep that afternoon, I was thinking of Zenn trapped in the Special Forces compound. He should be coming with us. Smoke clouded my head, but not the kind from the Fire Region. This smoke swirled and turned blue, forming into people.

Zenn and I were walking. Little things weren't right. The Abandoned Area loomed in front of us, which meant we were out of bounds. He wasn't wearing his hat. Deep shadows bordered his eyes.

"You look tired," I said as we walked through the pre-morning light.

He caught my hand in his on the next step. "I don't sleep anymore."

I glanced behind me, afraid that someone would see us touching. "Ever?"

He shook his head sadly. "If I sleep, I have to plug in. If I don't . . ."

I nodded, a silent confession that I didn't plug in anymore either. He'd stopped listening to the transmissions way before me. He'd still been chosen for the Special Forces. The way he glanced at me, the careful way he touched me, told me he still wanted to be with me.

Another memory awakened, but someone elbowed me before it could play out.

"Vi! Wake up," Jag said.

Opening my eyes, I could only see white. "Holy tech overload."

"Zenn's here," Jag whispered.

Silence pressed into my ears. The techtricity advanced slowly, causing bolts of lightning to ignite in my brain. I couldn't see anything.

"Shoes," Jag whispered, handing me my sneakers.

Blind, I pulled them on. "How do you know about Zenn?" I wondered if he'd tell me the truth—that he's known Zenn for years.

"You were talking about him just now," he said. "Something about the transmissions and the Forces."

"How do you know he's here?" Thankfully, my vision started to clear.

"Someone called his name."

My heart leapt. "I'll talk to him. He won't hurt me." I crawled toward the exit.

Jag seized my arm. "Yes, he will. He's one of Them now." His words carried a hint of bitterness. Obviously Zenn wasn't a spy anymore, and part of me felt relief. At least he wouldn't be in danger from playing both sides.

But if he was all good now, he'd do what he'd been trained to do—take out the Baddies. It didn't matter that it was me— the first girl he'd kissed and his best friend for five years. After all, he hadn't told me about working for Jag's Resistance.

And the Special Forces trained the humanity out of a person. Even though he'd only been there a few months, the Zenn I'd walked with in the park had been different. A brainwashed different.

I needed to see him, talk to him. He could come west with us, be free from the Forces, become my Zenn again. "Is Zenn alone?" I asked Jag.

"No." Jag helped me put the backpack on. He took both my hands in his. "We have to stay together. We have a better chance of surviving if we stay together."

"What does that—?" I began.

"Later. We've got to climb higher."

"Higher?"

"Yeah." He helped me with the backpack as it jammed against a limb. "All the way."

So much of me wanted to go down, go to Zenn, especially since heights aren't my thing. But up I went.

"That's good," Jag said after what felt like an hour of climbing.

"Where am I supposed to sit?" I gripped the branches so tightly the bark pierced my fingertips. If I fell, I'd kill the stupid bad boy for making me climb up here.

Jag scooted around the trunk of the tree. He sat on a branch and leaned back like he'd done this many times. I chose the limb slightly higher than his and nearly fell as I tried to shrug out of the backpack. Jag took it and looped a strap over a broken branch.

"Now what?" I asked.

"Now we wait."

Yeah, waiting isn't my thing either.

"I think you better tell me everything," he said. Even though I sat above him, his gaze penetrated the navy darkness. We'd been living in the dark so much, my eyes had grown used to seeing without light.

"Like what?" I asked.

"Come on." He sighed. "Who Ty is, and Zenn, and just about you. I've told you everything—"

"Not true," I interrupted.

"Everything about *me*," Jag said, covering my protest, "and, well, bawled my eyes out, and you've only told me two sentences about your dad."

Yeah, he hadn't told me everything—at least not while awake. "I don't like talking about myself."

"Too damn bad."

 Knowing where to start in my
family history was tough. Every-
one has memories they'd rather
forget. I'd been screwed up for as long as I could remember,
so I started at the beginning.

"My birthday is in three days—"

"Shut up," Jag said.

"O-kay."

"June sixteenth?"

"Yeah. So?"

"Mine too." His voice carried a smile. "That's so interesting," he continued. "We have the same birthday."

"Yeah, interesting," I said, trying to figure out what he
meant by "interesting."

"Maybe that's why They don't want us together."

I frowned. "But we were sentenced to go to the Association together. They had us living in the same cell."

"Not together, together. I mean, *together*, like, um, dating."

"Oh." *Together.* Several minutes passed while I wrestled with the togetherness I wanted. And who I wanted it with.

"So you were born," Jag prompted, bringing me out of the memory where he kissed me with the red light flashing behind us.

"Yeah. Ty is my older sister Tyson. She was like my dad. They knew tech, could invent it, improve it." I told him about Ty's talents with water and working with the rangers. About the man with the black hair. About how my mother hated me for not being Ty, and how we both hated the man for taking her away.

He remained quiet, even when my voice cracked. Even when I had to stop and wipe the silent tears away.

"And you got put in Ward D because you were . . . ?"

I cleared my throat. "Walking in the park with Zenn. After dark."

"Ah, there's the infamous Zenn." Jag was asking how I felt about Zenn and making fun of the Goodie rules at the same time. He waited patiently for the answers. I tried to decide how many he'd need. Probably all of them.

So I started again. I told him about Zenn and our friendship. About my birthday presents, and the kiss last year. About the Special Forces, and not listening to the transmissions, and finally the walk in the park. I tried to keep how much I adored Zenn from infusing my voice.

Yeah, I failed, because Jag said, "So he's your boyfriend."

He definitely was. We'd been matched. Part of me still longed for that, so I shrugged, which Jag couldn't see. A growl tore through his throat, which I interpreted as Jag-speak for, *Damn, I'm in love with you.*

Gathering my courage, I slid down to him. "Jag," I said, facing him. "Zenn's not my boyfriend." The words hurt, but they were true. Whatever life I could've had with Zenn wasn't available anymore. I found Jag's hands in the dark and squeezed them. "I'm with someone else."

"Anyone I know?"

"Just this guy with wicked cool hair." I felt his smile permeate the distance between us.

"Still doesn't explain why you got put in prison. Walking in the park after dark doesn't sound like that big of a deal— even in the Goodgrounds."

"You don't know much, then." I liked the way his hands felt in mine. His touch brought warmth and comfort, and all my secrets poured out of me.

Except for an occasional low chuckle, he didn't interrupt as I spilled the details about my eight rule-breaking episodes.

"You've been bad for a very long time," he said when I finished.

If that's what he wanted to believe, why should I correct him?

Zenn floated nearer. In this dream, the smoke was nearly black. It shifted into a moving sidewalk that had been stilled. Zenn walked next to me, his hands clasped behind his back. The silence in the twilight came easy.

"Well, now that you're here, I've got something for you," he said, smiling.

I angled my body toward him. Zenn's e-comm had said he had a surprise for me—surely something he'd tinkered with until it was absolutely perfect. Like he was.

"The Forces have kept me busy." Zenn didn't seem concerned about the circling hovercopters. "But we might not get to see each other again for a while."

He reached out and wrapped his hand around mine. His touch sent fear pounding in my veins. What if someone saw us?

But he smiled, and on the next step our shoulders touched.

The fear in my heart changed to anticipation. Zenn was my best friend, my match. I missed him like crazy, and I imagined the feel of his lips before they came.

"Nice," he said after he pulled away, and it struck a familiar chord with me. The memory swam in my mind. I pushed away the blurred edges, trying to fight off the rising awareness.

"I made you something special for your birthday." Zenn reached into his pocket. He grinned and held out his hand. A package half the size of my hand lay in his palm.

I took the gift. He'd wrapped it in green paper and written *For my perfect match* in his elegant scrawl. Those four words meant everything. He cupped my face in his palm as I stared at the paper. "Vi, I love—"

"You down there!" An electronic voice cut through Zenn's throaty tone. I flinched and took a half step behind Zenn. A one-manned tech-craft, the hovercopter was invented especially for ruining lives. No one ever escapes from one.

Not even me.

"Hide that," Zenn murmured.

As I knelt, something feathery touched my mind. A whispered word I couldn't quite hear stole through my ears. I disregarded the transmission as I crammed something into the tiny pocket on the side of my shoe. Zenn had a hidden slot like this in his old shoes too. We'd sewn them in when we'd realized only our eyes, fingerprints, and IDs were scanned and no one ever paid attention to our feet.

I stood up and studied the hovercopter. On the bottom rudder, a red rose winked through the twilight. My breath shuddered through my throat—I'd been caught by this hover-copter before. Maybe since Zenn was a Forces recruit and had invited me here, I wouldn't get in trouble.

Yeah, right.

Because he slowly took two steps away.

**19.**

"Come on, Vi, you're safe now," a smooth voice said in my ear. "Wake up, beautiful."

"Jag?"

"No. We got him. He won't bother you anymore."

"Zenn!" I threw my arms around him and cried into his neck, just like I had the day he left. His hands pressed on my back, but he didn't rub the way Jag did.

"Where's Jag?" I asked.

"Don't worry. You're safe."

I wasn't worried about myself. Jag's words rushed through my mind. *We have to stay together. We have a better chance of surviving if we stay together."*

"Where is he?" I asked.

Zenn didn't answer as he tied a rope around my waist. We shimmied down the tree in half the time it took to climb it.

When we landed, an entire squad of Special Forces waited with tasers—pointed at me. I glanced at Zenn.

He wore a black suit, to go with his Forces-issued haircut and stern frown.

"Vi!" Jag struggled against a pair of tech-cuffs.

Two SF agents were rummaging through our backpack, tossing the medical supplies onto the forest floor. "It's not here," one said.

"Then she's still got it," Zenn said.

"Got what?" I sidestepped, but Zenn's hand shot out and gripped my left wrist. Fear hit my heart. He would feel the tag. SF agents are trained to feel and see and hear everything.

Sure enough, his fingers stalled on the miniscule bump. A smile formed on his face. "Tagged."

"It's not activated," I said, yanking my hand out of his. I looked at Jag, and for the first time he looked truly scared. He shook his head, trying to tell me something. Sure, I knew Jag-speak, but I hadn't graduated into the body language department yet.

"Where is it, Vi?" Zenn asked.

"Where is what, traitor?" My voice cracked.

"Don't make me use my tech against you."

"Like you used your mouth?"

He shifted uncomfortably. Zenn was one of Them—the ones who took Ty away. A government spy. I couldn't believe it. He'd kissed me in the park! His e-comm had said how much he missed me, how he was trying to get me out of prison. He'd sent his *love*.

Disbelief blossomed into anger. Anger spiraled into full-fledged fury.

"Vi, please."

"Please what?"

"Give me the tracker."

My mouth dropped open and, "Tracker?" came out. No way was I carrying the tech that would broadcast my position to the world—something that would lead Thane right to me. No. Way.

Jag swore and thrashed. The other agents pressed closer, pushing Jag in front of them. He looked everywhere but at me.

"I didn't," I said. "Jag, I swear I didn't."

"Give it to me." Zenn grabbed my arm again.

"Don't touch her!" Jag yelled, kicking backward. Two men fell down. I punched an agent in the stomach. When he doubled over, I grabbed his taser and pointed it at Jag's tech-cuffs.

I flew backward from the blast of three tasers.

"Vi!" Jag's anguished voice rang in my ears. I stared straight up, unable to move. The canopy of trees created an umbrella that blocked out the stars. A single taser beam should have knocked me out. With three, I should be dead.

The fire in my chest needed cooling. Hot pain spread into my lungs and I couldn't gulp enough oxygen to put out the flames. A rushing white noise like water falling hundreds of feet clogged my ears. I closed my eyes and wished for death.

Air moved over and around my face. The crackling of dry leaves echoed through my head. Slowly, the rustling was drowned out by something much worse. Words.

Thane's voice infiltrated even my death. *So many choices,* he said. *Good or bad? Zenn or Jag? What's it going to be, V?*

Only one person called me V.

My dad.

The voice belonged to my dad.

I could only come up with one explanation: Thane Myers was my dad.

 I entered a dark place. The sun didn't shine. No smiling. No hugging. No happy reunions.

Only betrayal.

That man had taken my memory. Of him.

That man was controlling everything.

That man—*my dad*—had controlled *me* and persuaded me with his voice.

Inside, I felt like a raging storm, strong enough to destroy anything in my path. Too bad I couldn't move. But my voice still worked.

And so I screamed, desperate to drain the debilitating feelings. Anything to get the shock and hurt out of my mind.

"Help her." That voice soothed. Jag's tone always did. "Please, Zenn."

"So. The rumor is true," Zenn said, disdain dripping from every word. "You two *are* together."

Endless pain screamed through my senses. I couldn't rid myself of it.

"Zenn, don't. Our argument doesn't involve Vi."

"*Everything* involves Vi. Everything I've done is for her."

"*You* betrayed her."

A rustling noise joined the shrieking in my ears. "Just because I dropped out of the Resistance doesn't mean I stopped working for our cause. I've been protecting her for a long time. And not just because I want to use her for something. But because I love her."

"Let me get this straight." Jag's voice took on the strange quality that made my eyes heavy and the truth float to the surface. "You defected right when she needed you most. Is that what you're saying? That you turned Informant to *keep* working for the cause?"

Zenn exhaled, a heavy sound full of fury and frustration. "I didn't defect. You want her to die?"

"Of course not." Jag clipped the words out.

"Well, Thane doesn't take no for an answer. It was either help him or watch her die. What would you have done?"

A long pause followed, filled only by the wailing torment in my soul.

"Help her," Jag repeated, softer this time. "Please."

Time crawled by. Finally, whispers of cool air flitted across my face. "Vi," Zenn said. "Settle down, beautiful."

The wretched screaming stopped. Every cell in my body raged with fire. "Here, can you drink?" Zenn asked. Water trickled into my mouth, cooling the deception.

"Jag, listen," Zenn continued, his voice following his footsteps as he moved away. "I didn't—"

"Stop," Jag commanded. "I already know everything."

"You never heard my side."

"Whatever. I heard every single word." Jag's words carried grief amidst the fury.

Silence descended, trapping their conversation in my ears. Half of me wished I knew more about what they were discussing. The other half was fine with the ignorance. At least then I wouldn't have to choose sides.

"She's carrying a tracker," Zenn said, his voice foreign and far away.

"No," I croaked. "Not true." I staggered to my feet. "Jag. I—I didn't. He's lying. I don't have a tracker. Promise." I coughed and blood dripped down my throat.

Hope entered Jag's blazing eyes, but Zenn strode forward

and seized my arm. He motioned to the other SF agents, who'd retreated into the forest. As they came forward, Zenn dragged me back toward Jag, who looked like the sky might swallow him. "Empty your pockets."

I dug my hands in my jeans and came up empty-handed. "I don't have anything."

"*All* your pockets," Zenn said, nodding toward my feet.

Toward my shoes that had a secret pocket, something only Zenn knew. Betrayal tasted like metal, thick and tinny in my throat.

I knelt down and probed the tiny slot with two fingers. I felt something papery. Slowly, I withdrew it and cupped it in my palm, unwilling to believe that the dream could be true. That I'd been carrying this in my shoe for the past two weeks, that Zenn had brainwashed me.

Zenn wrenched my fingers apart and a green-paper package sat there. *For my perfect match* in his handwriting glared up at me.

"Ah, you do still have it," Zenn said. His eyes looked cloudy and distant. "My birthday present. Happy birthday, Vi." He laughed in his precious voice, the one that used to heal my agony and calm my fears. The one that had said the three most important words on earth just a few minutes ago.

But he'd invited me to take a walk with him so he could

trick me. "No." I shook my head, looking only at Jag. "Stop."

"It's coated in protectant." Zenn unwrapped his gift, peeling back an inner filament layer surrounding the tech. Before I could process the word "protectant," my vision blurred, my chest burned, another cough tore through my throat. Through it all, I saw the ring, golden and shiny and beautiful. What would it have meant to me if I'd opened it that night in the park?

Honestly, it would have meant everything. It would have meant I was good enough for Zenn. That he loved me and thought of me during his Special Forces training. That we would be *together* when he was finished. Jewelry means something in the Goodgrounds, remember?

"Oh, Vi," Zenn said. "I can't believe you didn't open it. This breaks my heart." His eyes were clear, his voice held no sarcasm. "We're matched." He held up his right hand, where he wore an identical band of gold around his pinky finger.

Then his eyes clouded over. He seized my right hand and slid the ring on my pinky finger. Tech sizzled through my flesh—definitely a tracker.

Through my tears, the betrayal showed on Jag's face. "Zenn, stop it. Please."

"I guess you aren't *totally* in tune with tech." He pushed me toward another agent, who cuffed me. Twice.

"Vi?" Jag asked, the question hanging between us.

The words in my mouth tripped over each other. My mind raced, trying to find the exact thing to say that would take the pleading out of his eyes, remove the accusation in his voice. The explanation stalled and gathered in my throat.

Jag's mouth tightened and his eyes hardened. "Nice."

21.

Memory modification is an extremely advanced form of control. Much more than suggestion, which is what the transmissions do. MemMod is only done to those who have a memory They need them to forget. I know, because the one time Ty came home, she'd told me she couldn't find her way. She'd suspected They'd been performing MemMod on her, but she couldn't remember what for.

Her eyes were cloudy—like Zenn's. Ty said she couldn't see, and I'd had to lead her to her bedroom. I brought her lunch and then dinner. And the whole time, all I could think was how I was going to kill the Thinker that had erased my sister's memories.

I begged her not to go back, but she said she had to. I'd never see her again. After that, I stopped plugging into the transmissions. I dyed my hair. Zenn and I snuck out and stayed up all night just to watch the sun rise the next morning. We skipped rocks in the lake. I went to parties and stole shoes and anything else I could think of to show that no one—and I mean *no one*—could control me. Through it all, Zenn had been there with me, my silent partner. My perfect match.

But now I wasn't sure of anything. My memory of that day in the park had been modified, stolen. They'd taken my memory of Zenn and his birthday present—and I use that term loosely. Even boiled cabbage is better than a kiss of betrayal, a gold-plated tracker, and a whispered word of MemMod.

And who'd done that to me? My match, the person I loved and trusted the most after my dad disappeared.

Jag stood straight, his eyes boring into mine. So cold. Finally the agents pulled him away.

Zenn pushed and prodded me in another direction. Two agents walked with him, and they joked about how easy it had been to find us. I tuned them out and thought about what might happen to Jag.

"Worried about your boyfriend?" Zenn asked when he caught me looking back.

"Yeah. When did you go all Green?"

He looked shocked, but quickly wiped the emotion away. "Please. I saw you with him."

"Oh?"

"Yeah. Sleeping in a tree with him. Vi, are you really so desperate?"

"At least I didn't kiss him to cover my ass."

He flinched like I'd slapped him. He blinked a couple of times and fell back with his squad. The thing is, the words hurt me as much as him.

The facility was a lot farther away than it looked. It took most of the night to get there, mostly because I kept tripping on purpose.

"Knock it off," Zenn said, pulling me to my feet once again. "My mission needs to go smoothly."

And there it was. I was Zenn's mission. Probably his first, and he needed to make a good impression for the big boys in the Association—for Thane.

The facility stood five stories tall, shiny and silver, made with seamless tech. Zenn led me inside with his traitorous hand on my shoulder. He kept glancing from left to right as if he expected an ambush, but none came.

Icy air blew in my face. It didn't cool the heat spreading

from my chest into my limbs. The tech felt different here. New. Bad.

The stark walls lay bare: no art, no color, no hint that anyone had ever been here before. An alarm sounded, and four Mechs whizzed out of a door in the far left corner.

"I thought you said she was clean," Zenn hissed to another agent.

"She is."

"Where's Jag?" I demanded.

"Who?" Zenn's eyes looked like he'd had an optical-enhancement that didn't turn out so well. Blurred. Foggy.

Each Mech's siren erupted as they scanned my left wrist.

"I thought you said it wasn't activated," Zenn shouted over the *whoop-whoop-whoop!* of the Mechs.

"That's what that guy said!" I yelled back.

"What guy?"

"Him!" I pointed to Baldie as he appeared next to me, wearing his Greenie robes.

Baldie reset each Mech, silencing the alarms. "Thank you, Specialist Bower, you may go."

Zenn stood there, blinking fast. That obviously wasn't what he'd expected. "Who are you?"

"I'm invisible. You should go now." Baldie stood with a smile on his face that only touched his lips. The tech lights glared on his scalp. Tension and power emanated from him.

Zenn opened his mouth to protest. Then the defiance slid off his face, and he turned to the other agents. "We should go now." The way he repeated Baldie's words screamed of control.

I puzzled over exactly what Zenn had done on his own and what he'd been told to do. I wondered which of the words he'd said to me came from his mind or from someone else's. I wondered if he knew my dad was Thane Myers or not. I wondered if it mattered. I still loved him. I still couldn't stand idly by and watch him be controlled.

"Welcome, Violet," Baldie said after Zenn had gone. "We have a lot to talk about." He gestured toward the door in the far corner. His voice could definitely influence me—if I let it.

"Like I'm going anywhere with you. Where's Jag?"

He turned and took a step toward me. "Trust me, it's in your best interest if we move to a more secure location." His eyes darted around the sterile room, as though expecting danger.

"I want to see Jag first." I moved toward the exit. Baldie appeared in front of me in a flicker of light.

That was teleportation without a terminal. Way advanced in the tech department.

"How did you do that?"

He held up his left hand. He wore a wide silver ring on his middle finger. A symbol adorned it—two looping snakes with no beginning and no end.

"Jag will be fine. The Special Forces pose no threat to him—or you. Their job was to bring you safely here."

"Then where is he?"

Baldie stepped forward and held out an identical ring. "I'll give you this if you'll please just go through that door." He nodded behind him to the door in the corner.

Something didn't add up. He'd give me an advanced tele-porter ring just to walk through a door?

"Yeah, it's probably not activated," I said. "Like my tag. Oh, wait. That *is* activated. You said it wasn't."

"It's not."

"Then what's up with the Mechs?"

"They merely sense bar codes. All tags have a bar code, I believe."

Yeah, he was right, but I still didn't believe a single word he said. "I set off the alarm at the border. Explain that."

"We have Mechs stationed at each entrance to the Good-grounds." He glared back at me, then gestured toward the door. "Shall we?"

I folded my legs underneath me. "I'm not going anywhere until I see Jag."

"Fine." Baldie nodded to the wall. A projection screen brightened, and a picture of Jag appeared. He wore a blue shirt and lay sleeping on a bed under white sheets. Iron bars barely showed at the top of the screen.

"That's nothing," I said. "That looks like Ward D. No. I want to see him, in person."

"He's through that door."

"Then get him the hell out here!"

He glared down at me. For a second I thought he'd throw me over his shoulder and carry me through the door. I stared back, willing him to do what I wanted. His eyes glazed over, and he nodded again. A few minutes later, Jag walked through the door, wearing a black shirt. That lame projection *was* Ward D.

Jag didn't speak. He wouldn't look at me as I sprinted toward him. Tech-cuffs still circled his wrists, and his right eye looked puffy and bloodshot.

"Jag!" I flung myself at him, but he had no way to catch me. We stumbled backward together, landing in a pile on the floor. "I didn't know, Jag, I swear I didn't," I breathed in his ear. "Zenn tricked me. I didn't—*oof*!"

"No talking." Baldie shoved me away from Jag, using himself as a barrier between us.

Jag kept his icy gaze trained on the blank wall behind me, silent, as Baldie helped him stand.

"You've seen him, now go." Baldie pushed me behind Jag, who was already being herded through the door by two Mechs.

"Jag!" I yelled. "We have to stay—" Baldie slapped on a silencer and the rest of my words died.

Jag's left arm twitched, but he didn't break stride or turn around.

Baldie steered us down a long hallway (un)decorated exactly as the main entry. Doors bordered both sides. All white, all closed, all unlabeled.

At the end of the hall, a waist-high silver desk broke the monotony of the walls. Baldie tapped on an electro-board. Images flashed to life, filling at least a dozen projection screens simultaneously.

I moaned with the spike in techtricity. A moment later the fireball in my chest burned.

But I couldn't look away from the pictures.

A five-year-old Tyson and a three-year-old me played in the water, dipping our feet and splashing each other. I could almost hear our laughter. A sob broke from my throat, mingled with a smile.

A young boy—obviously Jag with his playful grin—played ball with his brothers Pace and Blaze. His blueberry eyes sparkled in the sun with freedom.

In front of me, Jag clenched his fists.

My dad, exactly how I remembered him, filled the screen. Clean-cut brown hair. Crinkly green eyes. Alabaster skin. The tears flowed freely now, and I raised my hand halfway toward the picture before letting it fall back to my side. He wasn't that man anymore. I wasn't sure who he was. The man on the back of Jag's book? Thane Myers? Or the man in my memory? He couldn't be all three.

A man and a woman appeared next. I'd seen the man in Jag's nightmares. His parents. Jag's shoulders shook as he broke apart again. The stupid silencer kept me from consoling him verbally. I laid my hand on his back, and he didn't shrug me off.

Another picture filled the screen. A man sat in a red armchair. The middle Greenie, wearing the black robes of a Director. And—now that my memory was complete—the man who'd taken Ty away.

Jag was still cuffed, so I slipped my hand around his waist in an effort to calm my rage.

The projection began to move and speak. "Hello, Mr. Barque and Miss Schoenfeld. Welcome to the Tech Production Facility, located in the Badlands. You're here to learn how you can serve the Association."

I reached up and removed the silencer, something not

lightly done. Pain ripped through my neck and shoulders, and I screamed.

"Now, Violet," the Director said. "Sometimes silence is called for."

"You killed Ty," I managed to gasp out. "Screw you."

Jag chuckled. "Ditto."

22.

We never let go of the ones we lose. Jag dreams of his brother Blaze. And even though Ty is dead, I can't help thinking about her. What might she be doing right now if she were still alive? Would my mother have been different? I know I would have been. Maybe I wouldn't have turned bad. Maybe I wouldn't be in the Badlands staring at the Director on a p-screen. Maybe I wouldn't have met Jag. Maybe Zenn and I would have been married in a few years.

So many maybes.

As I looked at the Director, I thought of Ty. She was dead, she wasn't going to come back, but I'd never had the chance to say good-bye. No closure, no funeral, nothing to seal that chapter of my life. No wonder my mother is the way she is—angry, bitter, mean.

But killing the Director wouldn't bring Ty back. Wouldn't erase the years I'd lived with a hole in my heart that only she could fill.

I rubbed my neck where the silencer had been. Sticky, warm blood trickled over my shoulder.

"Oh, come on." Disgust dripped from Jag's voice.

On the screen, another man had joined the Director. I forgot about the blood and pain.

"Dad," I whispered, moving forward.

He didn't look anything like Lyle Schoenfeld's photo on the back of Jag's book.

At the lab, Thane had kept his eyes covered and his skin had been shimmery, pearly. I realized he'd probably teched it up in the Goodgrounds so I wouldn't recognize him.

Because in the projection, my dad's lopsided smile looked familiar. He watched me intently, as he always had. His brown hair was neatly trimmed, just the way I remembered.

But he had *stained skin*.

"Hello, V." His words didn't hold the fatherly quality they should. "I see you made it to the Badlands. It's about time." His voice sounded the same, low and crackly. He looked so *happy*. "We've needed you for a while now," he said.

"You should have pulled a better prank a long time ago."

"Thane," the Director said. "We couldn't arrest her for petty shoe thefts and unauthorized teleporter use."

"But a walk in the park—"

"She was up to eight offenses."

"Seven," I argued. The rage woke, smoldering through my veins.

"That you were arrested for," the Director said, his eyes all-knowing.

"Still, the park?" Dad asked. I wondered what in the world he needed me for. And would he protect me, like he always had? Or was he Thane-posing-as-Lyle-Schoenfeld, and I'd never really known him?

Dad and the Director argued over my lack of serious offenses and whether or not walking in the park was severe enough for removal.

Jag and I looked at each other like we were watching a comedy that we weren't quite sure was funny or not. I opted for not.

"Um, I hate to break up your little argument," I said. "But . . . what the hell?"

"Yes, yes," the Director said. "We won't discuss it over a projection. We have some business to conclude, and we'll be there tomorrow."

"Where are you?" Jag asked at the same time I yelled, "Discuss what?"

"The Goodgrounds." Dad eyed him like he knew Jag's lips had tasted mine. "Tomorrow. Cam, you have my orders."

"I do, Director."

The screen faded to white. Some of the burning in my chest lessened. Except now my heart felt like it might bust open. My dad . . . with sun-kissed skin. My dad . . . addressed as Thane. Being called a Director.

Seeing him hadn't answered any of my questions, which fueled my anger. I turned to Jag. "What the hell is going on?"

"Hey, don't yell at me. Ask your buddy over there." He thrust his chin toward Baldie who was busy nodding at the walls.

"Jag, don't be such a high-class jerk."

"I'm not. You're obviously on better terms than me. I'm the one who's cuffed."

"Like that's my fault."

"Get him to take them off."

I was about to turn around when something clicked in my mind. *Get him to take them off.*

I'd gotten Baldie to get Jag by willing it.

I'd silenced that Mech at Jag's house.

I'd forced the crowd to part when I ran away from the iris recognizer.

I'd broken tech-cuffs in the prison bathroom.

I can get what I want just by thinking it.

The room spun in a dangerous kaleidoscope of colors and feelings and patterns.

I am one of Them. I steadied myself by leaning against the desk. "How do I do that?"

"Mind control." The stupid bad boy rolled his eyes at me.

"I—I can't. You'll have to get out of this by yourself."

"No way. I don't use my control like that."

"Oh, but it's okay if I do?" I wiped the blood on my neck again. "Wait a second. You have the ability to control?" I tried to think back over the past few weeks with Jag.

He looked away for a second. When he met my gaze again, a blush colored his face. "It's not really mind control. My voice ..."

His voice? His damn *voice*?

He'd put me to sleep.

He'd told me he was a great liar.

He'd told me I could touch him.

He'd told me *lots* of things.

"Oh man, Jag. You're dead." I took a step away from him so I could swing with more force.

He stumbled backward, unable to defend himself because of the cuffs. "Stop, Vi! I didn't mean to, and you—you resisted most of it anyway."

"Don't talk to me anymore," I said. "And I'm not helping you get out of your stupid cuffs. Do it yourself. You've got such a *nice voice.*"

"*You* led them straight to us."

"That was an accident! I didn't know I had that damn ring! They did MemMod on me—you can't blame me for that."

He shrugged. Apparently he could.

I sank against the nearest wall, closed my eyes, and wished for a hot bath and a warm bed.

"Come on, Violet," Baldie said. "You can shower and then rest."

Jag smirked. "Nice."

"Shut up. Don't talk to me." Horrified, I watched Jag battle with himself. He really couldn't speak—because of my command. This was so bad. I reached for him, but he turned away.

"Are you ready, Violet?" Baldie asked.

"No. Yes. Let's go," I said, following him around the desk and into another barren hallway. Five doors down on the right, he paused and pushed open the door.

A large bed sat in the middle of the room, with warm red blankets and puffy white pillows. Next to the dresser, another door led into the bathroom. Thick blue rugs covered the floor and heavy curtains fluttered at the open window. Breakfast was the only thing missing.

"I'll bring you something to eat," Baldie said. As he left, my mouth watered for hash browns and watermelon and ten protein packets.

I ran a hot bath, and nothing had ever felt so good in my entire life. I wished all my problems would swirl down the drain with the dirty water. Yeah, they didn't.

After eating breakfast—hash browns, watermelon, and ten protein packets—I changed into the pajamas I found in the top dresser drawer. Just as I was pulling down the soft covers, Baldie opened the door. "Sorry the accommodations aren't spectacular. Are you comfortable?"

"Sure," I said. "Everything's fine." He turned to leave. "Wait, where's Jag? Can I see him?"

Baldie shook his head. "His room is down the other hall, and my orders are to keep you two apart—at least until the Directors come."

"What's gonna happen to us?"

"I'm surprised you have to ask. Jag figured it out already."

"Yeah, well, Jag is just *wonderful*, isn't he?"

Baldie didn't answer. He looked at me blankly until I shooed him from the room.

The ten protein packets turned out to be a big mistake. Sleep wouldn't come because I had to use the bathroom every fifteen minutes. My mind raced through the events of the past twenty-four hours.

First, everything with Zenn. A fake invitation. A real kiss. A traitorous birthday present. A modified memory.

Then Jag. His voice. His nightmares. His Resistance.

The accusation each harbored in his eyes when he looked at me.

Everything was upside down. Dad had been in the Goodgrounds—with brown skin. He'd controlled me. Whispered lies in my ears, in my mind. His name was Thane. And Jag said Thane was the bad guy.

But he was my dad.

Now it wasn't my bladder keeping me up. More like the bitter taste of anger. Seven years worth of abandonment. Of living without a dad. Of having him steal my memories, brainwash me, control me.

But my dad loved me. He'd always protected me. Maybe this time hadn't been any different. Even though my dad was Thane, he still could've used his control to help me.

I fell asleep with tears on my cheeks, thinking that no matter how I spun it, my dad wasn't quite the hero I needed him to be.

When I woke up, darkness drenched the room in shadows. "What time is it?"

"Eleven-thirteen," the walls answered.

"A.M. or P.M.?"

"P.M."

"What day?"

"June fourteenth."

"Where's Jag Barque?"

"Hallway eight, room four."

I had no idea where that was, or how big this facility was. I didn't even know if I could open the door without forty Mechs whizzing down the hall, alarms blaring.

Just shut them down, I told myself, thinking of the Mech I'd disabled at Jag's house. I slipped out of bed and pulled on my sneakers. No sirens sounded when the door opened, nobody came down the hall when I stepped out, no Mechs intercepted me as I made my way back to the lobby with the silver desk.

I couldn't see another hallway. "Where's hallway eight?" I asked, turning in a circle.

The walls shifted and moved, revealing another corridor. Glancing behind me, I hurried toward it.

"Show me room four," I said. A yellow light pulsed around the second door on my right.

Jag's room had the same blue rugs and drapes on the windows as mine. But his bed was at least twice as big and covered in fuzzy blue blankets.

He sat propped up by a mass of comfy pillows, reading (of course).

"Jag," I whispered as the door closed behind me. "You still need me to get your cuffs off?" I asked, hoping he could still decipher Vi-talk.

He looked up and ditched the book. "Vi, I'm sorry too." Then he ran to me, the same way Sloan had launched herself at him a few days ago. He held me tight, swinging me around in a circle until my feet came off the ground and I laughed out loud.

He put me down, and he looked *fine*. He wore dark jeans with a white tank top, which contrasted nicely with his skin. He climbed back into bed and picked up his book. I sat on the other side, staying on top of the blankets. Something felt wrong about being on his bed with him. But I was bad now, so maybe it was right.

"Tell me what you know," I said.

He remained silent for a while, his gaze lingering first on me, then on his book, then the bedspread. Just when I thought I couldn't wait one more second, he spoke.

"The Association wants me to make their transmissions. They have for a while now. I can . . . sorta make people do whatever I say."

Talk about a lot to digest. I think I did a pretty good

job, because my voice sounded normal when I said, "What about me?"

"They need you for the mind control. What you want, you get. You can bend the will of the people to your own. You can Direct."

I couldn't answer. Because I didn't want to Direct.

"You don't really have a choice, Vi," Jag said, cutting into my thoughts. I looked at him, wondering how he could see inside my head.

"I can sense feelings in others. Yours especially. I think because we're both free. Maybe our birthdays . . . I don't know." He paused. "But we may not have a choice. Help Them or die."

"You're wrong," I said. "That's exactly what makes us different. We do have choices. It's everyone else who doesn't." Something about Jag's parents clicked in my mind. "Your mom and dad. They had choices too, didn't they? They knew what we know."

He stiffened. "Yes, they knew. They tried to tell others, but Thane was too strong and he countered them with louder transmissions and harsher rules. The people allowed themselves to be told. Changed."

Everyone knows about the change. We're taught the sequence of events in school until we want to puke. You see, the first change started out subtly. The Thinkers recruited and controlled those They wanted on their side. At first, people resisted having their minds taken over, but They became too powerful. Wars between races and religions started, and people grouped together behind the Thinker they believed in.

War spread through the world, Thinker against Thinker, brainwashed army against brainwashed army. The fires marked the beginning of the Great Episode, and it killed almost everyone. That's when the General Director organized the people into cities to establish peace and rebuild the human population. He set up the Association of Directors, a governing council to oversee regions. Regional Directors governed ten cities. Each city had a Director who reported to the Association. We were told that the General Director was our savior—the only reason humans survived the thick smoke and years of darkness during the Great Episode.

Receivers were implanted in our ears. Transmissions were recorded about loyalty and trust and how wicked awesome the Director was. Another reason I stopped listening—I don't think Director Greenwood is all that great. Because I pretty much hate all Thinkers.

And now I am one.

"Wait a second," I said. "Thane made the rules? Didn't your parents live in the Badlands?"

Jag held up the book. "According to Lyle Schoenfeld, the good and bad used to be united. Thane split us up twenty-five years ago. My parents were the leaders of a movement against your dad that triggered the separation."

"So . . . who's Lyle Schoenfeld?" I asked.

"I don't know, but I think Thane stole his identity to go into hiding."

I rubbed my forehead, trying to order my thoughts. "Hiding? Thane's clearly not hiding, Jag. He runs everything."

"Now, babe. He runs everything now. He's from the Association, and they have so many identities no one can keep them straight."

"How do you know?"

His face closed off. "Let's just say I know," he said, meaning it had something to do with either his brother Blaze or the Resistance (or both), but I couldn't push it because, technically, I didn't know about either.

"We need to stay together," Jag continued. "I can feel your fear about controlling others. Alone, we can be influenced by the Thinkers with more training and experience. But together, we can remind each other of the injustices that have happened. Maybe we can finally be strong enough to do something about them."

I touched his cheek. My fingertips traced over his eyebrow

and down his jaw. "I don't want to be like Them." I couldn't mask the terror in my voice, but I didn't feel embarrassed. "Promise me we'll stay together."

"I would never leave you, Vi." His voice sounded forced. He leaned back against the headboard, and I couldn't search his face.

"I can't control anyone," I said, settling my cheek against his chest so I could hear his heartbeat. "I just can't do that."

He finally tilted his head down to look at me. "I don't want to use my voice to brainwash people to live a specific way, with a thousand stupid rules." The muscle in his jaw twitched.

"Me neither."

"Then we won't do it. I'll never control anyone, not even you."

"Deal."

The edges of his mouth softened. "I knew there was a reason I loved you."

 Before I processed the L-word,
Jag's mouth caught mine. He
moved with precision, slipping
his hands around to the small of my back. His touch felt
dangerous.

He kissed my jaw up to my ear and murmured, "Violet."

It didn't bother me; if anything, I loved my whole name
when he spoke it in his velvety voice. I forgot everything
except that he was here with me, and we would always be
together. I shivered at the thought.

"You cold?" he whispered, his lips brushing mine.

"A little," I said, but the shaking came more from nerves.
I'd never thought beyond kissing. Good girls don't even go

that far. Stealing and trespassing tops the list of Bad Stuff I've Done.

His blanket lay thickly between us, a barrier I couldn't cross. His hair slid through my fingers like silk.

"You're nervous," he murmured, and that raised the embarrassment factor.

"How do you know?" I trailed my fingers along his jaw.

"I can hear your heart racing," he said.

He could hear my heart? Like superhearing to go with his supervoice?

I pushed him away. "What does that mean?"

His hands rested on my waist. "I can hear your heart beating, that's what it means."

"Nobody can hear a heart beating," I said. "I can't hear yours."

"I can feel your feelings too."

"Do you have high-class smell as well?"

He laughed, and I curled into his chest to feel the reverberations from that wonderful sound.

"I'm not a superhero."

He was to me. It felt safe to lie in his arms, his hand massaging my shoulder. I closed my eyes and inhaled the scent of his skin. He smelled musky and clean. Very *guy*. He hummed a soft melody, sending sound waves from his chest into my cheek.

"I love you, Vi," he said, kissing my forehead. "I really do."

Knowing I loved him too, I wanted to tell him, but my voice didn't work the way his did. Those three tiny words choked in my throat, and I couldn't get them out. I pulled away so I could see him better.

"Jag, I—"

"I know. Lie back down. That was nice."

Jag fell asleep. I lay next to him, thinking about what we needed to do next. I wondered what business the Director and my dad needed to finish, afraid it might have something to do with me. My dad could've invented who knows what over the past seven years—and I knew from firsthand experience that his tech-inventions aren't always pleasant. But they do require extensive testing. Could that be why he hadn't immediately teleported here?

After a half hour of listening to Jag's steady breathing, I took his book with me into the bathroom. With the tub full of steaming water, I settled in to read what Lyle Schoenfeld— whoever he was—had to say.

I plowed through a mind-numbing chapter analyzing the effectiveness of tech in the daily life of an average person. Boring.

I flipped to the second section, which detailed how to break tech. Teleporters can be damaged so nothing can be received or sent. Silencers can be reversed, amplifying sounds. Walls can be reprogrammed to keep secrets and reveal incorrect information.

Tags can be removed.

As I read and reread that chapter, I decided that Lyle Schoenfeld was not my dad. A book like this was dangerous, and no one in the Goodgrounds would allow it to be published. No, Lyle had to be part of Jag's Resistance, a Baddie, someone who wanted Goodies to question their Thinkers. Thane could've assumed his identity during the separation, but he and Lyle were two very different men.

I thought about the farmhouse where Jag had stolen the book. How did that farmer get it? Was he a Free Thinker too? Or someone like Zenn—an Insider?

I wanted to ask Zenn—or my dad. There were so many things I needed to ask them. So many uncertainties swirled inside my mind. Zenn loved me. I knew he did. I'd heard it hiding between his words, seen it in the careful way he'd acted around me.

My dad loved me too, even if he watched me with more interest now. Even if he was a Director.

I shook my head to erase the questions that kept piling up. I'd see them both soon enough, and I'd get my answers one way or another. I focused on the book, on how to remove my tag.

The procedure required a special tool—also a feat of tech—a pair of shock scissors. I wondered if I could get my hands on something like that here. Of course I would need some surgery skin to eat away my flesh, and then some kind of regenerator to grow it back, but—

"Vi?" Jag's soft voice called from the other room. I'd been soaking so long, the water in the tub was cold. I stepped out, careful not to get the book wet, and wrapped a towel around myself.

"In here," I whispered. He had switched the lamp on and was rubbing his eyes when I came into the bedroom.

"Hey."

I slipped the book back onto the table next to his bed. "I didn't get it wet."

"Not. That." His eyes raked over my only-towel-covered body with a hungry expression.

"Knock it off." I pulled the towel tighter and returned to the bathroom. He followed me, putting his hand on the door before I could close it. I looked anywhere but at him. Lying fully clothed in bed with him was bad enough.

I couldn't help it when I drank him in, starting at his

feet and slowly creeping up to his neck, past his chin, lips, and nose to his eyes. When I finally reached them, my heart clutched almost painfully. I swallowed hard and cleared my throat, playing with the end of my towel.

"Vi, babe—"

"Don't talk like that," I said.

He smiled his Jag-winner. I took a shuddering breath and tried to focus. "Don't smile like that either. It's not fair."

"Okay, then. Let's talk about being fair." He carefully wove his fingers through mine. The way he studied the ground was adorable. He took a few slow steps back into the bedroom, pulling me with him.

"Jag—"

He suddenly stopped, his fingers fumbling along mine. He looked up. "You're still wearing it?" Anguish drowned out the shock in his voice.

Zenn's ring glinted in the lamplight.

24.

Things have a way of working themselves out. Ty always said so. Nothing has ever worked itself out for me—at least not in the way I wanted. A month ago I would've died to get a kiss and a ring from Zenn. Now I probably *would* die—literally.

Jag dropped my hand like it was on fire. "Well?"

"It doesn't mean anything. I just forgot, that's all." I wanted to rip the ring off and throw it down the drain, but I didn't trust the towel to stay up.

Jag folded his arms and glared. "Take it off."

After adjusting the towel so it was tucked tightly under my arms, I twisted and pulled on the ring. It seemed welded to my skin.

"Jag, I can't get it. Help me."

He stepped out of my reach. "No way. If it's a sticker, I don't want it to touch me."

"It already has," I said, rolling my eyes.

"Damn you," he said, his voice laced with danger.

"That's nice, Jag. It's not like I knew this thing was a sticker."

"Well, it will follow us wherever we go. It records things, Vi. *Records* them. You can't just throw a sticker away."

Like I needed him to school me about stickers. My dad invented them. They're put on undercover agents as well as criminals. They record conversations, feelings, temperatures, everything. The data is beamed back to headquarters, or wherever, for analysis. I did not need a lesson on stickers.

"We can break it," I said, desperate to make things right. "I can break it."

"They'll know everything anyway. I said I loved you. You practically said it back. We— They'll know everything!" He started pacing, throwing me a murderous look on every turn.

"This isn't my fault," I shot back. "You're being a jerk— again." I turned to get my clothes from the bathroom. I would not cry in front of him.

"Yeah, you should go, Vi. Go get that damn thing off. Don't come back until you do." For a moment I didn't even consider disobeying him. Until I remembered his promise.

"You said you wouldn't control me." I spun to face him, my fists clenched. He wouldn't look so perfect with his nose broken.

"I lied. If you can do it, why can't I?"

The heat rose to my face. He stood there, glaring, daring me to hit him. Which meant I totally wouldn't. Calmly, I strode into the bathroom and closed the door. Somehow I got dressed through the flood of tears pouring down my face. The ring still wouldn't come off, even in hot water, even when I wished it would.

When I went back into Jag's room, he was gone. I grabbed the book from his side table as I left. I locked my bedroom door and made the lights as bright as the sun at noon.

The book didn't outline how to remove stickers. I knew they were advanced, specifically made for use in the Special Forces. Agents wore them on their covert missions—there had to be a way to get them off.

I closed my eyes. My thoughts wandered to Zenn. My eyes flew open.

Zenn was a Special Forces agent.

He'd given me the sticker. He'd also given me the way to get it off.

Zenn knew how to do just enough without crossing the

line. He'd saved me countless times. He'd done something this time too, I knew it.

He had kissed me. I strained to find the word I'd heard during that forbidden activity.

Remember.

Oh, I remembered, all right. I remembered the pressure of his mouth, the warmth that had spread through my body with his touch.

And that had been more than just a birthday kiss from Zenn. It was his act of betrayal. One the Association wouldn't suspect.

I glanced at the walls. I'd just read they could be programmed to lie, which meant they were as good as alive, listening and watching my every move. Concentrating on the smooth plaster, I could almost see through it to the electronics underneath. The heat in the room increased, the buzz in my head grew louder, so loud I couldn't believe I hadn't heard it before. The tag in my wrist throbbed in response to the now unhidden techtricity.

I nodded, and the wall shut down. I stumbled to my knees from the release of the tech, still reeling with the knowledge that it existed so close and I couldn't feel it.

Coated in protectant. Zenn's words rang in my ears. The Association had a way to bypass my sensitivity now. By the time I had all the walls in my room disabled, my throat ached and my stomach felt heavy. Breaking tech was hard work.

In the bathroom, I adjusted the mirror until it pointed at my mouth.

I stuck out my tongue. Nothing.

An array of labeled bottles lined the shelf under the sink. I selected a mouthwash melter. I puckered at the bitterness as it dissolved on my tongue.

I opened my mouth again and peered inside. Still nothing.

I grabbed a blue teeth-cleaning tablet and chewed it.

Smiling widely, I examined my tongue. Through the blue foam, a message swam. I willed it to stay still so I could read it.

> Stickers only stick when there is danger.
> To remove the adhesive, use a ranger.

I copied it onto the first page of Jag's book and rinsed my mouth out. "Use a ranger . . . what does that mean?"

Of course, no one answered since I'd just turned off all surveillance in my room.

A ranger . . . a ranger . . . I didn't know who that meant. Ty had been a ranger, but she died a long time ago.

A knock sounded on the door. I shoved the book under my pillow before answering it.

Baldie waited with an army of Mechs. "So. You found Jag." He pushed past me into the room. The Mechs crowded in also, their silver canister bodies clinking together.

"Yeah," I said. "So what?"

He faced me, his arms folded. "And you turned off your walls."

"Yeah." I didn't mean for it to come out as a challenge.

He waved off my attitude. "I told you Director Myers didn't want you two together. Now he has a record that you spent time *in his bed*."

"We didn't—"

"I don't care what you did or didn't do, Miss Schoenfeld. What I care about is the fact that he now thinks I am incapable of doing my job." Baldie's voice was crisp and low. "I'm here to help you. I've worked for years to be in this position, Violet. I don't need you and that hormonal boy to screw it up. Stay away from him."

I scrutinized his angry eyes. He wasn't lying. Thinking quickly, I asked a Mech for a cup of hot chocolate. The mug materialized on a silver tray, and I plunged my stickered hand into it, hoping to interfere with the reception. I bit back a cry of pain so I could speak. "I need to find a ranger."

The anger in Baldie's face evaporated. "What did you say?"

"This ring is a sticker and to get it off, I need to find a ranger. Please, you've got to help me."

Baldie stepped closer to me and held my hand under the near-boiling liquid. "Around here, rangers only live in the Goodgrounds."

"Tell me how to find them," I demanded.

Baldie's eyes glazed over and then quickly cleared. He pulled out a tech device and deactivated his army of Mechs. "You don't have to compel me to help you." He locked the door, and somehow that didn't make breathing any easier for me. I wasn't even sure how I'd "compelled" him.

Then my comm beeped with an incoming message. From Cameron Blaus.

"You sent me an e-comm?" I asked.

Baldie's impatience rolled across the space between us. "Be careful. The walls here have eyes and ears, but I'll make sure they're set on reliable. Go alone. The rangers arrive at seven." He checked his phone. "It's five thirty." Then he clapped, reactivating the Mechs, and fled with them in his wake.

I pulled my throbbing hand out of the hot chocolate, wondering if I could trust him.

25.

Cameron Blaus's e-comm contained directions to get to, well, wherever the rangers were. For some reason, I decided to trust him. Maybe because he'd given me what I needed without being compelled.

I couldn't go gallivanting off to the Goodgrounds in my pajamas, so I checked the dresser in the corner. I found jeans and a T-shirt and changed before sneaking down the hall and into the sterile room with the silver desk. Crouching, I recited Baldie's instructions to myself: *Hallway one. Hallway four. Descender three. Teleporter seven—which requires a code.* Never mind that I despised descenders and had no idea what the password for the teleporter could be.

Baldie hadn't been that thorough. Or maybe he didn't know.

I crept toward the main entrance. My soft shoes made no noise and I felt like I was back in the Goodgrounds, doing what I did best. Breaking rules.

Once in the lobby, the hallway behind me closed and a new one opened on the opposite wall.

"Is that hallway one?" I whispered.

"Yes." The mechanical voice boomed in the stillness. Bright tech-lights reflected off the silver front door. I commanded the walls to power down, and the tech-buzz decreased. I wished the lights weren't so bright, and they immediately dimmed.

I ignored the fact that I was controlling everything with my mind. Just a fleeting thought, and I got what I wanted. My empty stomach clenched, and I pushed the thoughts of control away.

Come on, Vi, I coached myself. *Find the rangers.*

Sprinting toward the open hallway, something banged behind me. I didn't stop to look and willed the walls to close as I passed. They did, forcing me to run faster to avoid getting squished.

I ended up in another room with a silver desk. Techtricity burned hot and fast in my bloodstream. Several doorways led into unknown corridors with hidden problems.

"Hallway four?" I whispered. The middle door flashed

yellow. Baldie said he'd set the walls on reliable, and I slipped through the door before powering everything down. My trust only extended so far.

This corridor stretched with no end in sight. I started out running but slowed to a walk after only a few minutes. "Give me a break," I said, my breathing ragged and my pulse throbbing behind my eyes. "Where do I go?" The walls didn't answer because I'd nodded them off. Just when I needed the tech, it was gone. I considered turning them back on but didn't want to draw attention to myself by switching them on and off too much.

I couldn't see the room I'd come from. A small wave of panic surged at the thought of being stuck in this endless white tunnel. I leaned against the wall, gulping lungfuls of air.

I slid down the wall and leaned against it, my head in my hands. There had to be a way out of here. *Descenders . . . descenders . . .*

Descenders go down, just like ascenders go up. Sure, Thinkers can control people, but They suck at coming up with creative names for tech.

I examined the smooth concrete. It had been painted gray to prevent cracking. Further down the hallway, a purple eight shimmered. I wanted the lights to be darker, and the tech responded.

The eight grew brighter. Beyond that, a nine sparkled in blue lights. I spun around—a seven lay maybe twenty yards behind me. Striding quickly, I crossed back to the green three.

I stood in the middle of it and waited. Nothing happened. "Um, down?" I guessed. The floor vanished, as it always does in the case of a descender. I screamed, forgetting that I was on a secret mission and stealth counted.

Hot pain shot through my foot when I landed. Hobbling, I hid behind another desk. I rubbed my ankle and counted six open doorways in front of me. I needed to find teleporter seven. Staying low, I peered over the counter into the room behind me.

Ten teleporter terminals stood against the far wall. I couldn't believe they were here. I wondered where they went—I hadn't seen any terminals in the Badlands.

I moved across the room and stood in front of terminal seven. Now for the sticky part. The password. *Laboratory. Ranger. Zenn. Ty. Schoenfeld. Thane.* What would it take to get into the lab?

I'd only get one chance. Tech doesn't accept mistakes. "What's the password for laboratory four?"

No answer. They were personalized. Just great.

Several minutes passed, my heart thumping more wildly

with each one. I made a decision, took a deep breath, and stepped into the terminal.

"Violet," I announced, closing my eyes. I expected to be spit out on my butt amidst a shrieking alarm.

Instead, my particles shook and separated in a blitz of light and heat.

26.

Teleporting is the best—and worst—way to travel. The best part is the speed. You simply say where you want to go and your molecules evaporate, fly across space, and reassemble there. In a few seconds, any distance can be covered.

The bad thing is the reorganization of your particles. It isn't exactly painful, but it takes several seconds for your body to start functioning again.

Sometimes my lungs scream for air, and sometimes I can't see. Sometimes both. Everyone experiences different symptoms, so you should experiment with a partner until you know what yours are.

"Time," I said as soon as I could draw breath.

"Six forty-two," the walls said. I sucked at the air and kept my eyes closed until the bright lights in the room infused my eyelids.

My skin crawled with the intensity of the tech. I nodded off the walls and the buzz faded to a tolerable level. I had no idea where I was, because the same white walls and gray-painted cement surrounded me. Several doors led off into dark hallways. Two closed doors had nameplates pasted on the walls next to them.

The first one read: DR. ELLIANNA KREMPT, GREENIE LEVEL 9. The Hawk. I wondered what kind of doctor she was. I tried opening the door, but it didn't budge. Hey, I'm not above breaking and entering, but I didn't have time.

The second nameplate said CAMERON BLAUS, GREENIE LEVEL 10. Baldie. The trust that had blossomed for him withered, even if he had said he'd worked for years to be in his position.

The Hawk, a doctor, *and* a Greenie. Baldie, a level ten Greenie. That sure didn't seem to benefit me.

I surveyed the rest of the lab. Besides a wall of p-screens, counters glinted with silver tech instruments. It certainly felt like the Goodgrounds, and the middle Greenie's words came back to me. *You're not to come back. Ever.*

If I got caught here, I'd be in some real trouble. Some *control-others-or-else* kind of trouble.

Maybe I was still in the Badlands, still in the facility. After all, that place had some high-class tech.

I stepped to a window set into the wall next to the offices. My breath caught and I ducked. The neighboring room was the lab where I'd been tagged. Great—I was back in the Goodgrounds.

I pressed my back into the wall and brought my knees to my chest. Several deep breaths later, a whirring sound filled the lab as a cover descended over the window. All it took was a simple thought.

With the room secure, I stood. I spied a stack of phones and picked one up. A soft moan escaped my lips. The techtricity vibrated through my whole body. The phone had voice recording capabilities, a camera for still shots and video, lie detector software, iris recognizer options, surveillance security features, bar code scanners, and a GPS.

And a distance taser.

It was a weapon.

I flipped it over. The same insignia as on Baldie's teleporter ring—one swirling eight on top and one on the bottom—twisted on the back.

A thief since age twelve, I slipped the phone in my pocket.

On the next counter, small cylinders filled two white

trays. I picked one up and turned it over. Tiny bumps dotted the bottom, meant to be stabbed into the skin.

Yikes, another weapon. The same double figure eight wound around the cylinders. I recognized the symbol as two square knots, one tied over the other. Water girls know all about knots.

A handful of bio-cylinders went in my pocket. After that I didn't stop to examine the tech items. I just took as much as the cargo pockets in my jeans would hold.

While I was pilfering through a bin on the far side of the room, a teleporter ring slipped through my fingers. "Come on." I dug deeper, but it slid into the mishmash of tech items.

My eyes watered with the intensity of a fresh wave of techtricity. I spun and faced the terminals. Blue lights flashed along the top of one. Crouching down behind the counter, I waited.

But not alone.

Oh, no. Dad's voice roared into my head, filling it until I couldn't think my own thoughts.

Choose wisely. There's more at stake here than just you. The Association needs you. I can protect you, V.

I bit down hard, tasting blood. I hated to admit it, but he'd said exactly what I hoped he would. Because I certainly needed his protection about now.

27.

A man stepped out of the fifth terminal, followed by another from the second. The first kept his eyes closed as the other twitched violently.

"Odd," Mr. Twitchy said. He wore a short-sleeved shirt with black pants and shiny shoes. The second man wore a brown sweater, tan slacks, and a pair of leather sandals. Such strange clothing.

They had their silver hair pulled back into ponytails. Their gray eyes darted around the lab.

"The walls are off," Brown Sweater said.

"Maybe they turned off over the weekend?"

"Never before."

Their voices rolled and floated through the air. Their skin

glowed golden in the increased tech light. I thought for sure they were rangers.

Purple lights flashed on another terminal. My chest felt like it would burst into flames at any moment. The two rangers moved out of the way, their briefcases swinging. I swallowed hard, wondering which one of them could help me.

The Hawk stepped out of terminal ten. She retched into a bag—the worst side effect of teleportation—before straightening.

The sight of them erased the line between good and bad completely. I understood now. They allowed the sun to touch their skin, they wore whatever clothes they wanted, they traveled between the Goodgrounds and the Badlands, because they were free. They didn't break rules. They made them.

My dad was free. Again, I wondered if he could be on my side. I mean, I didn't want to be good or bad—just free. Surely the label didn't matter.

Of course it matters.

And those infuriating voice words were right. I clenched my fists and ordered Dad to *Get out of my head!*

"Morning, Brine," the Hawk said, nodding to Mr. Twitchy. "Hans."

"The walls are off," Hans said.

Nobody spoke, but the tech increased in the room. I muffled a moan as blinding pain consumed my stomach. I willed the tech to decrease so my internal organs wouldn't spontaneously combust. My control must have superseded theirs, because it worked, and I drew a cool breath.

"Hello?" the Hawk asked, looking around. She started nodding to the walls, but I wouldn't let them turn on. Controlling tech with my mind was easy, almost natural. And very sickening.

"Who's here?" the Hawk asked the wall.

It didn't answer.

She spun back to the other rangers. "Show me everything."

Hans, with gray eyes as cold as steel, clicked a button, and projections sprang to life on the walls. One screen showed a home with a small boy, maybe five years old, playing on the floor. His skin was stained by the sun. With bright eyes, he looked directly into the surveillance tech. He waved, and his mother smiled.

"What are you looking at, Surge?" She turned toward the camera. She obviously couldn't see it.

In another projection, a woman worked on something in the corner of the kitchen. A man, decked out in a crisp business suit, sat down at the table. The woman—complete with her Goodie hat and long-sleeved shirt—turned and put a plate of food in front of him. He didn't wear a hat, didn't have a receiver behind his ear, didn't have tanned skin. So was he good or not? He stared straight at the camera as he ate. He knew he was being watched—what was the point of that? Of course he wouldn't break the rules if he *knew* he was being monitored.

Then it hit me. Both the boy and the man were uncontrollable. Like me.

How many times had I "forgotten" to wear my hat indoors? Lots. How many times had I gazed out the window, wondering what it would feel like to have the sun coat my skin? Too many. How many times had I noticed the increase of tech in the corner of my kitchen, the flicker of a white light in my bedroom, or the hint of a red flash on my porch?

Every freaking day.

I'd already stopped breathing by the time I saw the projection of Jag lying in bed. He had a different notebook open and was writing in it.

"Strange," Hans said. "We've lost the connection to Violet's room." He pointed to several blank screens on the far side of the wall.

The Hawk swore. "Can you rewind?"

Brine stood there, half-turned away from the screens, a

definite curve sitting on his lips. I felt like I should know him, but he wasn't in my memory. Of the three people in the room, I was drawn to him the most, but I wasn't sure if I could trust him to help me.

Hans punched some keys, and my room filled the screens. He stopped the image, and I watched myself close my eyes and concentrate. After the slightest nod, two screens went blank and I fell to my knees. A moment later, all the screens were blank.

"She shut down her walls," the Hawk said, more awed than angry. "Rewind Jag's record." The image of Jag's room wavered as the time ticked backward. "Go back twelve hours," she said. "I want to see everything."

Oh, she'd see everything all right, including our conversation and me wearing Zenn's ring. Closing my eyes, I focused on the tech in Hans's e-board. I felt my way through the reader port and saw the electronic circuits and tiny pins. Willing it to freeze, I watched as the wheels and gadgets slowed and stopped. The electro-current faded away.

I opened my eyes and fell back, exhausted. A fire burned behind my eyes. But the screens where Jag had been writing had turned white. My mind raced with what I'd just done.

Hans started typing furiously, as the Hawk barked, "Status report."

"Completely down," Hans said. "The whole facility. The Special Forces. The wanted. Everything."

The Hawk's eyes sparked with an energy not entirely human. I reached in my pocket, gripping the phone as I decided that Hans and the Hawk had to go. I'd take my chances with Brine over the two of them.

I have no other choice, I rationalized as I activated the weapon.

Yes, you do. There's always a choice.

Shut up, Dad. I don't need parental advice right now.

28.

I peered around the corner to see a pair of shiny shoes loitering nearby. Brine knew where I was, but he just stood there. My mind raced with what to do next. Would Brine help me take out his team?

The Hawk and Hans remained close to the e-boards, both of them talking on a phone. Hans barked, "Get Thane Myers."

A scrap of paper fluttered to the ground—with my name on it. I snatched it up and cowered behind the counter. *Destroy their phones. Take them out.* The handwriting was unfamiliar and written in a hurry. I made a snap decision to trust Brine, even though he'd just written me a note.

Using my mind, I jammed their phone signals.

"Dammit!" the Hawk yelled.

Letting out a roar of frustration, Hans threw something against the wall. I seized on the shattering noise and stood, aiming my phone at him. I pressed send, and he fell with a loud thump.

The Hawk turned toward me, her hands up in a gesture of peace. She glanced at her phone. "Your dad is—"

I fired again, unwilling to hear what she had to say, especially about my dad. She slumped forward, her eyes still open. Her phone smoked, that conversation over. I felt the seconds tick by, each one long and painful, full of fear and the possibility of Dad showing up. Part of me wanted him to, desperate for answers. But mostly I didn't want him and his control tactics near me.

I faced Brine, pointing the phone at his chest. "Who are you?"

He raised both hands slowly, his eyes crinkling as his mouth curved up. "Impressive. Very nice." The way he said "nice" sounded too familiar. I knew him but couldn't find the memories.

"Who are you?" I asked again. The phone slipped in my sweaty hands. My gaze flickered from his hair to his face, trying to match his name with his features.

"Don't move." Brine stooped and dug something out of a cupboard. Then he pinned my stickered hand and pulled a silver glove over my fingers. It latched onto my wrist with tiny teeth. I cried out as the metal melted into a second skin. The sticker on my pinky bulged out slightly.

"There," he said. "Now that thing can't transmit anymore." He took a step back and regarded me with eyes like polished silver.

I looked at my hand and then back to him. "And you are . . . ?"

"Pace Barque," he said. "Jag's told me a lot about you."

The room spun. The walls threatened to crush me. Now I knew why I couldn't place him—the memories were Jag's. I dropped the phone as I swayed on my feet.

Pace helped me move to a chair where he spoke the same way Jag did. Not really an accent, and not with control, but more like a specific way he formed his vowels and how he clipped certain words like "sit" and "drink."

I sat.

I drank.

After a minute, I looked at Pace. He grinned, making the resemblance between him and Jag obvious. My stupid lips curved up just as they had the first time I'd met Jag.

"Look." He turned an electro-board toward me. Jag's face filled the screen. Then he held up his notebook. He'd written, *Hi Pace and Vi.*

"How the hell does he know everything?" I asked.

Pace laughed. "He can see and hear us, but we can't hear him," he explained while Jag scribbled in the stupid notebook.

"Just tell me what's going on," I said, refusing to look at the e-board. "I need to get this sticker off. I, uh, well, someone told me a ranger would help. You're a ranger, right?"

Pace crossed his arms, unsmiling. I looked away, but my gaze landed on the still forms of the Hawk and Hans. I swallowed hard, noting that their chests were rising and falling. But that didn't erase the images of them falling to the floor.

Some things are necessary, aren't they?

I hated that more and more, my dad was right. But how could he be right when what he stood for was wrong?

Maybe what I stand for isn't wrong.

Go away! I thought, needing the command to keep Dad at bay while I finished talking to Pace. And I needed to decide for myself if what my dad stood for was good or bad, but I didn't know how.

So I looked back at Pace, anger meshing with the uncertainty inside. He pointed to the e-board and walked away. Jag held the stupid notebook again, his fingers gripping the sides. This time the words spelled, *Sorry Vi. I was a high-class jerk. Please don't be mad. I love you.*

Of course my stupid mouth betrayed me. I smiled and leaned forward as if he would know that of course everything was forgiven, and yeah, I loved him too.

"Now that we've gotten that bit of embarrassing business out of the way, we can talk." Pace whipped the e-board around, said, "Later, brother," and slammed it shut.

"So. You're Vi. I can see why Jag likes you." His words were laced with more than one meaning, none of which I liked.

"Jag said you were gone and he was all alone," I said.

"Well, you've told lies before," he said with the patented Barque-shrug as if to say, *Jag did what he had to do.*

As if I didn't know I was a liar. What, was it a genetic trait in the Barque family to call people on every little fib they tell?

"Besides, it wasn't really a lie. Jag is alone. I left for the rangers four years ago."

"Good for you," I said. "Help me get this damn thing off."

He touched the slightly bulging ring with one fingertip. He closed his eyes and stroked the ring and then over my whole hand and up my arm. His hands reminded me of Jag's. His touch didn't.

Suddenly he let go, and his eyes flew open. "The ranger you seek is not here," he said, his voice strangely robotic. Then he slumped forward on the table.

"Pace? Pace! Wake up." I placed one hand on his shoulder and tucked a stray lock of hair back in place. He opened his eyes slowly and shook his head.

"Vi," he said as the color came back into his face. "You're in danger here. The sticker can't be removed in a situation of danger. Didn't your clue tell you that?"

"Yeah . . . but I don't . . . Wait a second," I said. "How did you know about a clue?"

"We have spies too," he said. "The Goodgrounds has been declining for years. Haven't you ever wondered why?"

No, I hadn't. They still seemed to have ultimate control over the population. I thought of my mother, still following blindly. But that farmer had a contraband book that screamed of freedom . . .

I shook my head, unsure about pretty much everything.

"The Association allows some places—like the Goodgrounds—to be on 'low alert' so they can find those with the gift of control." Pace didn't say it, but he meant people like me.

"What about the Badlands?" I thought about Lyle Schoenfeld's book, and Jag's parents, how they'd separated from the Goodgrounds twenty-five years ago.

"Places like the Badlands spring up whenever control is relaxed. It's human nature to fight for personal freedom.

People without gifts are allowed to live in uncontrolled cities, somewhat monitored by the neighboring land that's still controlled. But only for a little while."

"So what's Seaside? Frec?"

"Seaside is in the oceanic region, which is currently involved in a treaty with the Association. They have a Thinker, but they don't control the people. It's more like an appointed leader, and he allows the people . . ."

"To live freely," I supplied.

"As free as you can get in our world," Pace agreed. "There's a ranger there that offers political asylum to people with abilities. She'll help you."

I rubbed my eyes, wishing I could lie down and sleep for the next ten years. "What's the ranger's name?" I asked.

"Gavin." He eyed my bulging pockets. "I see you've raided our weaponry. You'll need it. Tell Gavin I'll be there as soon as I can." His tone radiated pure urgency.

"I'll tell her . . . if you tell me what you know about Thane and the city of Freedom."

Pace's eyes hardened. "Thane works for the Association. He's here, there, everywhere."

"And Freedom?"

"The homeland of the Association. Anything but free.

Imagine the Goodgrounds, but ten times worse." Techtricity started to vibrate in the air, but Pace didn't seem to notice.

"You're in a lot of danger here," he continued. "If you get caught in the Goodgrounds, it will mean your deportation to Freedom for Thinker training. You can't stay at the facility either. Thane's been running final tests on a wicked new piece of tech and is scheduled to arrive in the Badlands later today. You must escape before he does. If he can get you to Freedom, you'll be imprisoned."

The techtricity in the air caused my eyes to water. My barriers were coming down. The walls were coming back to life. I wanted to ask Pace a dozen more questions about Baldie and the Hawk and who I could trust, but instead I flung my arms around his neck. "Thane's coming, I've gotta go. Thanks, Pace. Stay safe."

"You too, Vi. My brother's had a hard life. If he lost you, he'd die."

I pushed away from him and studied his face. He smiled sadly. "He's never said as much, but I know how he feels about you. You're his Choker."

I had no idea what that meant. But I didn't have time for questions right then, so I filed it away for later.

"I haven't had time to sneak this to Jag yet. Can you

take it?" Pace handed me a bag loaded with more tech, and I barely had time to think about when he'd had time to sneak things to Jag as I slung it over my arm.

"Vi!" Pace called as I headed toward the terminal. "You need to tase me."

**29.** Tasing someone you don't like is really hard. Tasing someone you like is unthinkable. It hurts. Real bad. Sure, the Hawk and Hans probably deserved it. But Pace? Jag's big brother? Yeah, that was torture.

But I did it. I aimed horribly wrong and barely grazed his arm. He still fell like a sack of rocks. His pulse was beating strong in his wrist. I tucked Pace's hair behind his ear thinking that at least Jag had a friend.

That's the last nice thing I thought about Jag. What a big, fat liar. *Ooh, I'm all alone. Kiss me, Vi, so I'll feel better.* Whatever.

I stepped into the seventh terminal as the one on the end began to vibrate. I said my name and dissolved into particles before anyone appeared in the room.

Back at the facility, I raced down the quiet halls, my irritation growing into a living, breathing thing. Zenn had tricked me with a kiss. So had Jag. My dad used to hug me. Maybe that was his way of betraying me while I thought it was a gesture of love. How had I been so stupid? How could I not have known? About any of them—Zenn, Jag, Dad.

By the time I arrived at Jag's door, my fury was ready to be unleashed.

I knocked at the same time I entered. Jag sat at a desk under the window, writing in that loser notebook. He glanced up, all light and joy—until he saw me. "Um, you're pissed."

"You think?" I dumped the bag from Pace on the floor, my fists clenched at my sides. "I think you better tell me everything before I explode."

"Well, we wouldn't want that." His mouth twitched in an annoyingly sexy way. If he didn't look so good, I probably would've punched him. But I didn't want to mess up his face. Well, maybe a little.

"What the hell is a Choker?" I asked.

Jag's eyes flashed with fear before he smiled. "Did Pace call you that?"

"Yeah. And what's with Pace anyway? Why didn't you tell me about him? You two have been having a great party while I've been bawling my eyes out, sneaking around, and fighting with Baldie. Oh, and—"

"You've been crying?"

I ignored him. "—then I had to blast the Hawk and another tech ranger, and then your brother, who is very cute, by the way. All while wearing this stupid sticker that apparently I can't get off until I find—"

"Wait a minute. You think Pace is cute?"

Yeah, I'd said that just to see what he would say. "—Gavin, and I don't have the first clue who that is. And my pockets are loaded with weapons. Weapons, Jag! Like we're gonna have to fight or something. Assuming we can even—"

"Gavin? And what do you mean you think Pace is *cute*?"

"—get the hell out of here before my dad arrives and hauls us off to Freedom for a life of Thinking." Even as I said it, I wondered if maybe things would be different if I could hug my dad. Actually look into his eyes. Talk to him. He'd been in my head long enough, said things that blurred which side of the line he really stood on.

But I didn't want to find out for sure my dad wasn't on my side. Because if he bled good, that'd be like losing him all over again.

"Why are you just standing there? Haven't you heard anything I've said? Get packed up."

He remained standing there, staring.

"You'll have to carry your own tech crap. It's heavy." I couldn't sense my dad nearby, so I flopped on Jag's bed and closed my eyes. I hadn't slept and now we were headed off into who knows where. My head hurt, and I needed a pain stick. The bed shifted when Jag sat down. I expected his touch, but when his cool fingers brushed my arm, I still jumped.

He handed me a pain stick (damn him). "Vi, a Choker is someone who fills you up," he said, his soft voice reaching to the furthest parts of my soul. "Fills you up so full, you feel like you could choke."

Well, that was the absolute perfect thing to say (damn him to hell).

He wrapped his arms around me and cradled me against his chest. "You've been crying?"

"You looked like you were going to kill me last time I was here."

He chuckled softly. "You think Pace is cute?" His voice took on a distinct jealous edge.

I shrugged. "He looks a lot like his brother."

He kissed my gloved hand, right on the sticker. "So, we gotta go see Gavin."

"Yeah. She's a ranger in Seaside." I groaned. "Rangers! I

tased three of them. That's got to be like, I don't know, the death penalty or something."

"Yeah, we better get out of here." He got up and started shoving the clothes from his dresser in a backpack I'd never seen.

"Where'd you get that?" I asked.

"Pace. He's, uh, beamed in a few times since I got here."

The words going through my mind were so inappropriate, I bit down to keep them from spewing out. He tossed me an identical bag. "Here's yours. Go get your stuff. Don't forget that book."

"Fine," I said. "But you're telling me everything on the way there. You think I'm a liar? You're ten times worse than me. And you have to carry the weapons, Mr. Muscles."

He grinned at me without remorse. "What can I say? Baddies are born liars. Just look at you."

It took maybe two minutes to transfer the weapon-tech to the backpack and stuff in the extra set of clothes from the dresser. I had just powered on the wall to request a water bottle and protein packets when the door creaked open.

"Vi? Come on, we gotta go," Jag said.

Sighing, I shouldered my backpack and shoved the weapon phone in my pocket. He reached for my hand, and when we touched, an electric charge pulsed from his hand into mine. I didn't think that signaled something good. Or rather, it did mean something—or someone—good was very near. We needed to leave and fast.

"We can't teleport," Jag said, and he was right. Each terminal has to be programmed with a specific location, and we didn't know where we'd end up. And we didn't have time to reprogram them.

"What about the window?" I strode over to the billowing curtains and swept them aside. A blank wall stared back. "A projection," I whispered. Our options had dwindled. I wished I'd taken that stupid ring from Baldie when I had the chance.

"Come on, babe. Front door." I followed Jag into the hall, both of us running. I tried not to look at the walls, but my eyes lingered on them as they filled with faces.

Greenies.

My dad.

The Director.

Other Thinkers I didn't know.

They moved and spoke. Typed into c-boards. Glared at me as I sprinted into the lobby.

Zenn and his team of Special Forces formed a wall in front of the only exit. Zenn smiled, and I imagined his controlled eyes behind the dark sunglasses.

"Tell them to let us leave," Jag whispered.

"You're stuck," Zenn said as we approached.

Let us go. We have clearance. Director's orders. I repeated the words in my mind, telling each one of them individually.

One by one, they stepped back until only Zenn remained. "Vi," he said, and something desperate hid inside my name.

Jag pulled on me, but I jerked my hand away. Reaching up, I removed Zenn's lenses. His eyes held nothing but agony.

"Help me," Zenn pleaded. "I can't . . . I'm not strong . . . Your dad . . ." His voice became lost in his throat and tears leaked out his eyes. I cradled his cheek in my palm, remembering how much he once meant to me—how much he still did. I wanted nothing more than to bring him with us to Seaside.

"I love you, Vi. Don't forget about me." When Zenn opened his eyes, they clouded over again. He stiffened and turned toward the exit.

"Come on, Vi. He's being controlled. We have to go." Jag hauled me away from Zenn. I felt a part of my soul stay with him. He deserved that much.

Jag inhaled sharply, and I slammed into him before I realized he'd stopped.

"Thane," Jag said, his voice low and full of warning. "Or is it Lyle?"

My head cleared when Jag spoke that name. I peered around Jag's shoulder to see Dad standing in the doorway.

"Violet, I can help you get that sticker off." Dad's voice cascaded over me like a fountain of icy water. It zinged through every cell, a confirmation that he was a Thinker. I don't know how I'd missed it growing up. I hated him then, for the way he was controlling Zenn.

"She doesn't need your help," Jag growled.

"She certainly doesn't need yours," Dad shot back. "You're deliberately making this harder than it needs to be."

"And I always will." Jag took a tiny step backward, crushing into me even further. "I will not work for you. I will not serve the Association. Not now, not ever."

"It is your duty."

"I told you once, *Lyle*, I'll take death over duty."

I slipped my hand into Jag's and squeezed. My dad's gaze followed my movement, but he ignored Jag's use of his alias. "Violet? What is your choice?"

Seeing him in person didn't make anything easier. It only made the truth that much harder to shoulder. "I don't know what you're talking about." My throat scraped with the effort it took to speak.

"Jag refuses to use his voice, something he knows the Association of Directors desperately needs. And you, my talented offspring, you have the gift of control. So what will you do with it?"

Excellent question. "I won't help you," was all I could come up with.

"That's really not the best choice." His eyes shone with anger, with hurt, with disgust. "You have a responsibility to use your talents. How can you turn away the people who need your help?"

"By 'help' you mean controlling them?" Jag clipped out the words. "Brainwashing them so they live in ignorance of the world around them?"

"No, by giving them the structure they need so they don't pollute the water. So they don't cut down all the trees. So they don't neglect the sick and poor. So they don't destroy themselves with their selfish choices." Dad spoke in a calm, rational voice, but his face grew bright red. His fists clenched and he seemed to swell until he towered over me, the same way he had when I was a child. And I knew: he was good, through and through.

"Let us leave," Jag commanded. "Now." He squeezed my hand, which I took as Jag-speak for *Help me*.

I repeated his words in my mind and imagined a scene where my dad stepped to the side. Teleported back to the Goodgrounds. Took a long afternoon nap.

"I mean it, Thane. Let us leave, or I'll really use my voice on you."

I felt fierce desperation to make my dad let us leave; Jag's voice was that powerful. Again, I played through the scene where Dad let us go. Jag commanded, "Step aside."

Dad's eyes clouded. He stepped to the side. A moan escaped as he attempted to fight both Jag's voice and my mind control. He dropped to his knees, his head cradled in his hands. Something pulled in my heart. He was my dad. Family bonds and all that.

I'd taken two steps when a heavy hand landed on my shoulder.

"Remember me, Vi," Zenn wheezed. "I'm on your side."

Then Jag was pulling me out the door and my dad was cursing the day I was born. My eyes wouldn't focus in the bright sunlight. I stumbled along, tangled in painful thoughts of Dad and confusing memories of Zenn.

A sob raked through my throat as I ran.

30.

Only sand and betrayal existed. The desert landscape repeated endlessly, as did my tortured thoughts about my not-so-great—and not-so-missing—father.

Tall plants with strange limbs dotted the horizon. The arms grew at funky angles with sharp spikes covering every inch. They stood guard, protecting an unknown secret of the barren wasteland. The sun beat down on me until I poured with sweat.

"Jag," I panted. "I have to stop." I fell to my knees, gasping for air. Thankfully, Jag seemed just as winded.

"Okay," he said. "But only for a sec. One drink." He pulled off his backpack, revealing sweat stains where the straps had been. He produced a bottle of water and drank the whole thing. He handed one to me and I copied him, slopping a good part of it down the front of my shirt.

Jag took out another bottle and dumped half of it over his head and then did the same to me. The warm water cooled my skin, which felt like fire.

"Let's go," he said, repacking his bag and standing up. "Oh, your arms."

The T-shirt I wore left most of my arms exposed. I touched the bright pink flesh on my forearm. It hurt. Maybe the covering clothes were a good idea too.

Jag rifled all the way to the bottom of his pack. "Here, babe. Put this on. You might be hot, but it's better than burnt." He tossed me the long-sleeved prison shirt.

"I thought they took all our stuff away." I pulled the shirt over my head, waiting for an explanation. A look of supreme annoyance flashed across his face, like we didn't have time to talk about this. "Well?"

"Pace got it all," Jag said. "Food and everything. Let's go. There's a stream at the bluff, and some trees we can take cover in. Thane can't arrest us once we cross the gorge into the demilitarized zone." Lines of worry appeared around his eyes. "Come on, we've still got a long way to go."

I suppressed my questions about the treaties and how

Pace had the authority to get our stuff back. Better to be confused than caught.

And so I ran.

Somehow my lungs kept working, but every muscle complained. I'm sure I slowed Jag down, but he never said anything and matched my (s)low-class pace.

The crooked-armed trees and reddish sand blurred together until I could have passed the bluffs without noticing. Finally I fell down and couldn't get up again. Jag said something about going over the next hill to scout ahead. I think I grunted before he left.

I prayed the outcropping of rocks was nearby and that I would have the strength to get there.

"The cliffs are another mile or two," Jag said, collapsing next to me. "We can make it by full dark."

My voice scraped through my throat in an animal growl. That's Vi-talk for *Okay, but then I'm sleeping and you can't make me take another step.*

Jag smiled as he helped me stand up. "I know, babe. We'll sleep when we get there." He took out the weapon phones and handed me one. "But we have a welcoming committee."

I sighed. "Wonderful."

Halfway up the dirt swell, he crouched and slithered on his stomach, pushing with his feet and clawing with his hands.

I copied him, feeling like an idiot. But the intense techtricity drowned out the embarrassment.

"Tech," I whispered. "Tons of it."

"Who's in control?"

We reached the top, and I blinked back the white spots caused by the tech buzz. In the distance, orange cliffs stretched into the sky. A golden flicker of fire licked at the base, just before a dense stand of trees—and water. My mouth grew even drier.

I focused on the glow of the fire and found the minds of the people crowded around it. "Greenies," I whispered, relieved to feel that my dad wasn't there. "Mechs too."

"What do we do?" Jag asked.

"Well, I think I can power down the Mechs." I closed my eyes and extended my mind across the sand. "There're maybe . . . twenty of them. High-class ones that require decoders, but, well, I'm pretty sure I can do it without the code."

"Yeah, I'm pretty sure you can too."

A flicker of irritation sparked in my mind. I wished he would've told me about my talents a long time ago. I sure could have used that information to cross the border.

"Earth to Vi. Come on, babe. Stop blaming me for everything."

I took a deep breath to quiet the perfect comeback.

"Twenty Mechs present a lot of problems," Jag continued. "We can't have them following us into the desert. They never stop; the sun doesn't bother them. And, technically, they're immune from the treaties. Man, I hate Mechs. How many Greenies?"

I still needed a course on what the treaties entailed. Seemed to me that if Mechs could enter the desert, then it wasn't safe.

"I'll explain later," Jag said. "How many Greenies?"

Anger smoldered through my veins. I hated how he was inside my head, listening.

"Vi, how many Greenies?" He didn't sound sorry.

"Ten," I said, swallowing another insult. "Five men, five women."

"That's nothing. Why so few? Hmm, maybe they think we won't fight back. Weird."

"Jag, *everything* is weird to me, including every damn thing you just said." Yeah, the biting-my-tongue-thing only happens once in a lifetime, and I'd just used my quota.

He shrugged in response, which pissed me off even more.

"Okay, here's what we can do," Jag said, rolling over and staring at the sky. "Option number one: stay here and wait until morning so we can see better. That sucks. Forget that as option number one. New option number one: Get as close as we can, turn off all the Mechs, and fight the ten people." He didn't wait for me to reply. "Option number two: Get as close as we can, listen to see what their plans are, and then act at the best time. Hell, that sucks too. Okay, option number three: Well, I don't really have an option number three." He looked at me, like I was supposed to ramble on to myself about insane options too.

"Okay, why don't we just start west now?"

Jag sat up and rubbed sand out of his hair. "The road goes straight west from the bluff. There is no other way."

Why couldn't we just walk up like we didn't know they were there, turn off the Mechs, and tase everyone else? Maybe use those bio-canisters I'd taken. Jag could just tell them to sit down or something. I mean, the guy has *voice control.*

"Yeah, let's do that," Jag said, standing up.

I grabbed his pant leg and pulled hard. He fell, sending sand into my eyes and mouth. I coughed and spit. "Wait just a minute. Do what? I didn't say anything."

His eyes betrayed him—the guy could do a lot more than simply feel emotions.

I punched him, hard. In the shoulder—because I'm partial to his face. "I'm so sick of you reading my thoughts like they're your personal journal."

"I don't—"

"Shut up. Just shut up! Don't you realize that's what

Thinkers do? Read my thoughts? Get inside my head?" Fury and frustration combined with exhaustion and sparked behind my eyes in a beam of crimson light. "Since you're so fond of plans, here's mine: You leave me the hell alone. I'll get to Seaside on my own." I stood and marched over the hill, scanning for cover as I went. Stupid, stupid guy. Just because he could didn't mean he had the right to read my every thought.

Now that I'd let the anger out, it consumed me, driving all rational thought away. Only fury existed. Every injustice of my life piled up until I was pissed at the world—and determined to do something about it.

I slipped behind a plant and got a little too close. One of the spikes stabbed me in the back. I stifled a cry as an idea formed in my mind. Using tech this close would alert the Greenies . . .

I pulled out a bio-cylinder and stabbed it into the flesh of the plant. The explosion puffed out a cloud of dense smoke. The plant shook and white flowers descended from above. Several spines smoldered and fell off.

The Greenies gathered, looking toward me. Dashing to the next plant, the tech from the Mechs nearly blinded me. I closed my eyes and concentrated. I took out my phone just to be ready. I deactivated all twenty Mechs simply by telling them to power down. I imagined how still they stood, how quiet the night would be without their whirrings.

And what I thought came true.

That really got a rise out of the Greenies. Their shouts of concern could be heard from my position at least a half mile away.

There's nothing wrong. Violet isn't coming tonight. Thane arrived in time, and he apprehended her. I thought this, I thought it hard, sending it to each Greenie. As one, they turned away from the open desert and took a seat around the fire.

I squashed the rising nausea and snuck from plant to plant, careful to avoid being impaled by the spikes. The silhouettes of the Mechs shone silver in the firelight. I shivered. The sight of twenty high-class robots—that I'd made still, silent, dead—gave me some serious creeps.

The cool air pierced the thin fabric of my shirt and kissed my sunburned skin, making me hot and cold at the same time. My head throbbed with the effort it had taken to deactivate the Mechs and brainwash the Greenies. My own thoughts, what I was capable of, tortured me. The landscape swayed, and I threw up.

A hand touched my shoulder. I spun and fired the taser. Jag flew backward into the sand, arms and legs sprawled, eyes closed.

I swear I didn't know it was him.

31.

My mind raced while Jag's clothes smoked.

Jag or the Greenies? He wasn't dead, but we both might be if I helped him first.

My fine display of tech hadn't gone unnoticed—the Greenies abandoned the fire and began to fan out. Quickly, I took the phone from Jag's limp hand. I refused to look at his peaceful face.

The Greenies were moving steadily out into the open dirt. I scampered west and then darted toward the stand of trees littering the bank of a small stream, sending my *Everything is fine* transmissions again. These trees had green leaves and familiar bark. I crouched behind the first one I came to.

There were ten Greenies. One me. I couldn't just start

firing at random. I crawled from tree to tree until I lay hidden a few yards from their camp. Night settled in, silent and comfortable, but I was scared stiff. I controlled the Greenies, telling them there was no danger, and nobody was going to come that night, and hey, just relax and enjoy the company.

They did. They all resumed their places around the fire. "We need to train Violet," a man said. "Her natural talent exceeds even the most powerful Director in the Association. No wonder Thane was so persistent in waiting until she divulged her full scope of abilities."

"Breaking tech cuffs was pretty impressive."

"She almost escaped, simply by mentally telling that hovercopter pilot to let her go."

I couldn't get my heart to settle back in my chest. Listening to them talk about the things I'd done using my control made my stomach coil into a tight ball. My dad had been watching me for years. Waiting.

The beautiful rage awakened, spiraling through my blood until it coated my mouth.

"White Cliffs or Bloomington or perhaps Seaside will protect her. And even Thane must honor the treaties with the oceanic region."

"And Jag Barque has formidable talents as well. Remember how he talked the council to sleep last January? Don't underestimate him just because his talent is in his mouth." That voice belonged to Baldie.

"We never should have let these cities lapse so far."

"Reports have been sent to the Association every month, as required." Baldie sounded a little too defensive.

"I know. But the recruiting department hasn't found any-one new for a year."

"Except the Bower boy."

I inhaled sharply at the mention of Zenn's last name. What was this recruiting department and how had they found him? What exactly could he do?

"Don't forget about Surge Pennington, either. He watches the camera like it's a projection. His ability to sense tech is amazing."

"Nowhere near Violet's, though."

"Definitely not. But he was transported to Freedom for training this morning," a woman said. I stiffened at the casual way she spoke about the child. Like he wasn't a person with choices, but a pawn in their sick mind-control game. And now he'd been captured, and according to Pace, would be imprisoned in Freedom (how ironic) while They trained the humanity out of him, taught him how to brainwash others. I swallowed back the anger so I could continue eavesdropping.

The Greenies talked in turn, more gibberish I didn't

understand about how it was time to tame the west. How the Goodgrounds had enjoyed twenty-five years of freedom, but now They needed to re-establish control. If they called life in the Goodgrounds free, I didn't want to experience control.

"Freedom can be easily taken."

Baldie was right. Freedom can be easily taken. Men are easier to control than women, so I targeted them. Each man moved his hand to his pocket, extracted the tech-phone, and pressed send when I commanded. A moment later I stepped from behind the tree, firing both of my phones at the closest men.

The women fell at the hands of their fellow Greenies, and I had three men tased before the other two realized that anything had happened. I pressed the send button, and another man fell. The remaining Greenie—Baldie—stood gaping at me.

"I'll do it," I said, moving forward. My voice sounded stronger than I felt. "Put your phone down and empty your pockets."

Baldie lowered two phones, several bio-canisters, a golden key, and a teleporter ring to the ground.

"Now back up," I commanded, moving one step forward for each one he took back. I gathered the tech and put it in my pockets, trying not to look at the fallen Greenies.

"I can help you. I'm not working for Thane. Please, listen to me Violet."

"Whatever," I said.

"I've been protecting you for years. You have to believe me."

"I don't."

"Who do you think covered up all your rule-breaking in the Goodgrounds? Viol—"

I willed him to be silent. His expression glazed; his mouth hung open in defeat. I played with his teleporter ring, twirling it in my fingers to buy time. *I can silence without a silencer.* The thought brought hot tears of anger to my eyes. And what if he was telling the truth?

"Sit," I said.

He sat.

"Stay." I had no doubt that he would stay. I controlled him completely. Easily. My legs shook as I hurried out into the flat expanse to find Jag.

Kneeling over him, I tried to shake him awake. I said his name. Nothing worked. I took a deep breath and called to him in his mind. After a few moments his eyes opened and he moaned.

"Jag! Jag, I'm so sorry."

He sat up slowly, and I brushed the sand off his face and back.

"I don't know why I keep comin' back for more," he said, his voice thick and slow. "You're gonna kill me one day."

I laughed. It came out shaky and much louder than necessary.

"That wasn't a joke."

"You shouldn't sneak up on people in the dark," I said, my attitude resurfacing.

"I thought you'd sense me."

"I did, but I didn't know it was you, I swear."

"I thought we had, well . . ." He trailed off and stood up.

"We had what?"

He wouldn't look at me, not that I could have seen his expression in the dark. "Nothing." He threw the word over his shoulder as he stalked away.

I expected him to be mad. I didn't know it wouldn't be about getting tased.

As I followed him back to the fire, I came to the conclusion that boys are impossible to figure out. It seemed like everything I said or did was wrong.

Which reminded me of my mother. Nothing I did was ever good enough for her either.

Jag stood in front of Baldie, taking in the scene around the fire. "You did this? By yourself?" He looked at me and cocked one eyebrow.

I shrugged and rummaged through a backpack. I found a length of orange rope. When I turned, Jag was rifling through their food and supplies. I moved to tie up the fallen Greenies.

"Leave them," Jag said. "We're not staying."

"What?" I asked, looking behind him where he'd put Baldie to sleep.

"Night is the best time to travel," he said, dumping the contents of a backpack onto the ground. He threw two teleporter rings into the fire before gathering the rest of the tech and protein packets.

"Hey, those are teleporter rings," I said. I still had Baldie's in my pocket.

He looked up. "We're walking. Seaside doesn't allow unauthorized teleportation, and we don't have time to contact the right people. Hell, I don't even know who the right people are." He straightened and shouldered his bag.

"You said we could sleep," I complained, annoyed that I sounded like a three-year-old who wanted a sweet.

"We can," he said, not bothering to look at me. "Later. It'll take several days to get to Seaside on foot. We'll have plenty of time to sleep."

I wanted to scream, tell him how unfair he was. I wanted to tell him I hated him, but my voice wouldn't allow the words to be spoken.

"You wouldn't mean it anyway, Vi." He spoke in his *tell-me-everything* voice and stepped toward me slowly, his eyes trained on mine.

Refusing to let him see me cry, I picked up my backpack and left.

Using the GPS on the phone, I found west and walked along the bank of the stream. I heard him behind me, but I didn't wait because I didn't care.

Jag caught up and fell into step beside me. He walked close enough to hold hands and far enough away that words could never repair the damage we'd done to each other.

We came to the edge of the ravine, and Jag said, "After you."

Yeah, thanks, I thought, eyeing the barely there land bridge with only darkness underneath. We'd have to go one at a time. Across the gorge lay the jagged landscape of the demilitarized zone.

My legs felt waterlogged as I shuffled along the narrow path, and when I reached the other side, I hurried behind an outcropping of rock. *Let's see how Jag likes it when he's left behind.*

Rage simmered in my veins as I chose random paths that seemed like they'd take me farther west. I couldn't trust anything that came out of his mouth. He'd said he'd help me, but he hadn't. He blamed me for the sticker and the tag and who knows what else. When he told me he loved me, he'd probably been lying about that too.

That hurt. A lot. Because, yeah, I'm a liar too, but about that, I hadn't. I really loved that stupid Jag Barque.

But what about my dad, with all his aliases—did I still love him? I didn't know. Blood was thicker than water, right? But was blood thicker than love? Than choice? Than freedom?

I reran my dad's speech at the facility through my head. Maybe he was right. Maybe people do need someone to keep them in line.

The images from primary school repeated in my head. Elderly people living in the streets.

The bones of children practically popping through their skin because they didn't have enough to eat.

The hollow, worn-out faces of those who had no one to take care of them.

The Association of Directors had fixed all that. Would it be so horrible to use my control to make sure our society didn't lapse back into poverty, ruin, and starvation?

It seemed like an easy choice. It wasn't.

Just as I forced one foot in front of the other, I forced the disturbing thoughts out of my head, fumbling for one good memory.

I remembered my tenth birthday, when Ty made me a pink birthday cake with purple frosting. My mother was angry because Ty used her last ration of cherries to tint the cake batter.

But Ty didn't get punished. My mother adored her, and Ty showed her how the cake had risen perfectly. My mother smiled and got out the replicator to take the only picture I had of any of my birthdays. And I wasn't even in it.

When the sun started to rise, I looked behind me for Jag. Most of me wanted to see him, following me to make sure I was okay—or at least headed in the right direction. But a tiny part didn't want to find him. That part needed more than a night to reason through the confusing mess of good and bad and free and safe and betrayal and love.

He emerged like a dark shadow from the awakening sky. "You hungry?" he asked, spitting out the words like it was my fault hunger existed.

My stomach roared. "No," I lied, barely forming the word in my dry throat.

"Come on, Vi—"

"I don't need your help."

"I have protein packets."

Ignoring him—and the protests of my belly—I found a cave amidst the rocky landscape big enough to lie down in.

I did not need Jag Barque to survive.

**32.** I couldn't sleep with all the growling in my gut. Just when I'd drift off, my insides ached as if they were about to collapse.

I finally couldn't take it anymore. I sat up, feeling weak. I had to eat. Across from me, Jag slept. I slipped over the rocky surface, cringing when the grating sounds of my movement echoed off the cave walls.

Jag's backpack unzipped easily, quietly. The silver protein packets glinted underneath the orange rope. I reached for them, cursing silently when they slid further into the pack.

I had just managed to trap a packet between my fingers when Jag muttered in his sleep. I jumped and backpedaled away. The lines on his face smoothed as he settled back into his dream. I wondered which one it was this time. Part of me longed to be asleep so I could experience his memories with him. Another part hated that I could enter his mind at all. And still another part wanted nothing more than to eat. Now.

Tucking the lone protein packet in my back pocket, I pulled on my backpack and stumbled in the direction of the river. I twisted through the canyon down to the water's edge. My head felt detached and everything was turning white.

I drank greedily, not caring that the water needed to be purified. A few brush trees and scraggly bushes grew nearby, but nothing like the bulbs I'd eaten in the Badlands. I dumped out the contents of my first aid kit so I could mix the protein packet. Nothing had ever tasted so good as that putrid drink.

But I was still starving. One packet wasn't going to sustain me for very long.

I dug through the clothes and tech supplies, laying them on the ground to see them better. The three tech-phones were incapable of making food. That seemed like a good feature to have. The stupid phone could do everything else.

I had a dozen bio-cylinders. Two round platters lay next to them. After picking one up, I felt the tech twitch inside the sliver of metal. My fingers shook at the same time.

The now-familiar insignia of the two square knots snaking around each other adorned the back. Maybe this was another weapon. Maybe you could throw it and it would grow nasty edges and cut enemies down. Who knew?

Jag, probably.

I pushed the plates away along with the annoying thought of Jag. I turned my attention to the two cubes of pure silver. They didn't bear the double square knot. I picked one up and the techtricity infiltrated my mind, almost whispering instructions. I pressed with my thumb on one side and my forefinger on the other.

The cube shook and started to unfold. I dropped it and watched as it flopped into a square big enough to stand on. I didn't think it was a teleporter pad, though it looked like one.

The tray looked familiar . . . like the one my hot chocolate had arrived on at the tech facility.

"Pink birthday cake with purple frosting," I said. It appeared on the square. I smiled, picked it up, and stuffed it in my mouth.

"Happy Birthday to me," I sang softly to myself. "Scalloped potatoes." A large plate of potatoes and onions with cheese sauce appeared. I ate it in about two minutes even though it burned my mouth.

"Milk," I said next, but the square remained empty. "Fine. Whole milk." With the clarification, a large glass of creamy white milk appeared. Nothing had ever tasted so good as that milk.

I sighed happily and wiped my mouth. A flicker of light beamed in my mind, a signal that someone with power was drawing near. I started stuffing everything back into the pack.

I glanced behind me to the path through the canyon— the only way out. Pulling on my pack, I ran parallel to the river, toward the safety of a small cluster of rocks. Just as I crouched behind them, Jag emerged from the canyon and crossed to the water. He bent down and drank from the stream.

Then he moved toward me slowly, his eyes trained on the ground. He stopped in the exact spot I'd been eating my solitary birthday meal. Today was his birthday too. I wondered if he felt as alone as I did, if he also longed to have a party with his sister—the way it should have been.

"I don't have a sister," he whispered. I hadn't seen him approach. Hadn't heard him, he was just suddenly there. "I only want you."

The stupid tears pricked the back of my throat. When had I become such a baby? Anyway, now I knew why I hadn't seen him: everything swam in my vision, including his perfect smile and caring eyes. But he wouldn't trick me again.

"Liar." I pushed past him and retraced my steps to the cave. Jag followed me, and I knew him, felt him, almost became one with him. Not in a physical way, but emotional.

Our connection. This was what he thought I should have sensed last night before tasing him.

"Vi, wait," he called.

I paused just outside the cave, the swirl of emotions threatening to engulf me.

"I'm sorry," he said.

"Whatever."

"Why are you so mad?"

"Why am I so mad? *Why am I*—? Look, if you don't know, I'm not going to fill you in."

"Because I said we couldn't sleep?"

"Because of everything! You act like it's no big deal to raid my thoughts. You think I'm something special, but you don't tell me anything. You say you love me, but you don't trust me." I paused, not wanting to get too carried away and spill everything I'd been hiding from him.

His shoulders slumped. "I'm sorry. There's so much I want to tell you, but I need you to make your own decisions."

I put one hand on my hip. "Whatever you have to tell yourself to sleep at night, Barque." I turned toward the cave.

He touched my shoulder. "I don't want to influence you with my voice."

Damn him. He always *always* knew the perfect thing to say. I adjusted my backpack and lay down. He climbed into the cavity with me, and I was crying (yeah, again) before his strong arms encircled me and his velvety voice whispered in my ear.

"Shh, I love you. Happy birthday, babe." He could influence me with that voice any day. "And I can't hear your thoughts. Just what you feel. I didn't know what your plan was, just that it felt good, it felt like it—whatever it was—would work."

"What plan?"

Jag chuckled, and the tension between us disappeared. I lay in his arms, finally feeling safe. I shivered and he pulled me closer, only for me to push him away a few minutes later when I got too hot.

Finally, when I'd kept us both awake for an hour, he got up and retrieved the ointment from his first aid kit.

"Take off that shirt," he said. "I mean, if you want my help."

"Shut up. I won't die from a sunburn." At least I thought I wouldn't. I'd always been told there was nothing worse than a sunburn, but now that I'd seen so many Baddies, I wasn't so sure.

"Okay, then." He lay back down, stretching his hands behind his head and studying the ceiling of the cave like it held the secret to living an uncontrolled life.

"But I—want your help."

He grinned as he sat up. "Take off your shirt."

I peeled off the prison shirt. Because of the tee I still wore, only my arms glowed pink. But, damn, they hurt.

"No wonder you can't sleep." He gently rubbed the cream into my arms, neck, and face.

I flinched. "Cold," I murmured.

When he finished, he helped me put the long-sleeved shirt back on. "You'll have to get it wet to take it off, okay? Don't rip it. It'll hurt."

I nodded, so tired I couldn't speak. I simply curled into his embrace again, wishing sleep would take me so I wouldn't have to think anymore.

"Vi?"

"Hmm?"

"Will your dad give up?"

I didn't answer right away, even though I knew. Surely Jag knew too. He'd obviously had more experience with my dad—with Thane—than I had. Just as I was about to answer, Jag said, "I'll protect you. I promise."

Yeah, he knew. And I did too.

My dad was not the giving-up type.

 I settle into my desk chair and cross my legs. I can't decide if I want to hear what he has to say. I sigh. "Bring him in."

Zenn comes through the door, shrugging off the hands of his escorts. "Get off me." He strides forward, his eyes locked on mine. "Jag, man, come on. What's with the royal treatment?"

I regard him for a moment before waving away the others.

Zenn still has the softness to his face, though exhaustion has already carved lines around his eyes.

"Lay it out for me, Zenn," I say, steepling my fingers under my chin.

Zenn stands straight and glares at me from across my desk. I'll say one thing about him: he's got guts. "There are more important things in my life right now."

"That's it? That's your answer?"

"Yes."

"So you're telling me there're more important things in *your* life. More important than the work *we're* doing. More important than being *controlled*." I don't try to keep the malice out of my voice.

Zenn looks down. "Yes."

My jaw tightens. Inside, fury mixes with unrest. Okay, and a little fear. "Look, Zenn, you're the only Goodie I've got on the inside. You've done more for the Resistance in two years than anyone. I need to know you're with me. One hundred percent. All the way."

Zenn looks up, a fire burning in his eyes. I've seen it before. His mind is made up. "For now," he says.

I tilt my head, trying to hear the true meaning behind the words. Long after he's ushered out, I'm still thinking about it.

I have this sinking feeling Zenn's not with me anymore. He's gone Informant.

I can't trust him.

Problem: He already knows too much.

* * *

I sat up, my mind swirling with what Zenn knew about me. He knew pretty much everything. The dank air in the cave felt too thick to breathe. My chest constricted with the effort it took to inhale.

Next to me, Jag bolted upright. His eyes widened, staring right into mine. "What's wrong?"

I forced myself to exhale. "Nothing."

He studied me, much the same way I imagined he eyed Zenn. "Your emotions are all over the place. They woke me up."

"Bad dreams," I said. Hey, it wasn't entirely a lie. I let him take me in his arms. Let him stroke my hair. Let him whisper comforting words.

I closed my eyes and waited until he fell back to sleep. Then I got up and sat against the wall, the rocky ground grinding into my tailbone.

If I didn't fall asleep, I couldn't enter his mind again.

"You should take that shirt off," Jag said. "Let your arms get some air."

I knelt next to the river where he had finished filling our water bottles. The water looked like liquid ice, but I stuck my arms in all the way to the shoulder. The shirt billowed off the sticky ointment. Every time I removed my arms from the water, the fabric clung again.

"Can you help me?" I called over my shoulder.

Jag took the hem of the shirt and lifted, pulling it over my head before trying to peel it off my arms. The cold water and slight breeze soothed my burned flesh. I adjusted my T-shirt so it covered my stomach.

"Nice," he said, his eyes locked on my body. He tossed the wet shirt to the side and kissed me with a passion I now recognized as the hormonal-Jag style of kissing.

"Stop it. You're bad."

"For the love of all that's bad, you're beautiful." He planted a kiss just under my jaw. Then a little farther down on my neck. Good alarms sounded in my head. The rush from Jag's lips almost drowned them out.

Almost.

"Jag, I—"

"It's fine, babe. We're only kissing. It's fine."

And everything was fine. Kissing him was more than fine. Life was absolutely fine. Everything would always be blissfully fine . . .

The knowledge that he'd used his voice slammed into me like a heavy weight. I tried to sit up and pull my T-shirt down at the same time. "You're controlling me. It's not fine."

"Violet," he said, his eyes locked on mine now. "Vi, baby." His voice was soft, but not controlling. "I did promise, sorry."

"I don't want, well—" I clamped my mouth shut before I said anything too embarrassing.

He stood up and retrieved a new T-shirt. "Here. That shirt should be burned," he said, glancing pointedly at the one I had on. "I'll wait for you in the canyon."

I nodded, unable to speak. I checked to make sure he was really gone and then I changed. The cool air felt good on my arms, but nothing compared to how Jag's mouth had felt on my neck or my ear or my lips—

Jag laughed from wherever he waited. *Stupid mind-reading hormone-driven boy.* I hoped he heard that. I didn't care what he said—he could read a lot more than feelings.

He wore a clean shirt when I reached him. He chuckled again and slid his arm around my waist. "You ready? We have like, two weeks of walking ahead of us."

"I hate that you can feel what I feel," I complained. "Really, really hate it."

"I can stop. If you want."

"Yes, please." But I could tell he didn't want to.

His face fell and he started to remove his arm.

"No. No, it's okay," I said, taking his hand and replacing it on my hip. "It's fine, babe. Fine."

"You almost sounded like me right then!" He laughed, a clear sound that carried through the twilight.

I punched him and his laughter ended in an "Oof!"

"Don't control me again."

A little while later, Jag stopped walking and studied the starry sky. "We're adults now. Officially."

"Great," I said. Like it really mattered. So now I could get a job. Big deal.

"There are stricter punishments for adults," Jag said.

That brought a hollow feeling to my stomach. He took my hand and pulled me forward again. The silence rained down while I imagined what the Association might do to me now that I was of age.

I stopped walking. "Jag, what's going to happen when we get to Seaside?"

The moonlight emphasized the tension in his mouth. "Well, there's some protection with Gavin. But I don't know what Thane, uh, your dad, will do. The Association has pull everywhere, even if it's less in the oceanic region. And they want us." He moved forward again, but I stayed put.

"Do you know Gavin?"

"Course, she's Pace's girlfriend."

"What can she offer me?"

"I don't know."

"Liar. You never tell me anything."

"No, seriously. Every case is different." Jag threaded his fingers through mine. "Besides, you never told me why you went to see Pace or how you took out ten Greenies by yourself. You have secrets of your own."

"They're not secrets," I argued, striding forward. "You never asked. You're too busy being pissed off—or kissing me."

"Which would you like right now? 'Cause I could go either way." Danger lurked in his voice.

I stopped suddenly and grabbed his arm. I kissed him in the hormonal-Vi style. When he pulled away, I said, "I'll tell you if you promise not to get so pissy about things."

"That's a two-way street, Vi."

I kissed him again, tracing my fingers along his neck and into his hair. "Is it?"

"No," he breathed. "No, it's not." We kissed some more, his hands tightening along my waist.

"So you'll be nicer?" I whispered.

"Yes, absolutely."

"Good." I pulled away and strung my fingers through his. We walked for a few minutes before he spoke.

"You're really not fair," he said, his voice wounded. "If I

can't control you, you shouldn't be able to control me."

I giggled. Yes, giggled. "I didn't use my mind power on you. Just my body."

"That's twice as deadly."

As we walked, I told Jag about the message from Zenn's kiss, and he got all mad, like I'd known he would.

"You already promised."

"Kiss me again so I can remember."

"Nice try."

"Fine. Then I'm still mad."

"Listen, Jag. It's not like I cheated on you or anything. I don't understand why you're so jealous of him."

He looked at me, his gaze heavier than the darkness. "Vi, I can still feel your feelings for him. You've loved him for a long time. That doesn't disappear overnight. Even though he gave you that sticker, you'd go back right now and save him if you could."

I opened my mouth to argue, but he cut me off. "Don't. I can *feel* it. He's being controlled in the worst way and you want to help him. Because he's exactly like you. He stopped listening to the transmissions a long time ago too. He shielded you from some of the hardest things and comforted you during the worst times of your life. Those memories will *never* go away. You've loved him for five years, but you've only known me for like, a week."

I couldn't argue. Zenn had been my whole life. In many ways, he still was.

"More than a week," I said, just to be difficult.

Jag's grip on my hand tightened. "Fine. Two weeks."

I told him about sneaking into the lab after the e-comm from Baldie. Then I told him about dodging through the trees and as much of the Greenie's conversation as I could remember. I ended with how I controlled the five men so they would tase the women.

"Wow," he said.

"Yeah, men are pretty easy to control."

He slugged me in the shoulder. Like with his fist and everything. I hit him right back. Somehow we ended up holding hands afterward. Go figure.

"So Pace was beaming in to see you, huh?" I asked, with a heavy dose of *you-better-spill-your-secrets-too* thrown in.

"A couple of times. He had clearance."

"From who?"

Jag shrugged with one shoulder. "That bald guy, I think."

"That guy helped me get into the lab too. He said he was on my side. Do you think—well, how could he be helping us?" I watched Jag's face, but he kept his gaze on the horizon.

"Everyone has spies, babe."

"What does that mean?"

"Sometimes those who appear good are just pretending. I mean, look at you."

I thought about what he said. "My dad wasn't pretending."

"No, he was not." Jag spoke so softly, I barely heard him. After that, we walked in silence, the midnight sky surrounding us in cool air. My sunburned arms convinced me that traveling at night really was best.

We walked so much that when I slept during the day, I dreamt about walking. At least the tech-cube kept producing whatever we wanted to eat, and besides what came from what we carried, the air in the demilitarized zone didn't hold an ounce of techtricity.

Night after night, we trudged along, Jag regarding the stars while I wrestled with myself over who my dad was, with who I was.

With what my duty was.

Who I should follow.

If I should follow anyone at all. Maybe my brand of control would benefit people more than my dad's. Powers like mine could be used for good. Curing diseases. Purifying water.

I didn't want to take away the little things, the traits that made people unique, in order to provide that kind of life.

I'd seen Zenn at the facility. He wasn't himself. And that wasn't fair at all. I wondered that maybe if I joined Dad, he'd relax a little bit. Together, we could still work for the common good, but we wouldn't have to erase personalities to do it.

I'd almost have myself convinced of this golden future with my dad when I'd remember the loathing in his eyes.

Then I'd have to start all over again. I never found any answers, no matter how many different ways I looked at the situation. No matter how many stars I wished on.

"How much further?" I complained again the tenth night.

"Soon, Vi." Jag laughed and pulled me close. "Patience."

Yeah, I don't have much of that.

When the sun came up, my heart rose with it. The ocean loomed in front of me. I'd never seen so much water at once. It called to me, encouraged me to come closer. To touch it as it lapped at the earth. To taste the saltiness of it in my mouth.

A great city at least the size of the Southern Rim sat along the blue expanse.

Suddenly my throat tightened, my heart constricted. A presence—an incredibly strong and all-too-familiar presence—invaded my mind.

34.

Somehow "Dad" escaped my throat.

"Dammit." Jag pulled me down an embankment to a ditch. "Now what?"

I dropped to the ground next to him, as if I could hide my mind from my dad that way. "He's here . . . somewhere." I closed my eyes, trying to find Dad without inserting myself into his head. "Let's sneak around to the north."

Using the demilitarized zone was clever, V. Where are you going now? The way he called me V made my heart twist. How I'd longed to hear that. Now it only sickened me. I quickly forced him from my mind.

Jag gripped my hand, and together we stood. "Let's go."

As we ran I struggled to push the fear to the back of my

mind, the same way I kept pushing the sweat off my fore-head. It mingled with the dirt, creating mud that stung the corners of my eyes.

Then I couldn't see at all. "Jag! Tech!" I dropped to my knees, hoping to find cover from the unknown danger in the low bushes.

"Get your phone," Jag whispered from beside me. His beeped as he activated it, but I fumbled for my pocket, my vision still cloudy.

"Holy overload." My eyes streamed. My stomach boiled.

"Viii," he said, drawing out my name dangerously. "Who are they?"

I gave up the search for my phone and focused. "There're two people. Both men. Rangers. They can sense our tech."

"Rangers?"

Their minds . . . their minds were clear. Sharp. Uncontrolled. And focused on harnessing the power of the earth. "Definitely rangers."

Jag didn't move, didn't breathe. Then his fingers fumbled over mine and he pulled me to my feet.

"Jag?" The man who spoke had a deep voice. I couldn't physically see him, but his name floated through my mind: *Mark Kellogg.*

Surprise flitted across Mark's subconscious. He shifted

nervously while the other guy—his younger brother Jake—came up beside him. They both radiated advanced tech energy, and they wanted ours.

"We need to see Gavin." Jag's voice sounded odd, too breathy or something. He was afraid, and that terrified me.

"Everything's gone to hell," Mark said. "Some heavies arrived from the Association. Gavin is in a special session, and no outsiders are permitted to enter the city."

His words pierced the balloon of hope I'd been cultivating. "No outsiders?" I whispered.

Jag squeezed my hand, and I stifled a whimper of pain. Thankfully, my vision began to clear as I acclimated to the tech, but damn, that tag ached under Jag's viselike grip.

"We need to see her," Jag said, the fear gone. "Take us to her." His voice could command armies. Mark's mind turned to mush.

"Sure, she'll be done by lunch. Let's go." He'd have done anything Jag said. Hell, I would've taken Jag to Gavin.

The brothers moved toward the scrub forest. Jag bent down to retrieve his bag, and we exchanged a glance. I didn't like what I saw on his face: worry.

We caught up to the rangers and Jag made small talk with them. I moved in silence, a ball of anxiety growing in my stomach.

As we walked, the sun peeked over the horizon, and the first rays nipped at my healing-but-still-burnt face. The scrub forest gave way to towering trees. They were huge, and I mean like they-stretch-so-far-I-can't-see-the-tops-of-them huge.

Legends about tall trees had been passed around the Goodgrounds, especially in the City of Water, where the only forests grew. Old land and ancient trees supposedly harbored power beyond our tech. I felt a sense of peace and awe walking through the old trees, almost like they understood me.

". . . yeah, that's a good one!" Jag's laughter floated through my thoughts, causing some of the worry to unknot.

When we cleared the last of the forest, the rangers headed toward a small dock where a barge waited.

The tallest guy, Mark, pulled something out of his bag and checked it. I analyzed the brothers for the first time. They had bright blue eyes and luxurious waves of copper hair hanging to their shoulders. Jag looked like a complete freak with his black dye job and mess of spikes.

"So, we haven't seen much of Gavin lately," Jake said. "Even before the Thinkers showed up."

"Oh yeah?" Jag asked. "Why's that?" His voice sounded forced.

"Well, she likes to hang with her own crowd, if you know what I mean."

Jag cast a quick glance at me. "I'm not sure I do."

And if he didn't, I was completely clueless. Jake was trying to say something, something important.

"You know rangers," Mark said. "They like to stick to their own kind."

"Yeah, you mind rangers are especially clique-ish," Jake said, smirking at Jag and then me.

I stalled on the words "mind rangers." Jag was a ranger? And if he was, did that mean I was too?

"We are not clique-ish," Jag said, admitting his mind-ranger status. A few seconds passed as reality sank in, took root.

I am a mind ranger.

No wonder my dad wanted me so badly.

35.

"Are you okay?" Mark asked, looking at me. I realized a choking noise was coming from my throat.

I nodded, even though I still couldn't get a proper breath. If I couldn't enter Seaside and find asylum, well, I couldn't even think about what might happen to me.

Jag said something that didn't penetrate my ears. I wanted to spew everything out so I wouldn't get tangled up in the panic, but I couldn't order the words properly.

When I looked up, Jag and I stood alone on the dock. Jake and Mark busied themselves on the barge. Not knowing if Jag could hear my words in his mind or just feelings through, well, however he feels stuff. Maybe through his heart? Anyway, I tried to tell him the reason for my fear.

"Don't worry, babe," he whispered. "I know Gavin. We'll get you in."

"What if you can't?" I felt like I was six years old and needed reassurance that no matter what, everything would work out, that I'd be safe.

Jag gently pulled me toward the boat, his doubt voiced in his silence.

"Let me talk to them alone," Jag said, pointing to the steps that led below deck before moving to stand next to Mark. "You should hide out down there anyway, just as a precaution."

Precaution. Whatever. But as Jake untied the boat from the dock and joined Jag and Mark on the bow of the barge, I slipped down the stairs into the cargo hold. It was damp and smelly. Tech took up every nook and cranny. These rangers weren't kidding around. At least the tech hadn't been activated yet. I would've been writhing on the floor, blind.

The rolling motion of the ship calmed me. A few minutes later Jag stumbled down the steps, his face tinged with green.

"What's wrong?"

"Sick," he choked out. "The water . . . moves."

I tried not to laugh (yeah, that didn't work) as Jag bent over and threw up in a bucket. "Haven't you ever been on a boat?"

"No."

"Well, it's just like hoverboarding, right? You move on the air like this."

"Totally different," he said, "and you're not helping."

"Sorry." I patted him on the back as he lost his lunch again.

"You okay?" Mark shouted down. "We have seasick patches up here."

"Coming." Jag groaned and swayed as he turned, still clutching the bucket. "Mark thinks we can get you in to see Gavin." He wiped his mouth. "Let me worry about it, okay?" Then he disappeared up the stairs.

Right, let him worry about it. How was I supposed to stop stewing over the possibility of remaining a fugitive? Especially with my dad lurking in the city, waiting to swoop in and arrest me the first chance he got. At least I couldn't feel him anywhere close by.

After we docked, I tried to be invisible as I followed the brothers down a busy main street lined with brick, metal, and stone buildings. They were old, built without tech. I gaped at the ancient structures, drawn to how each one possessed a unique beauty.

Jag kept a firm grip on my hand as we moved through a rotating glass door in the tallest building on the island. We crossed the lobby to a row of ascenders. Jake and Mark stepped into a circle and disappeared in an upward flash of light.

Great. I hate ascenders almost as much as heights. They give you a none-too-gentle push upward. Usually there's enough time for your molecules to evaporate before you splat on the ceiling. Usually.

The lobby bubbled with a fountain and idle chatter. I placed my hand inside the circle they'd been in. The ascender vibrated with power, sending energy into my bones and making my tag feel white-hot under my skin.

Jag pulled me into the circle and said, "Lounge, sixteenth floor."

We arrived in a waiting room with soft chairs. A long couch separated a desk and a set of doors. Ancient pictures done with paint, not computer-generated images, hung on the walls. Jag set his backpack on the couch. "Let me talk to her first." He turned to Mark and Jake. "Lead the way, boys."

He left me sitting there next to his backpack. Waiting—which is so not my thing. I'd never felt so lost and alone in my life.

After about an hour that felt like forever, I made myself something to eat with the silver cube. Drained from the effort of simply breathing one more time, surviving one more minute, I lay down on the couch.

I woke up to two very deep, male voices. And someone touching my stickered and gloved hand. The brothers had returned.

"Sweet hair." Mark raked his eyes over my body, and I didn't like his appraising expression.

"Where's Jag?" I asked, sounding braver than I felt.

"He's still waiting for Gavin," Jake answered.

"Can I wait with him?"

Both brothers shrugged before leading me down the hall to another room with a blue couch and soft chairs. Jag was pacing when I entered, his gaze on the floor. He muttered under his breath and didn't notice that we'd come in.

"Hey, man," Mark said, "she wants to wait with you."

Jag's eyes flew to me, but his expression didn't change. "Yeah, okay. She can wait here." He sounded like he couldn't care less.

I waited until the brothers left before touching his arm. "Jag? What's going on?"

The corners of his mouth barely lifted before settling back into their original position. "Nothing. Nothing," he said, more to himself than to me.

"Sure, okay, because you only pace when you're nervous."

"I don't get nervous. This is anxious."

I worked hard to keep from rolling my eyes. "Okay, then.

I've never seen you so anxious." And it made me both anxious and nervous.

"Whatever, I'm fine," he snapped.

"Jag? Gavin is ready to see you."

My thoughts of punching Jag disappeared with those intoxicating words.

The man who spoke them swept one hand toward the hall behind him, pausing when his gaze fell on me. "Oh, hello. I'm sorry, we have no open appointments today."

I wondered what my name would sound like on his tongue. His voice was developed, carefully controlled, smooth and rolling like the sand dunes I'd spent the last two weeks hating. All the color was washed out of his hair and he'd spiked it the same as mine.

"She's with me," Jag said. "Hurry up, Vi."

I remained rooted in place, still staring at the Thinker. His eyes opened wider when Jag said my name. Surprise—maybe disbelief?—colored his cheeks.

"Come on." Jag grabbed my arm and pulled me past the type of person who could turn me in.

**36.** "Who was that guy?" I stumbled behind Jag, trying to shake his grip on my arm.

"Why? You see something you like?"

I blinked. "He's a *Thinker*."

"Of course he's a Thinker. That was Assistant Counselor Haws."

"I thought we didn't cooperate with Thinkers."

Jag marched down the hall at top speed. "Well, we do with certain types, obviously."

I ran to catch him. "Will you slow down? And stop biting my head off."

He stopped suddenly, and I collided with his outstretched

arm. "Let me do the talking." Then he turned and pushed open a door I couldn't see.

I rubbed my ribs while Jag settled into one of the over-sized armchairs. He crossed his legs and leaned back like he was expecting company that was beneath him. I'd only seen him look like this once—just before his little chat with Zenn. He gestured to the chair next to him, raising his eyebrows. His look said, *Sit the hell down before she gets here. Don't embarrass me, don't talk, basically don't be you, Violet.*

I sat, determined to keep my mouth shut. I'd show him.

"Jag!" A woman came through a concealed door beside the desk, and all I saw were the two long pieces of hair in the front that she'd dyed purple. I had instant hair-jealousy.

She bounded forward, a mix of nervous energy and hap-piness on her face. "Where's Pace? When is he coming?"

"Hullo, Gavin. Soon. Hopefully today." Jag smiled and stood to embrace her. He had a few inches on her, but she was probably a couple years older than him.

Her fingers moved over Jag's chest as if the fibers of his shirt needed adjusting and she had to touch him everywhere to do it. She leaned in and smelled him, her face inches from his neck.

"Ah, my gel," she said. "Smells nice on you."

He grinned and stepped closer to her, their knees almost

touching. Now a different kind of jealousy burned through me, hot and fast.

"Gavin, I brought a friend to meet you." Jag took a step back and gestured to me.

I stood up hesitantly.

Gavin radiated the same playful seriousness as Jag, with something intriguing hiding just under the surface. "Jag. Things are still unsettled. I can't—" She stopped when she looked at me, as if seeing my face meant she couldn't speak.

"You have to find a way, Gavin," Jag said. "This is Vi."

Minding my manners, I held my hand out. "Hello."

Gavin's face paled, her eyes hardened, her smile vanished. "Vi?" she asked, her eyes darting between Jag and me. "*The* Vi?"

Having "the" put in front of your name automatically increases your status. Like *The* President or *The* Director or *The* End. Think about it. It wouldn't be the same if it were just End. I felt like it was *The End* for me because it clearly wasn't a good *The*.

"Gavin," Jag warned. "We don't need to freak her out."

Annoyed that Jag knew something that would freak me out, I said, "Too late. Freaked-out-Vi, right here." My hand hung in midair and I pulled it back.

Gavin seized it.

My mind froze.

Gavin's eyes closed and her shoulders hunched. Several seconds passed. My lungs cried for air.

"Oh!" She released my hand and her control over my mind. She seemed faint and Jag helped her to his chair.

Gasping for breath, I had no idea what was going on. My stomach lurched.

"Let's go. Gavin needs a minute." Jag put his hand on my arm to guide me toward the door.

I stopped, sensing something in Gavin. "No. I'm not going." I moved across the room, and the memory became stronger. She was thinking about the pink birthday cake with the purple frosting.

"That's my memory," I said. "Did you steal it from me?" That was my favorite birthday memory, so strong that I'd re-created the cake just a few days ago. She couldn't have it. "Did you?"

"No, Vi," she said. "You still have it. You'll always have it."

"Then why do you have it?"

"Same memory," she whispered. "Different person."

"Huh?" I asked. My frustration and confusion boiled together, and I turned to Jag for an explanation.

"No way." He shook his head. "No *way*!" He knelt in front of Gavin and examined her face. "Damn," he whispered. But it was a good "damn."

He stood up and moved away from Gavin. "You better tell her. She's gonna start hitting in a minute, and I hate being her punching bag."

Gavin took a deep breath and let it out slowly. "Violet Schoenfeld. I always knew I'd see you again. You look great, little sister. Love the hair. It's different, but suits you."

I stared at the girl with the wicked-awesome hair and bright eyes.

"Remember when we bawled like babies the day I left?" she asked, my favorite smile arching her mouth.

Words battled to come out, but my voice died in my chest. My lungs stopped functioning. The room started to spin. Jag used his voice to convince me to breathe.

Tyson?

Impossible. But her eyes . . .

Tyson is dead.

I'd always believed that. Always.

My vision blurred, and Jag's voice became fainter and farther away until there was nothing at all.

No older sister who'd been missing for three years, eight months, and thirteen days.

No boyfriend who loved me and had reunited me with the one person I longed for the most.

Only darkness, and I was alone with myself.

37.

When I'm alone, I like to fantasize about what life might have been like if my family was still whole.

Would my mother have cooked fancy meals, or would I still have made my own lame baked potato?

Would Ty have helped me in school so I could get a decent job, or would I have ended up in the lame algae department?

Would I have depended on Zenn so much that I fell in love with him, or did I love him before the promise of a life together?

I didn't know.

Dad said I had to learn to be satisfied with what I'd been given, but I didn't know how.

Because I wanted more.

* * *

My heart doesn't seem to be beating. I can't get enough air.

"Jag, breathe, man." Someone touches my back.

I look up into Pace's face. His sharp silver eyes ease some of the tension in my lungs.

"I'm sorry, bro," he says.

"Don't," I choke out.

He glances over his shoulder. Gavin stands near the door. She must've seen everything. And she chose not to tell me.

"Blaze . . . died . . . Zenn . . . an accident . . ." My brother's words torment me. The fact that I won't see Blaze again slices into my gut. Coupled with the knowledge that Zenn— my best friend and most trusted Insider for two years—was involved and I can't stand up straight.

I square my shoulders, determined not to break down. "Okay, so what now?"

Pace clears his throat. I close my eyes against the worry in his.

"Gavin's seen something. We need you to return to the Goodgrounds."

"What?"

Gavin glides forward. I want to bury my face in her neck and cry. She's always been able to put me back together when I break apart. But I'm afraid to touch her. At the same time, I want to grip the sides of her face, invade her mind, and watch how my brother died.

"I can't tell exactly. I think it's a person," she says, her voice frail. "And whoever it is will tip the scale. Either for us or against us. You must find them. And soon."

I take a deep breath, feeling it shudder through my chest. I'm about to say I can turn things over to my second-in-command when Gavin hugs me, an invitation for me to see for myself.

Red light pulses in a dark space. Tall buildings strobe to life. The glare highlights Zenn's face every other second. His eyes are fierce, determined, terrified.

"Blaze," he says. "You can't. You go in there, you compromise the entire Resistance."

"Thane won't see me." Blaze claps Zenn on the shoulder in his typical *I-know-what-I'm-doing* fashion. I long to feel him do it to me one more time.

"And what if he does? How are you going to explain the fact that the Assistant Counselor of Seaside is evacuating Insiders?"

"Don't worry about it, Z." Blaze actually sounds like he's about to laugh.

Zenn doesn't get the joke. His mouth tightens. "Stay here," he commands.

The darkness pulses. When the world lightens, Blaze's eyes are glazed over. He stands as still as stone.

"I'll get the key code and meet you right here." Zenn uses his voice. It's powerful, controlling. Blaze merely nods.

I watch as Zenn abandons him. Leaves him there in the alley.

Sirens wail.

The red light doubles. Then triples. Dogs bark.

"Run!" I call, digging my fingernails into Gavin's back. I vaguely hear her cry of pain. But I can't stop now. Blaze is still in that alley. Still in danger.

And he can't move.

Because Zenn told him to stay.

The vision fades. My hands ache from their clenched position. Anger pounds within my heart.

"Jag?" Gavin wipes my face. Her fingers come away wet. I look at them, marveling at the fact that I'm crying. I can't decide if my agony is because Blaze died in an unknown alley in Freedom or because Zenn was the one who allowed that to happen.

Or because I sent them both there in the first place.

"He's still your brother," Gavin whispers. Her words and her breath cause goose bumps to erupt along my arms. I wonder who she means—Blaze or Zenn.

 "Are you up for breakfast?" My sister's voice echoed over the tech-comm. I sat up in bed, my heart pounding. Zenn's voice still caught in my ears. Jag's emotions still coated my nerves.

Next to me, Jag rubbed his eyes. "Yeah, sure. I just need to shower."

"Okay. Is Vi awake?"

"Isn't she in her room?" Jag asked, putting a finger to his lips. I smiled at the guilty look on his face.

"This *is* her room."

Jag laughed like he'd been caught, well, in his girlfriend's bedroom. "Uh, no, she's not awake yet."

"Jag, did you sleep on her couch all night?" Ty carried a hint of amusement in her voice.

Something like that, I thought as Jag glanced to the couch in front of a sliding glass door. A ruffled blanket indicated that he had slept there at some point.

"Yeah, I guess so."

"I knew you would. Did she ever wake up?"

"No, she never did," Jag said.

"Well, wake her up if you can. She can't sleep today away too."

"I'll try," he said, his face breaking into a wicked smile. The tech-comm beeped and Jag wrapped his arms around me. He kissed me and ran his hands through my hair.

"Jag." His name stuck in my throat. "Shouldn't we go eat breakfast?"

"No," he said, his lips brushing my neck. "Don't worry, I take really long showers. And I have to try to wake you up, that could take a very long time."

I tried to laugh, but I didn't have the breath. He murmured beautiful words in his sexy, controlling voice.

"No talking," I whispered. He fell silent for a minute before saying he couldn't resist telling me how pretty I was and how much he liked saying my name. I'll admit, I liked hearing it.

"So . . . you did sleep on the couch," I said, finally pushing him away.

"Yeah. I have some honor," he said. "But you had a nightmare. You wouldn't settle down. So I held you until you stopped shaking."

A blip of fear stole through me. I wondered if it was my nightmare or his that had disturbed me. "Thanks," I said, "for you know. Whatever."

Jag smoothed my hair off my face. "Don't worry. You didn't say anything embarrassing."

I laughed, glad (for once) that Jag knew what to say to make me feel better.

"I like it when you're happy," he said.

I curled into his chest. "When I'm with you, I'm happy."

"I know."

"What don't you know?"

He chuckled. "Not much, my pretty girl. Not much."

But he knew me. Better than anyone else. Better than Ty and Zenn and sometimes even better than I knew myself.

I tilted my face up to his and he rested his forehead against mine. "I mean it, Vi. Without you, I would die. You really are my Choker. I've never felt so full."

My life had always been empty, and I thought it was because my dad was gone or Ty was dead or my mother was awful. But that wasn't it. It was because I didn't have Jag. Did I tell him that, though? Nope.

But I think he knew.

Jag went downstairs while I showered. Meeting my sister, fainting, and then sleeping for twenty hours wasn't how I'd imagined things would go in Seaside. What would I say to her? I wondered if it would've been so hard for her to contact me. An e-comm or a simple projection or something. As a ranger, she could have found a way.

Nervously, I opened my bedroom door. Jag's voice filtered up from downstairs. ". . . was seen a long time ago. He won't be able to control me now."

"But Jag, Thane won't give up, that I do know. And now you and Vi—" A machine whirred, drowning out the rest of Ty's answer. When Jag spoke again, his voice was low and angry. I paused, waiting for Ty to reply. Her higher voice carried much easier up the stairwell. "Jag, I'm worried about you, maybe I can—"

"I said stop," Jag said, louder now. "Look, I know what has to be done. All Vi needs is to get that tag out. I'll go get her."

I thumped down the last four steps and rounded the corner. "Looking for me?"

Jag had started to move away from Ty, who was near tears.

317

She wiped her eyes with the back of her hand and poured something pink into a glass.

Before I could open my mouth, Jag moved in front of me and placed both hands on the sides of my face. "Don't worry, babe. Everything's fine."

I closed my eyes and nodded slightly before stepping away from him, half-aware that he'd used his voice control on me. But I felt too tired to call him on it. My brain filled with thoughts, emotions, random memories and wishes. Nothing fit together.

Jag led me to the table, where strawberries and cinnamon toast had been laid out. He poured orange juice and loaded a plate with food. He sat next to me and watched as I ate. Ty stayed in the exact same spot, sipping her shake.

My tension increased with every bite. Several times Jag glanced at Ty, his eyes narrowing for only a second before looking back to me. The silence pressed down until I couldn't take it anymore. "So, Ty, can I stay here?"

"I go by Gavin now. I wanted something with the letters of your nickname in it. Nice, huh?" She grinned at me like no time had passed. Like the conversation between her and Jag hadn't happened. But something big was going on. Something neither of them would spill. And a smile—even from Ty—wouldn't make everything better.

"That is nice," I said. "Did you do it so you could remember me? Because I haven't heard from you in over three years."

Her smile faltered. Remorse flashed in her eyes. She took a step toward me. "I know, baby, I couldn't. Mom had to think I was dead and gone."

"What? Why?"

Jag stood up to leave, and I threw him a furious look that said *don't you dare.*

"I gotta get the book, be right back."

Once Jag left, Ty sprang forward. "Let's get that tag out." She grasped my wrist and motioned to someone behind her. Mark entered, holding a black marker.

"No," I said, recognizing the surgery skin. I tried jerking my arm away, but Ty's grip was firm.

"It'll hurt no matter what, but less if you hold still," she said. "Don't worry, Mark's the best."

The best at what?

She pinned my left arm to the counter. As skillfully as a doctor, Mark drew the marker around my wrist. I squeezed my eyes shut and pounded my foot on the floor as the skin dissolved.

"This one's advanced," Mark said, his voice deep and rich. "It's not a problem though," he added when he met my startled gaze. "They've just gotten better, that's all." He took out a piece

319

of tech that looked like a pair of beefed up nail clippers with white tips. A blue spark jumped the gap between the blades. Shock scissors. He was going to cut me with those?

"Bloody hell," I whispered. This was going to hurt. A lot. I clenched my jaw.

"It's okay, Vi," Mark said. "Tell her, Jake."

I looked up to see Jake watching me. "Gavin's probably seen how this turns out. And she's never wrong."

Gavin had a slight blush in her face. "Thanks, Jake."

"Ready?" Mark asked. "I promise it'll be fine." I believed him. He looked so serene, so in control.

I nodded. He inserted the shock scissors into my wrist and snipped next to the tiny knot. A charge of tech sparked, burning a hot spot in my chest. A metallic clang echoed in the kitchen, and I saw the tag fall into Jake's hands before I went blind from all the techtricity.

"Sweet. Goodie tech. A tag, no less. I'll get right on it." His voice radiated the excitement that surely showed on his face.

Ty sighed as two sets of footsteps hurried from the room. When my vision cleared, she was holding out a glass of cloudy water. "Drink."

The solution tasted like rancid vitamins, but I downed it. "What is this?" I noted that the ache in my arm had already faded.

"Skin regenerator. Sorry, the boys only have it in powdered form. You probably got a shot at the facility, right?"

"I'd drink this nasty concoction any day over getting a shot, trust me."

Ty threw back her head and laughed. The sound awakened happy memories. She bandaged my wrist and drew me into a hug. I relaxed into her, clinging tightly and willing myself not to cry.

"Vi, I'm so glad you're here. Really. Will you stay?"

I inhaled deeply, finding the familiar scent of coffee with brown sugar. "Can I? Stay here with you?"

She smiled and looked like my mother. "I filed your petitions yesterday, back dating it to last week. Jag's too." She studied me like she expected me to spill my guts about Jag. Yeah, that wasn't going to happen.

"That's great. Will the petitions be approved?"

"These kinds of things move pretty slow, so I don't think anyone will notice the lag, especially not with the events of this past week." Ty didn't sound worried, didn't appear concerned about anything. She comforted me the same way she always had—with her confidence. "Jag agrees."

"What's your talent?" I asked, trying to steer the conversation away from him.

"Premonitions." She pushed herself up and sat on the

counter. She wore black soft-soled shoes with bright pink socks. Totally Ty. "I can see things. Usually the future. Sometimes the past, like I did with you. Sometimes I can just see what makes people happy or unhappy, or see the decision they should make that will make their life better, or anything really. I work here, helping the people in Seaside to see more clearly."

"Sounds nice." And it did. I glanced toward the stairs, hoping Jag would show. Both brothers stood on the landing, watching me. Jake smiled, and I involuntarily returned the gesture. Alarmed, I turned back to Ty.

"Don't mind them," she said. "There are different levels of mind control, and I can help you develop yours. If you stay, you can use your control to help people. That way we can protect you."

"What do you mean?"

"Well, you can't ignore your talent. You have to use it. But the Counselor can file a petition with the Association detailing that you *are* using it to help people—the way I do—in a much less controlling way. Then you don't have to go to Freedom and train to be a Director. Isn't that what you want? What you need?"

It was. But Zenn needed me too. I couldn't abandon him. I rubbed my gloved hand. "Yeah, but Mark said things have gone all wrong."

Ty waved her hand. "Don't worry. Dad can't come here." If she was lying, I couldn't tell.

"What's with the glove?" she asked, changing the subject as easily as I had earlier.

"I need to get this sticker off, and Pace said you could do it."

Her eyes flickered to my silver hand, where the outline of the ring bulged. "*Pace* did?"

"Yeah. So? Can you do it?"

Ty glared at me for second before she left the kitchen.

I followed. "Hey! Can you do it or not?"

Ty spun on the bottom step. "No, I can't do it. Only someone with extreme control can remove a sticker. I can't believe Pace told you I could do it. I. See. Visions."

"O-kay."

Like that cleared everything up. Thanks, Sis.

39.

Ty-Gavin-Whatever stormed up the steps calling Jag's name. I could barely keep up with my mad-as-hell sister. At the last door on the right, Ty didn't stop to knock, she simply barged in, bellowing for Jag. "Get out here and explain yourself!"

His room was clean and unused, with a bay window that opened onto a balcony. The ocean breeze ruffled the curtains amidst Ty's foul language.

"What's going on?" I asked.

"He's gone," she said.

Her words punched me in the gut, eliminating my ability to breathe. Ty banged open closet doors and metal drawers, like Jag might be hiding in one of them.

"Gone?" My voice sounded much too high. That wasn't true. Jag wouldn't leave me. Not again.

"Yes, Vi. Gone." Ty's eyes flashed dangerously. She moved onto the balcony and yelled obscenities toward the water. "See?" She turned, holding a metallic rope in her hands. "Gone." She flung the evidence away.

Jag had left me for, like, the fourth time. I felt lost without him. Numb. Empty.

I left Ty cursing on Jag's balcony and shuffled down the hall, down the stairs, down to the lobby. Outside, the sun shone guilty rays on my bare skin. My feet carried me toward the beach. I dropped to my knees and closed my eyes as a hole opened in my soul.

Then a voice entered my mind, familiar and fatherly. *Violet. You have the power to change the world.*

Dad's words echoed in my mind over the crashing surf.

I can help you remove the sticker. Zenn is desperate to see you.

A response formed, but I didn't allow it to leave my mind. Dad knew my weaknesses. Just because he'd been gone for seven years didn't mean he was stupid.

The Association needs you, Vi. Tyson has chosen a different path, but that doesn't mean you must follow her. We need Jag, too. You can help him see reason. You can be together.

I opened my eyes and blinked in the bright daylight. Dad was right. I *could* control Jag.

I realized that's what Dad wanted. I remembered the way he'd watched me in the tech facility. With interest. Like I could do something for him. And I could: get Jag to join the Association with me.

No way in hell, I thought. *Jag will not make your transmissions. Not as long as I'm alive.*

Dad's disappointment stole through me. *Your death would be tragic . . . Think of what that would do to me, V. I've lost you once, will you make me go through it again?*

The threat hung there, floating in the enraged space in my mind. I don't know if I blocked my dad out or he left, but I didn't hear him again. My shallow breathing washed in and out with the waves. The weight of my unmade choices pressed down on me until I felt like I couldn't stand up.

How does anyone ever figure out what to do with their life?

"Vi."

I looked up at the familiar voice. Right into Zenn's beautiful face. Tears stained my cheeks. "Zenn," I choked out.

He gripped me in a fierce hug before placing both hands on the sides of my face. "Shh, beautiful. Go to sleep now."

His voice spread thick honey over my senses. My eyelids drooped, no matter how hard I tried to keep them open. "Zenn," I murmured.

"Trust me, Vi. Go to sleep."

Problem: I didn't trust him. But I couldn't fight his voice, and the calming darkness swallowed me.

Everything moved. Strong arms held me close. It wasn't Jag, I would know his scent anywhere.

This person smelled like the wind, fresh and free and full of salt. My head bounced on a muscled shoulder. No color. No light.

"Put her down and get out." Ty's words carried a vein of fury.

"I'm here to help," Zenn said, sincerity written in every syllable.

"I don't believe that."

"And I don't care what you believe. If I hadn't taken her from the beach, Thane would have her right now."

Ty made a noise of disapproval in her throat.

"Besides," Zenn continued, "I'm the only one who can remove that sticker."

"That's not true," Ty argued. "Anyone with enough control can remove it."

"It's a new security feature. Only the one who put the sticker on can take it off. Thane reconfigured Vi's ring while she was at the tech facility. He didn't want her to be able to remove it herself." Zenn slid his hand into mine, and it felt familiar and safe. "I gave her the clue to get her here, hoping Jake could help her, but—"

"She made it here, didn't she?" Ty traced her fingertips along my eyebrows.

"I stalled Thane as long as I could, but she still almost didn't get out in time."

"She's fine, Zenn." Ty sounded exhausted. "Let's get this done. Vi?"

I wanted to move, speak, something. I couldn't.

"You put her to sleep." Ty sounded hysterical. "Wake her up. Right now."

"Let's get her unstuck first," Zenn said.

When I tried to open my eyes, I couldn't. Something thick lay across my face, creating a fierce blackness. I struggled against the binding.

"Lie still, Vi."

I obeyed. Anyone would obey his voice. "We've got to get your sticker off, and then we'll talk." Zenn laid me on a couch and set a pillow under my head.

"Sure, okay." My words slurred together.

"Go back to sleep." His words flowed into feathery ribbons, urging me to drift into blissful slumber.

I wanted to. But cool hands moved down both my arms. Then pain.

More hurt than anyone should ever have to endure. My right hand felt like it had been sliced off with a roto-blade.

Voices murmured around me. An intense orange light pulsed through the darkness. Two pressure points throbbed as someone pressed on my shoulders.

Someone close by was screaming. I wanted to make them stop. Help them. Anything so they would shut up.

Finally, the blinding pain in my hand receded. The screaming stopped.

"She has control issues," Ty whispered.

"Who doesn't when they first learn what they can do? She has more talent than anyone I've met. She'll be fine." Zenn's voice filled a void in my heart reserved just for him. "Her feelings for Jag are powerful."

"Jag has let his feelings cloud his judgment. He knows what I've seen. He won't—"

"Don't worry about Jag," Zenn interrupted. "He'll do what he thinks is right. He always does."

"That's exactly what I'm worried about."

A long silence followed. I almost wished for the physical pain. Anything to drown out this emotional burden swirling around me.

"I'm not sure we should remove the sticker," Ty whispered. "If she's stuck, she can't find Jag. He'll think he's finally pushed her too far. Then he'll do what he needs to do. And she'll be safe."

"That's up to Vi," Zenn replied. "We can't help her without her control. Let's try again."

I wasn't ready for the consuming pain this time either. The screaming started again as fire moved from my wrist down my hand, which was somehow still attached to my body. Bolts of hot pain tingled in the tips of my fingers. The light surrounding me turned redder. The glare became brighter.

And then a white light shone in the distance. On instinct, I reached toward it, called it closer so I could share in its glory. As it neared, I saw Zenn standing within the light. I wasn't sure if I should cry tears of joy or punch him in his traitorous mouth.

"Settle, Vi," he said. "You've got to help me." He took my hand and the pain faded. His eyes were the brightest blue I'd ever seen. No clouds. Only my sweet, wonderful Zenn, in complete control of himself.

"Zenn," I breathed out. "How come you never told me? I would've helped you in the Resistance." Tears slid down my cheeks. Lonely, heartbroken tears.

Zenn traced one finger down my face. "You mean that

here." He touched my lips lightly. "But not here." He placed his hand over his heart.

"I would've helped you," I insisted.

"I know. That's why I didn't tell you." He smiled, a gesture full of love and longing and sadness.

"Zenn, about Jag—"

He shook his head. "Don't." He cupped my cheek in his palm. His touch felt so light. "You don't have to explain."

He whipped his head around at a loud sound. "My time is gone." He faded from my sight, but his voice lingered in soul. "Good-bye, my lovely Violet. Ty?"

"Go," she said from somewhere beside me. "And Zenn . . . thanks."

"Tell her I miss her. And I love her."

"I'll tell her."

"No!" I reached for him, but Zenn was already gone.

40.

I told the girl inside to stop sobbing, stop screaming, stop feeling sorry for herself. A whisper of water touched my hand and all agony eased. The soothing darkness enveloped me.

Just breathe, I told myself. A cool draft washed over my skin. Voices floated around me. Familiar yet foreign at the same time.

"She needs to be trained," Ty said. "She knows nothing."

"Jag's been with her for almost a month," Jake said over the tech-comm. "He's been putting her through some tests. And he left her a note for the simulator."

"But she's had zero training. Jag said she didn't even know who she was—"

"She knows *now*. Jag told me how much she's already done. We don't have time for formal lessons. I trust Jag. You should too."

The darkness lightened and Jag floated in my mind. I reached for him, my Choker, the part of me I needed to feel complete.

Sitting up abruptly, I clawed the black cloth off my face. Ty knelt in front of me, an anxious crease in her forehead. No one else was in the room. I wondered if I'd just dreamt about Zenn or if he had really been there.

I flung my arms around Ty, the stupid tears falling again.

Her shoulders shook as she cried. "You're unstuck."

I examined my left hand. It looked like I'd submerged it in hot water for a long time. A small band of white scar tissue circled my pinky where the ring used to be. A permanent reminder of Zenn.

"Vi . . . how do you know about the Resistance?"

I looked up into my sister's eyes. "I've heard Jag talk about it . . . in his dreams."

"In his dreams?" Ty raised her eyebrows. "That's some wicked powerful mind control."

I shifted uncomfortably. "It's not like I enjoy taking a trip inside his nightmares." I exhaled as I ran my hands over my face. "What do you know about it?"

Ty smiled, the kind smile of an older sister. "I have an incredible talent—I can see things others can't. That's why I was taken away. When I wouldn't use my power the way he wanted, Dad let me rot in prison for a few months. I was allowed to go home—to check on you. See if you had any gifts. Remember that?"

I nodded, watching tears trickle over her cheeks.

"I was sentenced to Freedom. But Zenn came and helped me escape from prison. He had the proper ID card to cross the border. My new name. He gave me food and water for my solitary walk to the Badlands. He provided the code words so I could find and recognize Jag."

She paused, focusing on something only she could see. "Zenn saved me."

I knew how she felt. He'd saved me countless times. "But I thought he was working for Dad. Isn't he?"

Ty pulled herself out of her memory and looked at me. "It seems that way, Vi. Early last year, Zenn stopped all communication with the Resistance. I was already living here in Seaside, but Jag asked me to contact him. That's when we learned he'd switched sides." She exhaled loudly. "He said he did it for you, but you had no gifts and it didn't make sense. I've never seen Jag so mad. He was practically spitting fire."

She smiled, but it didn't extend past her mouth. "So, well, I don't know where Zenn is right now. Jag thinks he's solidly with Thane."

A long silence followed while I contemplated all I'd seen and heard in Jag's nightmares. Everything between Zenn and Jag. How Zenn had controlled Blaze. The way Jag blamed Zenn for his brother's death.

"So, what do you know about Blaze?" My voice sounded too hollow.

A steely glint entered Ty's gaze. "You know about Blaze?"

"I—"

"Does Jag know you've invaded his memories?"

"No. And you can't tell him."

A mixture of frustration and sympathy moved across Ty's face. "All right. I won't tell him. I told him to tell you everything."

"Everything? There's more?"

"Blaze died maybe a year and a half ago. During a job for the Resistance, with Zenn. I—I saw it happen." She ducked her head, her words fading into whispers. "Jag thought he was responsible. For assigning Blaze the mission to Freedom. I mean, he was already the Assistant Counselor here. But learning it was Zenn's fault? That broke Jag into so many pieces. He and Zenn were best friends."

I struggled through what Zenn had said in the forest. What I'd seen in Jag's nightmare.

"Ty . . . was Zenn really responsible?"

She cleared her throat. "I don't know the answer to that, Vi. No one does. Not Jag. Not even Zenn, I expect."

"I've seen it," I whispered. "I've seen what you've seen. Inside Jag's mind." I gripped her with a desperate look.

"Then you have what you need to decide for yourself." She stood and left me on the couch in her office.

Thoughts of Zenn clouded my head. Had he helped Blaze or not? Had he really helped me? Not only on the beach, but in the Goodgrounds? Had he really abandoned Jag's Resistance to save me? Or was he my dad's personal assistant?

Zenn is very loyal. Dad's harsh voice sliced into my thoughts. *You can still have the future you've always wanted with him.*

But—

Who do you think matched the two of you? Dad continued. *Zenn really loves you. Would do anything for you.*

I knew he would. Which meant Zenn *had* defected and joined my father. And for what?

For me.

But he knew I would suffocate under the blanket of a controlled life. He couldn't live that way either. Could he?

I trailed my fingers around the scar. *Dad . . . how can I get my sticker off?*

Only the person who put your sticker on can get it off. I invented that tricky bit of security tech myself.

So Zenn would have to remove mine.

Yes. And I would have to remove his.

Thoughts battled in my mind. The ring was gone. So Zenn had helped me. He was—

We all have methods of persuasion for our cause, Dad taunted. *Zenn . . . Jag . . .*

I squeezed my eyes shut. *Just stop. Please.*

It's all about what you choose to believe, V. So . . . who are you choosing to believe?

Good question, Dad.

41.

I returned to my room to retrieve my backpack. As soon as I opened the door, someone said, "Hello, Vi."

My emotions spiraled up and then down, as first I thought it must be Jag hiding out in my room. Then I saw the auburn-haired ranger, and my heart settled in my hollow stomach.

I folded my arms and cocked my head. "What are you doing here, Jake?"

His grin widened. "Oh, man. Jag was right."

My frustration resurfaced, and I couldn't contain it. "Shut up. I don't want to hear another word about that Baddie. What do you want?"

"Relax," he said. "I'm on your side here. It's a good thing

too. You look like you could easily kill me right now." He wasn't far off, but my murderous thoughts centered on a spiky-haired guy who was *gone*.

"Look, Jake. Just tell me whatever you're going to tell me." I waited. Quite patiently, I thought.

"Okay, I'm an island ranger—"

"Tell me something I don't know," I snapped.

He laughed again at my attitude, just like Jag would've done. I blinked back the annoying tears and looked away so Jake wouldn't see.

"My job is to equip the Counselor with the best tech. I know you've got some killer stuff in your bag. I'm here to bargain."

"What do you have that I could possibly want?"

With a knowing smile, he pulled an envelope from his back pocket. Even from across the room, Jag's handwriting made my heart pound. I took several steps forward, never removing my eyes from the two letters of my name. Jake could have anything he wanted. Kidney, liver, whatever.

"Jag really didn't want to leave you this way," Jake said softly. "You've got great control over him. I've never heard anyone talk about someone the way he talks about you. Not even Gavin with Pace. Choker-speak." His eyes met mine and he waited, as if I might deny it.

Man, I really wanted to. Let that get back to Jag. But I couldn't.

"Ah, I see. You feel the same for him." He smiled and extended the envelope toward me. "Jag wanted to say good-bye in person, but things . . . got complicated. He also said he's really, really sorry for leaving, and he hopes to see you soon."

We struck a deal. I kept the weapon phone and one food-generating cube; everything else went to Jake.

"Okay," I said once I had the envelope in my hand. "I know you know pretty much everything. So tell me what you know about mind rangers."

Jake glanced at his new tech haul as if he'd rather spend time with gadgets than with me. "They serve the Association as Directors. Gavin was the first ranger I met who doesn't. Then Jag started coming to visit."

"How long has Jag been coming here?"

Jake sighed and sat down on my bed. "Maybe three years? Something like that. He came with Pace shortly after he was made a tech ranger in the Badlands. Then every couple of months after that for lessons." Jake rubbed his hands through his hair. "He spends most of his time with Gavin."

"What do they do?" I asked.

"Gavin used to stay up nights training Jag to use his mind,

at least until they figured out that his weapon was his voice. Then they started studying how to develop it. I like the guy, but I hate talking to him."

Jag and Ty spent a lot of time together, I thought, not sure how I felt about it.

"But he's done with training now." Jake stared out the window. "He finished last Christmas. He came for two weeks, and Gavin didn't come out of his room once. Then she sent him back to the Goodgrounds to get something she'd had a vision about. Neither one of them knew what he was supposed to find, but he's been in enemy territory without specific directions before. And Gavin's never been wrong." His eyes finally locked on mine. "He left at the beginning of April, and we haven't heard from him since."

I looked away. Outside, the wind lashed against the window. Thunder crashed, mimicking the unrest I felt inside.

April. Six weeks in prison.

I swallowed and found my throat too dry. "What did he find?" I asked, but I already knew the answer.

A fierceness entered Jake's face. "He found you."

341

42.

I sank onto the couch, clutching Jag's letter and trying to organize my thoughts. I knew one thing: I didn't want to open the envelope, didn't want to experience him leaving me all over again. I took a long, deep breath and blew it out.

"Well, I'll be downstairs." Jake stood in the doorway, holding his bag of tech. "Come see me after you've read that note."

I nodded, but as soon as he'd gone, I shoved the paper in my back pocket. I stumbled into the bathroom, staring at my drawn face in the mirror.

Ty had said, *You have what you need to decide.*

I could still hear Jake saying, *He found you.*

And Jag said he'd never leave you, Dad mocked, his voice inserted into my thoughts.

Shut up! I screamed. I looked at myself with my newly colored skin and yellow short-sleeved shirt. Even the blue jeans I wore weren't mine. I hardly recognized the girl staring back at me.

I wasn't good.

But I wasn't bad either.

Those labels meant nothing.

I am Violet Schoenfeld. Armed with this knowledge, I grabbed my backpack and left my room. I found Jake sitting at the kitchen table. "Hey, where did Jag go?"

Jake glanced up. "I don't know."

"Big fat liar," I accused, glaring at him. "I know you talked to him before he left. Where did he go?"

Jake squeezed his eyes shut. "You're gonna be so mad. You know that, right?"

"Tell me," I said.

"He went through the tunnels." The answer came too quick. Because I'd controlled him.

I toned my emotions down. "Tunnels?"

"And he made me program the simulator with the most advanced profile we've got." He clenched his hands into fists.

"So . . . I don't get it."

Jake stood up, wiping one hand across his eyes. "Just come with me. You'll see." He started toward the stairs. But he didn't go up. Instead, he stopped in front of a blank wall.

"Okay, so you're gonna want to kill me. Before we go down, promise me you won't try to kill me."

I scoffed. "Come on. I'm not going to hurt you."

"You might. I've heard stories about you. Promise me."

"Stories about me? What kind of stories? Jake—"

"Just promise."

"Fine. I promise I won't hurt you."

"No, promise me you won't even *try* to hurt me."

I wanted to hurt him already. "I promise I won't even try to hurt you."

Satisfied, he turned back to the wall. I thought it would be the perfect time to elbow him in the gut, but I'd already made the stupid promise.

Jake tapped his fingers on the bare wall as if on a keypad. I frowned—until the wall vanished.

A staircase spiraled down into darkness.

Jake stepped into the shadows without speaking, like it was no biggie that he was moving into the great black abyss.

It was a big deal to me. "Um, Jake?" The murkiness had already swallowed him.

"Come on." His voice echoed off the stone stairway.

"I can't see."

"Feel," he called. And with that comment, Jake shot to the top of my To-Die List, with Jag in slot number two.

But I tentatively reached toward the railing. The metal felt icy, slippery. I edged my feet along the two steps I could see and then threw caution to the wind.

I descended farther and farther into darkness. I couldn't hear Jake in front of me. The steps simply went on and on, around and around. My breathing grew more rapid as the air turned colder.

Tech buzzed in my brain. I forced my foot down one more step. Then another. And another.

Now the tech burned. I leaned against the wall, relishing the bite of cool metal from the railing.

Step after agonizing step, I continued down the stairs. Until I couldn't anymore.

The darkness swirled. Tears stung my eyes. The air felt like cement.

"Jake?" I called. "I can't . . ."

Footsteps approached. A light bounced on the walls before blinding me further. "You coming? Don't tell me you're afraid. Jag said you don't get scared. He called you tough."

I couldn't recall a single time I'd been tough in front of Jag. But it didn't matter. Only breathing mattered.

"What's the deal?" he asked.

"Can't—breathe—tech," I stammered.

"Oh! Right." Jake dug in his pocket. "Sorry. Here." He held three purple pills in his hand. I blinked, and the three pills blended into one.

"What's that?"

"For the tech buzz. I guess you have some kind of heightened sense."

You could call it that. I reached for the pill and missed it completely.

"Here, sit." Jake helped me to the ground and placed the pill in my hand. "Swallow."

I didn't. I couldn't put my thoughts together. Taking a pill to control the techtricity seemed weird, though.

"Come on, Vi. It'll take the buzz away. I invented them for Ty."

"But I need the buzz," I slurred. "That's how I know if it's safe or not."

He scoffed and moved within inches of my face. His eyes shone with light, deep and golden like fresh honey. "You don't need to feel the stupid buzz. You have a brain. Use it."

Against my better judgment, I popped the purple pill in

my mouth and swallowed hard against the taste of ash and plastic. Almost instantly, the tech buzz faded.

Unfortunately, so did the light. Jake had turned and was already rounding the bend.

I resumed my downward spiral. Eventually the darkness lightened to gray.

Finally my foot landed on something besides stone. Jake sat at a counter in the back of a warehouse. A light shone over him in a pale yellow halo. I moved through the tech-stocked shelves to where he worked.

He didn't look up. "Take what you want," he said, gesturing to the aisles of tech.

"For what?" I didn't want any of it.

"You never know what you'll find in the simulator," Jake said. He wouldn't look directly at me. "Go on, take whatever you want."

A tiny alarm was ringing in my head. I wondered why I'd need any of this stuff for a simulation.

But I sighed and wished the room was brighter. Instantly the light increased. Jake snorted behind me. I ignored him as I turned my attention to the tech. It didn't look like anything I'd ever seen. Thankfully, each had a label with a name and a description.

Locator: helps find a person who's been lost.

That would've been nice three years ago when Ty went missing. Or when my dad disappeared. Maybe if I couldn't find Jag, this locator would help.

Not much bigger than the palm of my hand, the square of metal had a narrow screen along the top. A blinking red light told me the locator came equipped with an iris recognizer.

Further down the row, next to a spiky piece of tech that could drill a hole fifteen feet down, lay a bracelet.

Diminisher: reduces visibility so enemies can't see you. Warning: takes several hours to come back to full sight.

Nice. The diminishing bracelet joined the locator in my pocket.

I passed by the tech that turned skin green. I also left the spinning whirlwind and the shock spit on the shelf.

"Subtle weaponry," Jake murmured from the back. I almost told him I didn't need any weaponry, but I kept my mouth shut.

I wandered up one row and down another. Nothing else seemed important enough to take, because I didn't know what to prepare for. "I'm ready," I announced.

Jake stood and moved toward a corridor in the corner. "All right," he said, like I was anything but ready. "You need to get to the center of the city, where I've installed some wicked tech that scrambles directional devices."

He paused, like I should congratulate him on his achievements. I didn't.

"Okay, now here's the part where you're gonna be mad. Are you ready?"

"To be mad?" I tightened the straps on my backpack. "Totally ready."

Jake smiled. Then he did a most surprising thing. He pulled me into a bone-crushing hug. "Be careful, Vi," he whispered. "You're our only hope."

I wanted to ask him what he meant, but I couldn't.

Because in the next moment, he disappeared.

My arms hovered in the air where Jake had stood. I surveyed the tech warehouse. Empty.

When I turned back to the hallway in front of me, Jake stood there. Well, a projection of him.

"Vi, you must decide how you will use your power," the projection said. "This is the crucial decision all mind rangers face. If you don't decide, you can be easily swayed by others, especially others like you."

The simulation tech waited, as if it knew I had to think about what he'd said.

I still didn't know what to do. Zenn needed me. If he wasn't being brainwashed, he'd choose freedom, he'd choose me. I could help him live that uncontrolled life.

I needed Jag like I needed oxygen. But he'd ditched me so many times.

The ache for my dad was also strong. The image of our family—complete with Ty and both my parents—flashed behind my eyes. Maybe that dream could still come true.

No matter what, my talent would not be ignored. I had a duty to use it, to help others—not just when it was convenient for me. But Ty had said there were degrees of control. I could use my power for the Association or file a petition and stay in Seaside.

Minutes passed. The projection of Jake waited, his eyes fixed on me.

My conversation with Jag finally reminded me of my choice. *I'll never control anyone, not even you.*

I couldn't use my control to Direct. I would use it to help others, but I would not brainwash them into living according to my will.

"I'm ready," I said.

The projection of Jake smiled. "Your training continues, then. Remember the things Jag's told you, no matter how small, and you'll find what you need. Good luck."

He pointed down the hallway, as if that were adequate instructions for my next task.

43.

At the end of the hall, a light grew brighter.

It's never good to walk toward the light, but that's what I did.

The hall dead-ended in a tiny room with three doors leading out of it. A lamp in the corner cast shadows over the floor.

I closed my eyes, thinking this was just a bad dream and I'd wake up any second.

But it wasn't.

I sighed and opened my eyes. As much as I didn't want to, I had to read Jag's note. I pulled it out of my back pocket. His handwriting still made my breath catch, but when I opened it, I wanted to cry.

The paper contained two words: *Fly, babe.*

I shredded it into little pieces. Fly? The stupid boy wanted me to *fly*? I'd fly off the handle when I caught up to him. Then he'd see me *fly*.

A slight glow under the middle door caught my eye. I flattened myself on the floor and peered under the crack.

Blue light pulsed gently.

Under the door on the left, green light blared in a steady stream.

Only darkness existed under the door on the right.

I stood up, trying to think what the colored lights could mean.

I ruled the right door out. I was sick of living in the dark.

So, blue or green?

I tried to explore with my mind, but came up blank. *That stupid purple pill.* I knew I shouldn't have taken it. I couldn't feel anything.

Randomly, I stepped to the left door and twisted the knob.

Inside the room, an ascender ring stared up at me.

Right. Like I wanted to go up when I'd just spent who knows how long spiraling down those stairs. I turned to leave the room.

One problem: no door.

"I hate you, Jake," I muttered.

The upward thrust of an ascender always causes me to duck my head for fear of smashing into the ceiling. But I dissolved away without injury.

I landed in a featureless room with no windows. Gray cement stretched from wall to wall. Turning slowly in a circle, I looked for any sign that this room had an exit.

Yeah, it didn't. Fan-freaking-tastic.

I leaned against the wall. Definitely real. Keeping my fingers pressed against the plaster, I slowly approached the corner. Around the room I went—until my fingertips ran over a tiny bump in the third wall. I dropped my hand to where the doorknob would be. I twisted it, and the door swung outward.

I stood on the threshold of a towering building. The pale sand glittered far below, and my stomach clenched. I gripped the doorframe as the landscape started to spin. White lines crowded into my vision. I couldn't breathe.

But across the very windy channel lay the city of Seaside.

Fly, babe.

Damn you, Jag Barque! Damn you straight to hell.

I don't do heights. And floating with the wind? That isn't my thing either. Once upon a time I'd wished I could fly up to touch the stars. Now I just wanted to curl up in a bed on the ground floor and forget about everyone and everything.

"How the hell do I fly?" The wind didn't answer. No one

did, which only reminded me of how alone I was. The cruel breeze sounded like laughter as it whipped through my hair.

Suddenly my light backpack seemed very heavy. I pressed my body against the far wall. Taking a deep breath, I closed my eyes and tried to find the wind. I didn't feel anything.

A scream erupted from my throat. I ran as fast as I could and pushed hard with my right foot at the edge of the room.

I plummeted, face-first, toward the churning ocean waves. They didn't seem calm anymore. Now they threatened my entire existence.

The backpack pressed me down, urging me to go faster. I spread my arms and legs, trying to catch a current.

A strong gust pushed into me and I begged it to keep me aloft.

It ignored me. Time slowed down.

The water slapped me with enough force to render black sparks in my vision. The backpack dragged me further underwater. I twisted and tumbled in liquid darkness, trying to find the surface.

I couldn't.

Everything looked the same. Navy blue. Airless.

Refusing to give up, I kicked harder. The backpack grew heavier. I managed to free myself from it.

The bag drifted down—the same way I'd been swimming.

Salty water filled my lungs.

I twisted away from the sinking pack and kicked up.

Slower. And slower.

Until I couldn't kick anymore.

44

"End simulation?" a voice asked.

"No. Maintain possibility ten," Jake replied.

Fly, babe. The words echoed around me. Taunting.

"Scramble the doors. Heighten security on the directional tech." The spoken words cut through the ones looping in my nightmare.

"The subject is under great duress, sir," the computer said.

"Vi?" Jake put his hand on my back. His touch sparked something inside. I coughed. My lungs felt like someone had scrubbed them out with peroxibeads.

I tried opening my eyes, but they stung too much. My limbs felt heavy, weighed down with frustration. And water.

"She's reviving, sir."

"Resume stealth," Jake said.

Everything came rushing back. I pushed myself up and opened my eyes. The unyielding floor pressed into my tailbone. I could see the steady green light and the pulsing blue light from under the two doors.

I hated Jag then, more than anything.

Flying? I don't think so.

"Jake?"

No answer.

"Jake! I know you're here. I'm going to kill you when I see you again!"

"You promised." His voice came from everywhere.

"Screw that," I said, standing up. "I jumped off a freaking building. Someone has to die."

"Take it up with Jag. He forced me to set the simulation."

"I could have drowned."

"You're a water girl. You wouldn't have." Jake's voice carried a smile. I imagined it on his face.

My anger deflated. "Whatever. What now?"

Jake didn't answer.

I looked around the room, hoping for a big arrow to point me in the right direction. The hallway had sealed itself.

"There's no way out." Panic rose in waves. I suppressed it by taking a deep breath.

"Fly," I whispered to myself. "That makes no sense."

The green light now burned under the middle door. Darkness existed on the left. Blue pulsed on the right.

The equipment in my pack seemed to be in working order, so I slung it over my back. I placed my hand on the left door.

The force of the tech almost threw me backward.

My head spun. I tried to remove my hand, but it seemed welded to the metal. My stomach clenched. My chest burned.

I slid to my knees, finally able to break contact. I needed another one of those purple pills. I'd take ignorance over internal combustion any day.

I crawled toward the next door. I didn't even have to touch this one. The tech buzz filled my ears, my eyes, my mouth. I puckered as if I'd eaten something sour.

I moaned and pushed myself past the middle door. Once free of the debilitating tech, I stood up. This third door only held a whisper of buzz.

"Tech simulations," I said, the realization hitting me in the gut. "Jake, you're so dead! You tricked me with that purple pill!"

"But now you know you can't control the elements," he said.

Like that made me feel better. "I hope you have a will!"

"Blame Jag," he responded.

"Oh, I do," I snapped. "Trust me, he's going to die too." I imagined the way he'd smile when he saw me. He wouldn't even see my fist coming.

The only door without bucket loads of tech had the pulsing blue light. The doorknob tingled with techtricity, but nothing I couldn't handle. Certainly not an entire simulation's worth.

So I took a deep breath and opened the door.

45.

The blue light lingered at the end of a long corridor. The door clicked shut behind me but didn't disappear. This room was real. I walked toward the light (again). The corridor ended in a bulbous window. The color came from the sunlight shining through the ocean. Waves lapped against the glass, creating the rhythmic pulsing.

I retraced my steps, half-expecting the door to be locked or something. But it opened easily. The hallway loomed in front of me. Because the other two doors were gone, I concluded that the simulation had ended.

My heart hammered. I could simply go back up those ridiculous stairs. Hop on a boat. Sail to Seaside.

Why would I traipse around down here? In dark tunnels, no less.

Yeah, I wouldn't.

So I turned and headed back into the tech warehouse. I strode past the shelves full of gadgets and started up the steps.

My breath had barely started coming in gasps when a *boom!* sounded overhead.

I froze.

Somewhere far above me, people shouted. Ty. Jake.

And Dad.

"I know she's here. Your petition does not protect her." His voice sounded like it was inches from my ear.

Fly, babe.

I turned and fled back the way I'd come.

"You can't!" Ty screamed. "This is an insulated dwelling."

"Not for her," Dad replied. "Let's go, Zenn."

I flew down the hall, through the only door and toward the window. I felt along the glass, a sob threatening to break free. My fingers found nothing to latch on to, nothing to pry apart.

Frantic, I spun around. The corridor lay empty. The door remained closed.

I put one hand on the wall and sprinted back the way I'd

come. I had to get out of here. Halfway down the hall, my hand fell away from the wall.

No, that wasn't right. The wall ceased to exist.

I paused and looked into, well, the wall.

I reached out. My hand passed through the supposedly solid structure. My arm disappeared up to my elbow.

This wall was a projection.

The doorknob rattled. I leapt through the projection and pressed my back against something solid. I couldn't see the corridor from the secret room where I hid.

That did little to ease the panic rising in my stomach. Especially when the door opened and footsteps sounded close by.

They quieted the farther down the corridor the person moved. All too soon, they returned.

"Zenn, order a search of the tunnel system in Seaside."

I bit down hard to silence my cry. Dad was so close, I could practically hear his thoughts.

I submerged my control. My feelings. My breath.

Zenn repeated Dad's orders in a monotone voice.

"Every last tunnel," Dad repeated. "I want her. If she makes it to the center, I can't follow. Then it will be up to you, son."

"I'm not your son," Zenn said. His voice sounded hoarse, like he hadn't used it in weeks. At least he'd spoken the words screaming through my bloodstream.

"You're going to find Violet and bring her to me," Dad said. "Tell me, can you feel her down here?"

His words caused a surge of anger. Dad didn't need to follow me using tags and stickers—he had Zenn. He owned Zenn.

And Zenn loved me.

"N-no," Zenn choked out.

"Strange." Dad's voice dripped with disbelief. "Her readings are still in this area."

"Must be the simulators," Zenn said.

"Perhaps. But you will find her, won't you, Specialist Bower?"

"Yes, sir. Yes, I will."

"Station an agent outside this door. Just in case."

The door clicked shut as Zenn repeated the order, his voice foreign again.

I let out the breath I'd been holding. I found relief hard to come by as I scanned the hidden room. It sat empty except for a hovercopter resting in the corner.

Fly, babe.

I almost laughed out loud.

Like I know how to pilot a hovercopter. I scampered over to it anyway. With an agent right outside the door, I could hardly go that way.

I crawled inside, inhaling more dust than air. I wheezed, trying not to cough out loud. That didn't work. I sank into the pilot's chair while sneezing into the crook of my arm.

I froze, waiting for the spark of a taser. For an angry voice to yell, "Don't move!"

The door opened. Someone took a few tentative steps. I squeezed my eyes shut, as if that would make me invisible.

After a minute that felt like forty, the door closed.

When I opened my eyes, a large panel of knobs stared back at me. I wished I'd paid more attention to that pilot. I didn't even know where to put my hands.

Or how to start the stupid thing.

So I did the only other thing I could think of. I willed the machine to turn on.

And it did.

My right hand naturally reached out and gripped the joystick in front of me while the left one fiddled with a few knobs on the ceiling.

I had no clue what I was doing, but all my movements felt practiced. Precise. I flipped two more switches and the fans whirred to life. I eased the controls back and the hovercraft, get this, hovered.

I wanted to throw up. But something about flying this machine felt . . . easy.

I maneuvered it toward the simulated wall. Or at least where I thought it would be.

A grating of metal on metal caused a string of sparks. I yanked the controls to the left and around the corner just as the door flew open. I tapped three buttons in quick succession and pressed the joystick flat against the control panel.

The hovercopter shot forward, straight toward the glass.

I closed my eyes just before impact. Yeah, I'm that kind of chicken. I expected to bounce off the barrier, get bloodied up and then arrested.

Instead, the glass broke. The hovercopter sailed into the ocean, leaving the agent behind.

The machine didn't handle as well in the water. I made clumsy turns, following an unknown path. I just felt like I was going the right way.

Up ahead, a wall of coral shone brilliantly. A steel door beckoned.

I flipped a switch, and the door slid to the side. I quickly maneuvered into an elaborate tunnel of seamless tech, tapped the switch and twisted to watch the door slide shut. Ocean water glistened on the floor. Then my hand located another button and pressed it.

Tiny holes opened in the floor, successfully draining the

water. I focused on piloting the hovercopter, and before I knew it, I entered a cavern carved in dark brown rock.

I powered down the craft and got out. Four stalls lined one wall. Each one housed a hovercopter. What a great getaway cave.

A single doorway lay across the cavern. The walls were stone, built before the earth had burned and the Association of Directors was founded. The floor sloped downward, and the air grew colder with each step. My eyes adjusted to the darkness with ease, probably because I willed them to.

The light from the cave had faded by the time the hall branched in two directions.

Control or don't control.

Alone or together.

Zenn or Jag.

Duty or death.

I hate only having two choices. Really, really hate it.

Now, staring at the solid wall in front of me, with an option to the left and one to the right, I wanted a third alternative. I pressed my palm to the stone. It felt rough and smooth at the same time. Hot and cold. I closed my eyes. I leaned into the wall, willing it to move.

The stone sank into the ones surrounding it. Soon the rock had moved six inches and a loud noise shook the air around me. I stepped back as the wall slid to the side as if built on rickety old tech.

I moved through the opening into a cavern without a ceiling. Jag was very close; I felt the thrill of his touch in my mind.

Numerous hallways branched off the chamber where I now stood. More choices.

Rescue Zenn.

Join Dad and the Association.

Run away with Jag and live on the beach.

Save the world.

Before I could decide, Zenn's controlled voice echoed behind me. "She's here, sir. I can sense her."

I could almost feel the caress of his hands on my face. I paused, desperate to help him. He hated being controlled as much as I did. I knew he'd helped me remove the sticker. As much as he was able, he'd always protected me.

"We must find her before she enters the center." Dad's tone chilled me. I probed the minds of the people with him and found a dozen SF agents.

Violet, Dad said when he discovered me lurking in his mind. *Zenn loves you.*

Determined in my decision, I filled my mind with memories of Jag.

Zenn's voice grew louder. He called my name. I willed the wall to move back into position, blocking him.

Then, choosing a tunnel, I ran.

Jag stood in a circular chamber, his eyes shining like he was on the best adventure of his life. His pants hung too low, his shoes looked too big, his shirt faded into the blackness around it. The gems on his necklace glowed in the dark with a light that softened his jaw.

I ran to him and wrapped my legs around his waist when he caught me. He spun with me, both of us laughing.

Yeah, all right, I was in love with Jag Barque.

"Zenn's here," I whispered into his neck. "He's being controlled by my dad."

"Where's Gavin?" He set me down and wiped my cheeks. I hadn't realized I'd started crying.

"Gavin. We need to talk about Gavin." I stepped back. I didn't need to say more. Jag would pick up on my feelings.

He drew me into an embrace, leaning his forehead against mine. "She's nothing to me. Just my trainer."

"Jake said you spent hours in her bedroom." I hated the accusation behind my words.

"Jake talks too much." His eyes filled with adoration I

didn't deserve. "Vi, *you're* my Choker." He didn't use his voice.

I nodded slightly, stupid tears spilling down my cheeks. Jag wiped them away before kissing me.

"So what's with that stupid simulator?" I asked. "Jake said you—"

"Like I said, Jake talks too much. You needed that test." He chuckled. "So, where's Gavin?"

"I don't know. And what test?"

Jag strung his fingers through mine. "Jake has this elaborate system for discovering talent."

"Making people pick doors is his elaborate system?"

"Yeah. Works, too. See, he programs the simulator for three talents: tech, elements, and genetic adaptations. Every ranger falls into one of those categories. When you select the door with your true talent, you're led here."

"So it's not a simulator at all."

"Sure it is. For the two talents you don't have. Everyone gets a clue. I wrote yours." He sounded so proud of himself.

I wanted to inform him that his low-class, two-word clue was anything but helpful. He squeezed my hand hard, so I kept my mouth shut.

"So, did you pilot the hovercopter?" he asked. "Or ride

the wind? Or maybe you adapted. Sprouted wings, perhaps?"

"Sprouted wings?" I was so glad I didn't pick the door with the darkness. "You're insane. I flew the hovercopter."

"I know. You have a way with tech."

"What don't you know?" I hated how he was always right.

"I'm not always right. I've just seen you take out a Mech or two. Or twenty. So, where's Gavin?"

"I don't know. My dad—oh, no." I gripped his hand tighter. "My dad was at Ty's house. What if he arrested her?"

"Her place is insulated. He can't touch her." He moved his hands to my face, and his cool breath brushed my cheek. "You guys have such a powerful bond. And such strong gifts. I guess that's what you get from someone like Thane."

I looked around the cavern so I wouldn't have to think about my dad. It was empty except for the two of us.

"And Zenn?"

Jag's jaw tightened. He stepped back, scrutinizing me. I knew that look. He was checking out my feelings. I didn't try to hide them. Maybe he could make sense of the mess I had going on inside.

"Ty said he arranged her escape. He helped me remove my sticker." I held up my hand so Jag could see.

He traced the thin scar. "Zenn was my best friend for

years. We share the same goal, but believe in two very different methods for achieving that goal."

"You can't blame him for what he's done while being controlled. That's not fair."

"What if he's used his control in bad ways too? Then what?"

I searched Jag's face, finding the little boy inside who simply wanted to be told that everything would work out.

"He helped me remove the sticker," I repeated.

"Doesn't mean he's a good guy now."

"There are no good guys, Jag. That's just it. Good and bad mean nothing."

The fire entered his eyes. "I don't believe that. And neither do you. There are things we think are right and things we think are wrong."

Yeah, he was right. But my dad's words haunted me. *It's all about who you choose to believe.*

And I still didn't know what I believed.

"What now?" I asked. "Jake said I'd find what I needed down here."

"And you will." Jag picked up his backpack. "Use your connection to find Gavin." He stuffed something in his back pocket. "I gotta go."

I grabbed his arm. "No way. Where are you going?"

"We're sending our people to White Cliffs. There's a council meeting set for tomorrow morning."

"White Cliffs?"

"It's a couple of hundred miles north. Don't worry, you'll be teleporting with Pace. I have to help with the evacuation. If Thane shows up, I can use my voice to make sure everyone still gets out."

"I'll go with you." Everything I wanted to say but couldn't, everything Jag needed to know about how I felt about him, filled those four words.

He took both my hands in his and studied them as he spoke. "Pace and Gavin are coming here. Then you guys will all teleport to White Cliffs. I'll meet you there in a couple of hours. Please, wait for Pace."

"No. You won't make it to White Cliffs." I just knew, like I knew he wouldn't come out of his house in the Badlands, like I knew how to fly the hovercopter.

"Of course I will, babe. I told you I'd never leave you."

But I heard the lie hiding in that promise. After all, he'd left me before. I shook my head, fighting back angry tears. "No. Don't go."

He leaned down and kissed me with a new edge to his mouth I hadn't felt before. Something desperate and raw. It seemed like he'd never stop. Then he pulled back and whispered, "I'll find you. I love you." He turned quickly and disappeared down a tunnel.

I stood in the dark chamber—a place where I was supposed to be able to find what I needed.

But there was nothing there.

Just me.

46.

I checked my pockets for the phone. My fingers closed around something hard—the teleporter ring I'd taken from Baldie. Along with the diminishing tech, the locator, and my food cube, the phone completed my arsenal.

I closed my eyes and connected to Ty. She was a few hundred yards away, on the opposite side of the wall behind me. I crossed to it and put my hand on the stone. She did the same; I felt her touch as if we were skin to skin.

"Left," I whispered. Ty kept her hand on the wall to maintain our connection.

"Left again," I directed. A few turns later, she entered the chamber.

"Thanks, Vi," she said, grinning. "Well done." She had changed into jeans and wore her phone clipped to a holster around her bicep. "You're a natural."

She checked the screen on a piece of tech. "Hmm. No directional readings. No Directors." She pocketed the device and held out a purple pill.

"I don't want that," I said. "I jumped off a building last time I took one of those."

"That wasn't because of the pill."

"I still don't want it."

"You'll need them," she argued. "Thane will try to confuse you with the tech." Ty pressed the pill into my hand. "Take it. Trust me, you'll need it."

I studied her face. "All right." I swallowed the pill, but nothing happened.

Unless you count the fact that I didn't sense the tech buzz before the man appeared. I scrambled behind Ty as she took refuge in the shadows.

The man twitched. His silver hair fell in a ponytail down his back. One final shiver ran through his body before Pace Barque turned. His gray eyes didn't sparkle the way I remembered, and his cheeks were sunken into his face. Ty squealed and ran toward him.

"We need to go," he said as he hugged her.

"To White Cliffs?" I wouldn't leave without Jag.

He ignored me and frowned. "Thane—uh, your dad—will be here soon."

"Jake said he couldn't find us here," I said.

Pace reached into his pocket. "I know, but technically, Thane's the only one who can't enter. Zenn and his squad of agents can—and will—be here any minute. Here, take these. We'll be in White Cliffs in a couple of minutes." He passed a teleporter ring to Ty.

When he handed me a ring, I took it and slipped it into my pocket with the other one. "I'll get Jag and meet you there."

"You can't go to Jag," Ty said, her voice foreign. "He's going to Freedom. It's the only way to satisfy Thane."

The darkness in the stone chamber settled around me. The air thickened, too cold to breathe. "Freedom?" No way that was happening.

"We really need to go," Pace said, looking over his shoulder. "I promised Jag I'd get you to White Cliffs safely, Vi. Come on." He reached for me, but I stepped back.

"I'm not leaving without Jag," I said, turning.

Tyson clutched my elbow. "You can't go. Jag isn't going—"

"Did you see him getting caught?" I asked.

"Not exactly." She glanced at Pace. "He goes willingly."

"You knew?" I looked at Pace, who studied the ground. "You both knew and didn't tell me?" Hot tears pricked my eyes. I fumbled for the rings in my pocket.

"Vi, Jag's known his role since the beginning." Pace stepped forward, his smoky eyes glassy with tears.

"No." I shook my head. "No." This could not be happening. I would not abandon Jag. He filled my empty places.

Pace put his arms around me and drew me into his chest. His strong heartbeat pounded in my ear, the same way Jag's did. "He knew he'd be the one to go. He just didn't know about you until you showed up in prison. He almost ran away yesterday. He didn't know if he could give himself up. He did it to save you."

"Did what?" If I hadn't spoken the words, I wouldn't have recognized my voice. My breath came in spurts. My heart flopped against my ribs.

"He has to go with Thane," Ty said. "I saw it a long time ago. That's why he accelerated his training."

"What if you're wrong?"

"I'm never wrong," she murmured.

"But you didn't see me." Every breath fanned the flames erupting in my chest. Surely my heart would stop pumping, as though the thought of losing Jag meant it no longer had a reason to keep beating.

"I saw that Jag would find someone instrumental to the Resistance. He found you." Ty closed her eyes and took a deep breath. Then she merely shook her head.

"Vi, he knew he'd have to go," Pace said.

"Shut up!" I pushed him away. "You're lying. He would've told me. Tell me you're lying." I controlled them, willing them to tell me it was all a lie.

They didn't.

Instead, they shifted closer together, their faces grim.

I knew he'd lied when he'd said he wouldn't leave me. He'd known all along that he would. My mind sharpened with the anger coursing through my veins.

Jake's words came back to me as I gulped air. *Remember the things he's told you, no matter how small.*

Oxygen spread through me, forcing the rage out. My mind was calm as I recalled something Jag had told me: *We have to stay together. We have a better chance of survival if we stay together.*

And his last words to me: *I'll find you. I love you.*

He might have been willing to leave me, but I'd be damned before I'd leave him. I plunged my hand into my pocket and withdrew the rings. Fear spread across Ty's face. Pace almost smiled.

"He needs me," I said, placing one ring on my finger.

"No!" Ty lunged forward.

"Jag." I disappeared as Ty's fingers closed on nothing.

47.

I couldn't breathe and I couldn't see. But I could hear. People whispered and moved around me. Flickers of techtricity licked my senses every few seconds, and when my sight returned, I saw a line of people in front of me.

A man—Baldie—stood at the head of the line, handing out rings. People slipped them on, spoke, and teleported away. The crowd snaked around a cramped, square courtyard and then out through an archway.

Jag loitered in the shadows next to the entrance, his arms folded and his gaze trained on every person's face as they came into the courtyard.

I dodged through the line until I melted into the darkness beside him. "Jag," I whispered.

"Violet." Jag's voice healed the hurt in my soul. His touch sent a shiver through my mind. I wanted him to hold me, kiss me, tell me he loved me.

But I also wanted to live.

"I asked you to go with Pace," he said.

"Yeah, well, I asked you not to leave."

He went back to scrutinizing the crowd. "This is going to be much harder now."

"What is?"

His jaw clenched, and he didn't answer. The people shuffled forward, continued to teleport away. My plan: stay with Jag, no matter what. When he went to White Cliffs, so would I.

Jag straightened at the same time I saw Zenn's bleached hair, alabaster skin, and cloudy, controlled eyes. The crowd began scrambling away, but I stayed, pinned to the spot by desperation.

Through the pandemonium, Dad's emotions engulfed me: hatred and triumph, sadness and hope. *You have the power to change people*, his voice boomed in my head as if it had been amplified and broadcast into the courtyard.

I didn't ask for this power, I replied. *I don't want it. You don't control me—and I won't control others.*

Duty or death, he threatened.

I reached for Jag's hand. "Let's go," I whispered. "Please."

He gripped my hand, twisted the ring on my finger, and murmured something unexpected. "Badlands."

Dad's bellow of frustration rang in my ears as I dissipated into a thousand particles.

An evening breeze kissed my skin. Darkness stretched into forever. My lungs cried for air, my mind filled with fog. The teleportation symptoms had never lasted this long. The darkness turned white.

Air rushed at me. I took deep breaths, as if I could store the oxygen for the next time I teleported.

I opened my eyes to the soft glow of Jag's necklace. The colored gems radiated life the same way he did. In a swift motion, he removed his necklace and placed it in my hand.

I shook my head and pushed the necklace away.

"No, I want you to have it," he said, closing my fingers around it. "Please, babe, take it."

"I only want it if you're wearing it."

"I'll wear it again, I promise."

He was lying, but I put the necklace in my pocket anyway. The stones felt warm, even through the denim.

"Where are we?" I peered around the corner of a building. Lights illuminated the street, but it lay silent.

"Main Street." Jag hugged me. "Hey, this is where I first kissed you. Guess that made a lasting impression."

I laughed at the same time I suppressed a sob. It seemed like yesterday that we'd walked down this street. I couldn't pinpoint the exact moment I fell in love with him, but those overwhelming feelings filled me now.

I remained silent, still clutching Jag's hand. The air hissed with the beating of insect wings and the chirp of crickets. But that's it. No loud laughter. No lounging in the park. Nobody sat at the outdoor cafés, eating and living free.

Now the bad teens shuffling in the street wore long sleeves in one color—beige—and wide-brimmed hats. The little skin I glimpsed was still sun stained, but that would fade over time as the brainwashing continued.

Those who spoke did so in whispers. Girls walked with girls; boys with boys. No stolen glances. No shy smiles. No hand-holding.

The Baddies had been turned good.

"Jag—what's going on? Why are we here? What—?"

The fire in his eyes boiled into rage hot enough to scare me into silence. A muscle in his jaw twitched.

"This," he swept his hand toward the controlled masses, "*This* is what he expects us to do," he said, biting out each word.

A strong swell of nausea clenched in my gut. "I can't do that."

"Sometimes we have to do things we don't want to do," he said.

I saw inside his mind. He didn't have the option of asylum in Seaside. For him, it was all or nothing. It always had been.

Duty or death.

I opened my mouth to say something when a path of tech blurred in my mind.

"I love you, Vi," Jag said. "Don't forget that. Ever. I will always love you."

"Touching." Dad stepped out from behind a group of downcast Baddies. He wasn't wearing an *I-love-you-my-darling-daughter* expression. More like, *I-could-kill-you-without-even-blinking.*

But he was wearing his leather jacket. I remembered feeling it against my cheek, inhaling its polished scent. That jacket reminded me not of Thane, but of my dad. The alias of a man who hugged me and broke rules.

My heart pounded with a mix of fear and desperation. Another spark of tech and Zenn appeared a few feet away. He stood like a Mech, stiff and unnatural. His eyes held no life.

My sweet, wonderful Zenn.

Jag squeezed my hand, and I released my tension and hopelessness.

"Chokers." Dad sneered the word like it was dirty. "An unexpected inconvenience. You have a choice here, Violet." He smiled, but the expression held no fatherly emotion. "Zenn or Jag."

I'd already made that choice. A quiet corner of my mind wondered why neither Zenn nor Jag had told me anything.

"It's always the Voices who don't want to say too much," Dad said. "If Jag would've been honest, we wouldn't be here right now. Zenn too. But Voices are always worried about influencing people with what they say. Your dad went through the same thing, Jag. That's why I had to get rid of him."

A cruel smile marred Dad's face. "Stefan Barque made the transmissions you listened to for most of your life, Violet. He felt so bad about it, he actually became bad. He was dangerous, but at least he imparted his gift to his son."

Dad spread his arms and gazed around the city. "Look what we can do. We've turned this uncontrolled city into a haven of prosperity within a few weeks. Violet, you have amazing abilities. You could run a city this size—you could run ten cities! The world could be yours. There are precious few with your power. We could work together, be a family again. Please, V, choose wisely."

The word V stabbed through my heart. I was being torn in a million different directions. I could do what Dad wanted and serve the Association. I'd envisioned it a hundred different times on the trek to Seaside. But it had never ended well. Not for me, not for Jag, not for Zenn.

Maybe I could return to the oceanic region, where I could do something useful and respected with my control. And Jag and Zenn could come with me. We could all live a free life.

Choices, choices, I thought. *I hate making choices.*

"The Association has authorized the dictatorships here," Dad said. "We've moved our breeding and recruiting program to the southern region, an area that has produced great Thinkers in the past." He paused, pinning me with a dangerous look. "This is your last chance to join without consequences."

I stared right back at him. "Why do you care?" I asked. "Just go back to Freedom and leave me alone."

Dad took a step forward, anger painting his face with dark shadows. "I care because it's my job to find mind rangers and bring them to the Association."

I wanted to retreat, the rawness of discovering he was simply "doing his job" slicing into my heart. For a moment I convinced myself this man wasn't my father.

Jag's grip tightened and reality crashed down.

This man—Thane—was my father, my horrible, rule-following, brainwashing father.

But I didn't have to be like him.

"I have to return to Freedom with at least one of you," Thane said. "Violet, you can make this so much easier for everyone if you'll just come with me to Freedom. Zenn and Jag can both go free." He took another step forward. "Please."

"Did you even love Mom?" I blurted out, desperate to know that my entire life hadn't been a plan.

"I chose the most susceptible Goodie so that my genes would completely overpower hers. I got two mind rangers out of the deal." His smile sickened me.

Suddenly my mother became the victim. She must have known her husband didn't love her. And her daughters reminded her of that fact every day.

I sagged into Jag, who laced his arm around my waist and whispered, "Doesn't matter, Vi. I love you. Ty does too. Zenn always has. Even Pace adores you. You don't need Thane." I didn't care that he used his voice, didn't care if what he said was true or not, didn't care that both my parents hated me.

Jag loved me.

"I need you too, Violet," Thane said. "I've been waiting for you for a long time. I've worked my whole life to establish cities as places of refuge for the people, somewhere they could have food and water and a job. Somewhere they wouldn't die in the wild. We all need the guidance of the Association or our planet will die.

"Soon enough, Seaside will fall too," he continued. "The Association is waiting for my report before reclaiming the oceanic region. You could rule that region, Violet. Any way you want."

"He's lying," Jag whispered. "We have tech. Our methods of travel are clean. Nobody's going to die." Jag's eyes burned from within, the same way the jewels on his necklace did. He was right. Our world wasn't as bad as Thane made it sound. Do we have to control people? Can't they understand reason?

"No, Violet. They can't," Thane said, answering my thoughts. "They've always served themselves instead of thinking about their duty to others. They need someone like you to tell them what to think about, who to help, how to care about something besides their own selfish needs. The human race has always ignored those less fortunate than themselves, thinking that by ignoring the problems, they'll just go away." He laughed, the sound cruel. "But just look around. The problems don't go away. They just get worse until you've got people blowing up buildings, without consequences. That's what happens without a Thinker. Without someone like you telling those selfish people how to behave."

He took another step forward and gestured lazily to the statue next to him. "I have to return with one of you. So will it be Zenn?"

His laser-gaze bored into Jag. "Or Jag?"

When he looked at me, his features softened into the face of my father. "But I really need you, V," he whispered.

**48.** Before I could speak, Jag shoved something in my mouth. "Swallow."

I obeyed before groaning from the spike in techtricity. A moment after I choked down the purple pill, the burning in my chest faded. I blinked and saw Ty and Pace standing in front of me on the sidewalk.

"All you have to do is make a choice." Thane edged closer to Zenn, who stared straight ahead. "I told the Association you couldn't make choices. I asked for authorization to kill or capture any of you on sight. They wouldn't listen—and *I* obey the rules." He glanced at Ty. "Hello, daughter. So what are you two going to do now?"

No one spoke. Nobody moved.

"I can't believe my daughters have turned against me," Thane continued, his words sharp as steel. "I sacrificed everything for you two."

"Shut up," I growled. "That's the biggest load of crap I've ever heard. And believe me, I've heard some real shit."

Jag laughed and threw his arm across my shoulders. "That's my Vi," he whispered before kissing my temple.

Thane narrowed his eyes. "Get your hands off my daughter."

I laughed a little too loud. "Yeah, that's a good one. Like you give a damn about me. You just want to use me for my powers. If you cared, you wouldn't have left seven years ago." I slowly wound my arm around Jag's waist in an exaggerated gesture. I tucked my hand in his back pocket, and smirked.

"I had to. I—"

"Yeah, yeah. Your duty. I'm so freaking sick of that. Save it, *Dad*, for someone who cares." I glared at him, daring him to do something.

He glared back, waiting.

"Gavin?" Jag asked. I wasn't sure how many other unspoken words followed her name, but she looked at me and then him. She shook her head slowly, and I took that to mean that whatever she'd seen remained unchanged.

Zenn blinked and looked right at me. On the outside, he looked controlled. I studied him, finding his mind easily. He loved me. He hated my father. He was still resisting in his own way, but he needed my help.

"Jag." I tried to shake my hand out of his. "We have to help Zenn." He'd already been broken, but maybe he could be fixed.

"Let Zenn go," Jag said. His voice reached a new level of control. Powerful, well developed, commanding. I felt an overwhelming urge to get Zenn and drag him to Jag.

Thane's smile evaporated. The emotion in his eyes blanked out. Then the intense burning came back, hotter and brighter than before.

He laughed again, but this time it sounded low and terrifying. "That was very good. You almost had me there." His face took on a wild quality. Dangerous. "Now what?"

All I could think was, *Save Zenn*. I took two steps before my arms were pinned to my sides. Jag still had one arm, and now Ty held the other.

Zenn, save Zenn. I broadcasted my thoughts toward Pace as I struggled against the grip.

He met my eye before sprinting into the street. He let loose a wild roar and flung himself at Thane. They collided with a crunch of bone and a spattering of blood.

A sickening thud sounded, and Pace didn't move again.

Thane spit blood and wiped his mouth as he stood up. Ty had one hand on Zenn's jacket when Thane thrust his fist forward.

A jet of white mist hit Ty in the face. She choked and stumbled, knocking Zenn back toward Thane as she did.

I buried my face in Jag's chest so I wouldn't have to watch my sister die. "Stop!" I screamed. Everything turned still, silent. Thane waited—like I was the one calling the shots.

Because I was.

Oh. No. I was *in control* here.

No, no, no. Bile rose in my throat. The clenching in my gut wasn't from the bloodstained stones in front of Ty, though that would've done it. No, I'd become what I hated—a Director.

I'd finally found myself.

But I didn't like who I was.

Bright red blood stained Ty's stark face. I moved to revive her, tears already streaming over my cheeks, but Jag held me fast. "Let me go!" I thrashed against him, letting the rage blossom and replace the hurt inside.

"No, Vi," Jag said, his voice soft and soothing. "Stay with me." He spoke as a command. I sagged into him, but my eyes never left Ty.

Time slowed. The crickets became the loudest sound.

Thane took one step while I fumbled in my pocket for the tech. I hoped like hell I had the power to do what needed to be done.

I made my choice.

I spun toward Jag. His cheeks were wet.

"Jag, baby, take this and go." I pressed the diminisher bracelet into his palm.

He looked at it, defiance seeping into his eyes. "No way in hell. I won't run again. I'm not hiding—"

"Yes, you are. I love you, you idiot, and I refuse to watch you die. Now, go. This is my fight."

He shoved the bracelet back at me. "No. What's yours is mine. I won't—"

I squeezed my eyes shut and forced him to be quiet. "You have to go. It's the only way I know how to save you. Go, please."

His beautiful blue eyes glazed over. He fingered the device that would allow him to hide and escape. Just when I thought he was going to slip it on, he looked at me. "But I promised I'd never leave you."

"So you lied. I do it all the time." A hole opened in my soul that could never be repaired. I'd lose him, probably forever.

It's my choice, I thought when I felt the weight of my actions. *Thane said to make a choice.*

Jag wiped his thumb across my cheek, and I almost collapsed in on myself.

"I love you," he whispered. "I promise, I'll find you."

I nodded, desperate to believe him. "I know you will." I pried my fingers out of his. Focusing on his blueberry eyes, then his delicious lips, I mentally instructed him to put the bracelet on and run. I imagined him doing it.

A surge of tech burned my face, and I flinched away. Where Jag had just stood, a blank space stared back.

Feeling lost and alone, I sank to my knees. Exhausted and with my new power consuming me, I curled into a ball on the cold stones. Silence pressed down. Slow footsteps approached. I felt the careful caress of a father's hand. I sobbed at the touch I'd longed to feel for seven years.

"That boy has poisoned you, V."

I pulled away and staggered to my feet. "You're lying. Jag loves me."

He glanced at Zenn, who remained lifeless. "Well, I can see this is going to be a problem." His face twisted with determination as his hand shot toward me.

I tried to dodge, but he caught a fistful of my hair. The leathery scent of his jacket stained my senses with unwanted comfort. I twisted, but his grip was firm.

Icy fingers of control stabbed into my awareness, starting

where Thane's fingernails dug into my scalp. "Violet Schoenfeld, you will forget about Jag Barque. You will remember him no more."

I struggled against his hold. "*You* forget about him! Leave me alone." My command entered Thane's awareness. His grip loosened for a split second. It wasn't enough for me to get away before he regained control of himself.

I kicked, screamed, swung my arms. Thane stood resolute, holding me at arm's length where I couldn't reach him. An intense hatred resided in his eyes. "You will forget about him."

"No! I need him!" I clawed at his hand where he gripped my hair. "Let me go! I hate you!" Desperation overrode the control I might have had.

A cruel smile painted Thane's features. "I need the old you, not this new Jagified version. Violet Schoenfeld, forget about Jag Barque. Forget you even met him. Forget he exists."

I fought his voice, but a black weight slammed into my mind.

"You'll never make me help you," I gasped out as the darkness spilled into my memories, covering the guy's name, his face, his voice.

"I can do anything I put my mind to, Violet."

Pain rippled from my scalp to my neck and back. Thoughts fled. Memories darkened into sinkholes. Footsteps moved away. Coldness smothered me into a hole so deep and narrow, I couldn't move. Couldn't breathe.

"So can I," I choked out. "And you'll never . . ."

I couldn't finish, because I couldn't remember what Thane would never be able to do.

49.

I'm running. Fast.

Faster than I've ever run before. I'm chasing someone, and I desperately need to see his face. He haunts me. He has for months.

I have to catch him this time. I can't live through another night without knowing who he is.

He dodges into the doorway of a building. The night sky around me is bathed in red. I duck into the doorway too, but there's no one there. Something smells familiar. Pine needles and earth and . . . *guy*.

I've been here before.

With him.

He has no name. At least not one I can remember. A crushing hand of despair squeezes my fluttering heart. I touch the brick wall, expecting the cool bite against my fingers. Instead, it feels warm, like a body has lent its heat to the stone.

But no one is here. He's never here.

Like in the other nightmares, the doorway disappears and now I'm walking in a desert. It's so hot, and my face and arms are tender and pink. Someone holds my hand and rubs cream into my sunburned skin.

But when I turn to look at him, there's only a blank space. Walking next to me. Watching the stars. Chuckling. He says my name in a velvety voice.

I'm in love with the blank-space-guy.

Where is he? Why can't I remember his name?

Panic takes over. Fear. Crushing loneliness.

Because he's really gone. And he's not coming back.

This is where I wake up, almost like my dreaming self can't handle the weight of living without him. Like I can shoulder it while awake. If anything, it cripples me more.

I roll toward the wall, desperate to put the guy's face together and coming up empty.

When I can't stand lying in bed anymore, I step onto the balcony to watch the sun rise. A few minutes pass before I sense Zenn coming. Happiness pours from his mind because he has something exciting happening today.

"Morning, beautiful." He hands me a mug and slips his hand around my waist. I lean into him. His silk pajamas smell like toast and milk, the breakfast we eat together every morning.

The autumn sun rises, bringing with it a warm breeze from the coast. "I love it here," I sigh.

"Me too." He leans down and kisses me. My sweet, wonderful Zenn. "You've got two appointments today. We're meeting this afternoon, remember?" He inhales the scent of my hair before straightening.

I nod. "Are you meeting with the Director today?"

"Yes. I think he's going to—"

"You'll make an excellent Assistant." I smile at him.

Zenn's clear, blue eyes dance. "You think so?"

"Absolutely."

Something in Zenn's pocket beeps. He pulls it out with his right hand, where he wears a thin band of gold. I lightly trace the matching ring I wear on my pinky, proof of Zenn's dedication and love.

"I'll be right back." Zenn steps through the door and closes it.

I linger on the balcony. The wind plays in my hair, and the beach below brings comfortable memories. I've walked every inch of the coast with Zenn.

I touch the string of gems around my neck. They glow in

the weak morning light. The blank space beside me reappears. Someone gave me this necklace. It's important. He's important.

I retrieve a locator—something I found in my jeans—from my bedside table. Maybe I can try to find the blank-space-guy. Make him tell me his name and why I can't get him out of my head.

I flip the locator over and over. The screen at the top stays blank. Why can't I remember his name?

I stare a hole into the locator, desperate for a name to spontaneously appear. It doesn't.

Today is going to be a bad day. My appointments will have to be canceled. It isn't fair to tinker with people's minds when my own is so screwed up.

Zenn knocks on the door at the same time he opens it.

I almost launch the locator over the balcony. Then I won't have a way to find the guy. But . . . then I won't have a way to find the guy. And I'm not ready to give up yet.

"I'm going. I just need to shower."

Zenn stops me with one of his famous frowns. "How come you didn't tell me about your nightmare?" His adoring eyes usually calm me. Suddenly I don't want to look in them.

I slip the locator into my pocket, comforted by the warmth of it against my leg. "I can't remember anything."

"That's good," he says. "That journey is done. You should

forget all of it." He puts his hand on my shoulder. "Just forget about it."

I nod, my mind going blank no matter how hard I try to hold on to the slippery threads of memory. By the time I get out of the shower, I wonder why I thought today would be a bad one.

50.

After my appointments, I head toward the beach, making sure to pull my sleeves down to my wrists before stepping into the street. Zenn'll be waiting at the dock, ready to take my hand and walk south. We'll spend the rest of the day watching the waves and talking about anything and everything.

Suddenly someone hisses my name.

I freeze. Something like this has happened before. Not here, not in Freedom, but in the Badlands. I strain to grasp the memory, but it flees.

Zenn laughs. He pulls me into a shadowy doorway and removes his hat. "Surprise, beautiful. I thought we'd eat somewhere in today." He's handsome with his bleached hair and even whiter teeth.

"In?" I ask, feeling the coolness of the smooth stone disappear as Zenn pulls me so close our bodies touch along every point.

"Yeah, it's almost my birthday. I want to celebrate with you."

"Zenn, your birthday isn't until March. That's six months away."

"I know," he says, taking off my hat too. "But I want to be with you. I want us to be together." I imagine his next words before they come. "I love you, my lovely Violet." Zenn leans down, pausing just before kissing me. His mouth is warm and familiar, but that's all. It doesn't fill my soul with a choking desire or anything. I think it used to, but now his kiss feels, well, empty.

Then the blank-space-guy replaces Zenn. The doorway in the dream is similar to this one. Is that guy . . . Zenn?

It seems to fit, but at the same time, it totally doesn't. I remove the locator from my pocket. Vaguely, I hear Zenn say my name.

I run my fingertip over the screen. I need a name. Desperately.

"Let me have that," Zenn says, his long fingers closing over mine.

I grip it harder before letting him take it. A vital piece of my soul goes with it. I need that locator to find the guy. The one I'm in love with.

And it's not Zenn.

But I can't remember who it is.

"So . . . lunch?" Zenn asks, his voice false and bright. "Are you okay?"

I finally tear my gaze off my now-empty palm. Zenn's face is a picture of adoration. For me.

"Yeah, sure, lunch." My skin is the only thing holding everything inside. Still clutching our hats in his hand, Zenn steers me into the sunlight. The gentle rays feel like lasers, threatening to slice through my filament-thin defenses.

Because I have a hole inside that needs to be filled.

"Whatever is bothering you, you should forget it," Zenn says in his most soothing voice. "Today is about you and me."

I forget about the nameless, faceless guy and snuggle into Zenn's side. "You're right. Happy birthday, babe."

He tucks his hand in my back pocket and leads me to the nicest restaurant in the city.

ACKNOWLEDGMENTS

For DVR-ing my favorite shows, eating cold cereal for (breakfast, lunch, and) dinner, and waiting patiently in the queue: Adam, Isaac, and Eliza, my truest champions and greatest treasures.

For reading so many drafts of *Possession* and not gouging your eyes out: Christine Fonseca, Windy Aphayrath, and Amanda Bonilla.

For the friendship, beta reads, and late-night sob fests: Suzette Saxton, Bethany Wiggins, H. L. Dyer, Carolyn Kaufman, Mary Lindsey, and Patrick McDonald.

For providing a shining light through the maze of grammar and setting: Lisa Roecker, Laura Roecker, Beth Revis, Katie Anderson, Lisa Amowitz, Shannon Messenger, Jamie Harrington, Shelli Johannes-Wells, Danyelle Leafty, Cole Gibsen, Michelle McLean, Ali Cross, Jenn Wilks, Stacy Henrie, and Sara Olds.

For helping me stay hinged: Michelle Andelman, Anica Rissi, and the entire Simon Pulse team.

For bringing the awesome and making me spew beverages during chats: the ladies of WriteOnCon: Casey McCormick,

Jamie Harrington, Shannon Messenger, Jen Stayrook, and Lisa and Laura Roecker.

For holding back laughter at the idea, sending me amazing books, and cheering me on: the Bookanistas.

For raising me with the belief that I can do anything: Jeff and Donna Watkins.

For making me more beautiful than I actually am: Carol Johnson, Mary McBride, Amy Harris, Penny Welch, Jessica Cottle, and Brigitte Ballard.

For keeping me sane: all my blog readers, especially those whose comments buoyed me up during the floods, made me smile, or helped me take one more step. You know who you are.

And to my first teen readers, Haley Gallegos and Fabiana Fonesca; may there be many more like you.